SPECTR

Max Holden

DEDICATION

Spectrum is for those who take me away to think, and distract me when I've a creative block:

Angus, Bella and old Molly

(My three dogs)

CONTENTS

ACKNOWLEDGMENTS

My wife, Eileen, whose continued patience and support helped me through this second book.

Dawn, Kevin, Bev, and Andrea, who reviewed and commented on Spectrum.

Jeff, Morag, Alec, and my many other friends for their feedback.

All the technology companies, whose tools I've used to research, then polish the manuscript.

FOREWARD / PREFACE

The human mind is an amazing entity. Few, if any, are experts in its innumerable conditions. We label what we know to help explain and understand.

There are those (around me) who I know can reach higher than the ceiling a label places on them. Perhaps, it's wishful thinking on my part, but I hope not.

I wonder if this work of crime fiction might at least be thought-provoking.

I trust you'll enjoy (and hate) the novel's characters, live the action scenes, and be drawn into its ebbs and flows of emotions.

*** This novel contains some bad language, which I've used judiciously for those characters' personas that require it. ***

Author's aim – at least to be thought provoking
And if more to enjoy the action, be drawn into the emotion · enjoy ✓✓
the character, whether we love them or hate them. *Fulfilled /* *not?*

1. ENACTMENT

It was the end of a mild winter.

Emsworth weather! ✓

Now the second day of March, the flowers assumed spring was coming and started to pop their heads out of the soil; more fool them. However, they did bring some colour to the brown, wet soil.

Spring had sprung a leak. It had been raining heavily, making everything muddy and water-logged. The recent clear skies and beautiful sunny days would typically have brought out the gardeners and walkers.

Unfortunately, there was no joy with this weather. An icy north wind dragged a biting cold that froze all around. The hopeful buds would stay in suspended animation until the thaw decided if they would survive or die.

That evening, The Engineer, as he was professionally known, was dressed to kill, quite literally.

He'd normally wear loose-fitting clothes, such as dark tracksuit bottoms and a hooded top. However, here in expensive suburbia, that overly casual attire might get a second glance. When on a job, second glances were dangerous, so he dressed to fit in.

To keep out the vicious cold, his three-quarter length heavy coat was fully buttoned and the collar turned up. In addition to the warm collar, his neck sported a folded-down balaclava that also helped keep out the biting cold. *or style* ✗

Underneath were his smart buy-from-any-where chinos.

His gloves were thin linen and light brown. In this dim evening light, they looked like his skin. Wearing gloves on a cold night like this wouldn't be considered out of place, in any case.

He wore soft black trainers that one could buy from any High Street store or most likely online these days. In the dark, they looked like shoes.

Completing the ensemble, he sported an open umbrella to obscure his head and face.

7

✗ *Not well-written grammatically.*

He could have been anyone from around here out for a walk. So, if seen, he wouldn't stand out.

In his profession, it was always good to blend in, and he was skilled at that. His average height, average build, and pleasant yet uninteresting face also helped.

There was one thing that set him apart from normal people. He was extremely fit and strong for a man of his build, especially for one in his early 50s. This important contingency saved him on a couple of occasions when he'd only his speed, strength, and wits to escape from the authorities.

He liked contingencies and always planned for the worst. Via meticulous and accurate planning he fixed his clients' problems, hence the reason for his nickname, 'The Engineer'.

His wife would say that he sometimes over-planned, or in her words, "stop procrastinating and get on with it."

She never knew about his part-time career. As an honest, law-abiding citizen, she'd have been horrified to find out.

The Engineer had been following and monitoring his target for two weeks. The client assured him that the information supplied on the target and his movements were accurate.

Surviving so long in this business meant not trusting anyone. While pleased to receive whatever information his client supplied, he nevertheless painstakingly performed his own research. Every detail relayed to him was double- and triple-checked.

No matter how much his sometimes over-enthusiastic clients pushed for a swift completion, he would never enact any contract until everything flowed perfectly.

There were always last-minute issues, and he provisioned for those. This contract required him to rely upon agreed actions from the client's side to enable the kill. These people were not professionals. So, he had to provision for their errors, such as a backup emergency exit plan.

This evening the contract would be enacted, and everything was in place. The Engineer liked the simplicity of his plan, which followed his three Ss mantra. Simple Plan = Smooth Enactment = Safe Conclusion.

****

Judge Charles Davidson lived alone, at least to all intents and purposes.

His long-serving housekeeper, Mrs Marjory Taylor, occupied the top attic floor of his large three-storey house. There, she had a fully self-contained two bed-roomed apartment.

Both the judge and Marjory enjoyed their independence and privacy from each other. They lived apart, even though under the same roof, each having their own visitors and lives.

If and when they socialised together, it was by formal invite. When she finished the housework, their unwritten agreement was that each kept themselves to themselves.

They both preferred it that way.

Mrs Taylor's most regular visitor was her nephew, Alan Forrest. He lived on the nearby housing estate with his girlfriend and two children. Marjory doted on Alan. He was the son she would never have. He was also all that remained of her dear dead sister.

The judge tolerated Forrest. It wasn't only for Marjory's benefit; the nephew was useful to have around. He was the handyman they could call upon to fix the bits and pieces that go wrong in an old house like this.

Alan Forrest was also happy with the arrangement. The tax-free extra money from working there helped feed his gambling habit.

Judge Davidson knew about Forrest being a bit-of-a-no-user. Working in the judiciary, he'd many reports and anecdotes about the nephew's low-level criminal activities. However, the benefits outweighed the risks of having him around, and they mostly got along.

The judge was a man of habit, albeit not OCD-like pedantic. After hearing cases, he'd continue working in chambers, arriving home by 7 pm; his preferred dining time. From Sunday to Friday, Marjory would have his dinner ready and waiting, prompt at seven.

There were often exceptions when he might be delayed in chambers or socialising with friends and colleagues. He'd always notify her in advance of those occurrences.

Saturdays were a different routine for them.

For Marjory, Saturdays meant an afternoon with friends, followed by her regular bingo evening.

For the judge, Saturdays meant a roast sitting in the oven, awaiting his pleasure. She would set the table for him in the cosy kitchen. With the weather as cold as today, the large dining room would have been most unwelcoming in any case.

After his roast lamb dinner, a favourite of his, he retired to the living room. As usual, he sat in his comfortable winged armchair near the roaring multi-fuel stove that threw out a welcoming warmth.

When his wife was alive, each would sit in their own armchair, partly facing each other and partly facing the fire. She'd watch TV while he'd read his paper. After she died almost 11 years ago, the old TV was rarely on. He preferred the relaxation of classical music.

While reading his newspaper, he noticed an article on the case he was currently trying; the Crown vs. Mr Anthony Barker. There wasn't much detail, merely the basic facts that had come out.

Proceedings had gone well in court the previous week, and the case against Barker was in its final stages. All being well, by next week, the jury would find him guilty.

With all his years of experience, the judge could pretty much anticipate what their verdict would be. During the two long months hearing the case, he observed the individuals in the jury change opinion back and forth as the varying pieces of evidence were proposed and argued.

He knew the prosecutor would have a strong, if not clear-cut closing to present next week. He almost felt sorry for Anthony Barker's barrister now all the evidence had been laid out before the jury. There were no feelings of pity for Barker. The judge knew Barker was guilty, almost from the beginning of the proceedings.

"What a waste of time!" he grumbled.

As in this case, sometimes he wished the court process could be more prescriptive. If it was up to him, the guilty decision could have been made weeks earlier.

However, this was the legal process. And, he couldn't complain. After all, he'd enjoyed a good living from it over the years.

The CPS' key witness, June Mitchell, was potentially risky since she was a 'madam' running a prostitution ring.

There would always be prudes on the jury, prejudiced because of her profession. So, the defence barrister took every opportunity to discredit her based on what she did for a living.

The CPS' barrister did his best to get them to focus on the person. And he was the more successful. What swung it for him was that she was a credible witness who portrayed a warm and caring character.

Years of acting out various roles for her clients helped June Mitchell become a master actor. It was also a reason she was so successful in her profession.

The judge knew Mitchell professionally before this case; that is via her profession, not his. He'd often sampled her personal charisma and those of her 'girls'.

June had been particularly good to him, and he owed her. So, while he knew she'd perform well as a witness, he'd also reigned in the defence lawyer's excessive badgering to not unduly discredit his 'friend'.

He'd also used his position to help June and her staff, on several occasions, to get off with lowered sentences. In return, he received enthusiastic payments-in-kind.

Then, a feeling of remorse came over him. Not so long ago, there was that incident with one of her brothel madams. He racked his brains for the woman's name?

'Ah, *Sally, that's right, her name was Sally.*'

June accused Sally of stealing money, which she angrily denied. In a fit of pique, June threw hot oil over Sally, leaving her scarred down one side.

He did feel a bit guilty about helping June get off without charge. He was extremely fond of Sally.

"She was such a nice girl," he muttered.

Mitchell reminded the judge that they were good friends and that friends should always look after each other. She also dropped the unsubtle hint that she could ruin his career and reputation.

He could have recused himself from this case, but that would have meant admitting to using prostitutes; disastrous for a man in his position. Anyway, he and everyone knew Barker was as guilty as hell, so there was nothing to be gained from that course of action.

Judge Davidson flipped to the next page of his paper, drew on one of his favourite cigars, and took a sip of the expensive malt sitting on the small side table next to him.

During one of his most loved arias, Delibes' Duo des Fleurs, an uncomfortable chill came over him. It made him shiver. He suspected the old living room door lock had again sprung ajar.

"She needs to get her nephew to fix it properly this time," he grumbled out loud.

He let go of the paper from his right hand to check and draw on his cigar.

He couldn't believe what he saw!

****

No one was around, there were no security cameras in the house, and the target wasn't going to tell anyone. The Engineer had already pulled up his dark balaclava to hide his face before entering the house. Only his eyes and mouth showed. This was yet another precaution he took. You just never know what might happen or who might even be there.

The deep chimes from the grandfather clock, which stood in the main hallway, meant he was 'bong' on time. He liked that play on words. It was also another contingency. Even though he walked silently, the noise from the clock would cover any creaks he might make from the old floors and doors.

Most of what he could see in the dim light of his forehead-mounted lamp was old, quality, and expensive. He knew the target loved his antiquities.

He also knew the target almost always played classical music at this time in the evening. It was also when he read that day's newspaper while smoking his preferred make of cigar and savouring his favourite tipple, a 15-year-old

Speyside malt.

So, The Engineer needn't have provisioned for the grandfather clock's strikes. However, it was always prudent to take advantage of whatever added precautions were available.

The intruder followed the sound of classical music playing behind a closed door. As he approached, he pulled out his gun, a SIG P226. He extracted his usual suppressor from the inside pocket of his coat and screwed it on.

Performing that action made him think about his wife and it brought a smile to his face.

He'd often grumble to his wife about those TV programmes and films where the killer uses a silenced-cum-suppressed gun that just gave off a barely audible 'thwack'. It grated on him when people used the word silencer instead of the correct word, suppressor.

"What bollocks," he'd say to his ever-so-patient wife. "Don't they know that what they call a silencer only reduces the noise of the gunshot, not silence it? It's a damned suppressor!"

"Artistic licence dear," she would say, always wondering why he got so wound up about such a small thing.

For him, life was pretty near black and white; he had issues with the uncertainty of grey. Also, since this was a fundamental element of his part-time job, the reference always jarred.

He hated inaccuracies and misrepresentations.

The sound of an unsuppressed weapon would normally be at ear-damaging levels. His gun-suppressor combination was as quiet as one might reasonably expect, even though this combination would sound like a crack of thunder.

It wasn't only because of the noise factor that he used a suppressor. Other advantages outweighed its added bulk to the weapon.

The bright muzzle flash from an unsuppressed gun, which could interfere with his vision and be seen from the outside, would effectively be eliminated.

It reduced the recoil for improved accuracy. It was not just about the added weight of the suppressor to the barrel. The suppression mechanics also played their part.

Finally, a suppressed weapon would attract less attention and action from those hearing it.

Even when using a suppressor, neighbours and passers-by would still hear a loud bang with each gunshot. However, due to the lower level of sound, he knew from experience they'd take time debating whether or not they should make inquiries. Often they'd just wait, and if nothing happens again, they could settle back down to their normality.

People do not like their evening TV to be disturbed, even though there might be something untoward happening nearby.

However, he provisioned for the worst-case scenario, the time he needed to get away should someone call the police after hearing the gunshots.

Knowing the target didn't have close friends in the neighbourhood, the chances of a concerned call to the police would be low. In any case, his pre-planned exit would enable him to be miles away from the house before the police would arrive.

As The Engineer opened the living room door, the music grew louder. He could see his target sitting in his usual armchair, his right-hand side on to him. On the opposite side of the room, behind the window of the hot stove, the logs glowed and shimmered. The stove's welcoming warmth in that cold evening seemed to brush past him as it tried to escape through the open doorway.

His target was reading his newspaper. Or rather, he could see the newspaper and the target's right hand holding it. Between his index and middle fingers sat a smouldering cigar.

The intruder softly walked around to almost in front of the target and stood there, pointing his gun.

He realised that he shared the love of classical music with his target and was enjoying the moment. It would be a crime to ruin one of his favourite classical pieces from the noise of a gunshot. So he waited until Duo des Fleurs finished.

The target seemed to shiver.

To The Engineer's annoyance, the target lowered his paper and let it go with his right hand. The judge was about to look towards the door when he had a double-take at the man standing before him. He'd no chance to reconcile what the man in the balaclava was doing there.

The target killed this magical moment of music!

"Bugger!" the intruder cursed under his breath while killing the target in return. He shot him twice in quick succession; the second shot ensured success.

Additional shots or a longer interval in between would undoubtedly encourage neighbours to take action.

A bullet to the head and another to the heart was his trademark.

The contract had been enacted. The Engineer was now the killer.

After picking up the casings, the killer swiftly and carefully exited the house. He unscrewed the silencer and inserted the hot metal into a heavy canvas cloth before putting it back into his coat pocket. He placed the gun back into its shoulder holster.

The killer walked through the kitchen, where the judge had earlier enjoyed his lamb. He could make out the leftovers by the sink and an empty bottle of rather fine Chianti.

He exited the house through the large, sliding back door of the kitchen. From there, he walked around the edge of the back garden via a gravel path. There was a garage at the end of the garden. Next to it was a side gate that took him into an empty street. As he walked through, he lowered his balaclava, extended his collapsible umbrella, and calmly walked away.

The killer's car was parked thirty minutes away on foot in a street lined with terraced houses. It now had nose-to-tail parking. When he parked a few hours earlier, it was busy but still had parking spaces. That was when visiting workers to the area had finished work and were leaving for home, while residents would be heading back at the end of their day's work.

****

The weapon the killer used was ritualistically consistent. He knew his Modus Operandi (MO) would be documented and linked to his earlier kills. However, without evidence, and he never left evidence, the police would never be 100%

15

certain.

He rarely used a weapon twice unless there was a related need for the same client. Once he received full payment, he would always donate the scrupulously cleaned gun to the client.

Some clients liked keeping the gun from a special hit, for whatever emotional attachment it offered. For others, it was a tool to be used again or perhaps re-sold.

For the killer, giving the gun to the client signified the completed contract. It ensured the client had a stake in the hit by having to deal with the weapon; they were in the frame for that hit should they use it again.

It didn't matter to him. No one could link him to his client.

He also found that holding the gun pending payment was a reminder that the balance was due. And, if not forthcoming, there would be consequences. Typically this would stress his clients until they were clear of him and their current relationship. He was a dark figure to be feared.

Once, and only ever once, his balance payment wasn't paid, even though the kill was enacted as agreed. The follow-up killing of his client using the same gun was with his compliments.

That was earlier in his career. Word had gotten around, and since then, clients always paid on time and as agreed. With this contractor, once you had the gun back, you were clear of him; and he of you. That was the deal.

His priority after the kill was to safely hide the weapon. After fifteen minutes, he arrived where he'd planned to secure it. He removed the gun from its holster and hit it.

He always kept the holster since it was made-to-measure many years earlier; it still served him well.

He also withheld the suppressor, which he'd used for several years. Guns were relatively simple to source on the black market, yet suppressors were harder to get and more tightly controlled by the authorities. Guns were the tool that killed. Silencers didn't kill, they were just an accessory. The killer always found that to be a crazy situation.

"We truly live in a strange world," he mumbled to himself.

****

The Engineer had one more detour to make before driving home.

Killing a member of the judiciary, with the resultant ramifications, wasn't an action to be treated lightly.

So, this evening, he needed a reminder of why he'd taken up this second profession. He needed to visit his wife.

They all knew him at the hospice. Even though visiting hours were over, no one stopped him from entering. Instead, there were just smiles and welcomes from the staff as he made his way to his wife's private room.

"He's such a polite and gentle man," everyone would say.

He often arrived at all hours of the day and night but was always quiet and respectful.

His wife was asleep when he quietly entered, picked up a chair, and sat next to her bed.

With his specialist services background, he'd the skills needed as a contract killer. As a loving husband of a very ill wife who needed expensive medical treatment, he had the motivation to enter this dark realm.

His career in death started some years ago when he needed money for his wife's treatment. She'd a rare form of cancer. The initial hope for a cure, or at least remission, turned to realisation for all, except him, that his wife's condition was terminal.

She accepted her fate with grace, but he refused to face that reality. He loved his wife too much. There was no life without her, and he was desperate to find a cure; no matter the cost.

To please him, and without complaint, she bore the agonies of the continued expensive treatments, sometimes pre-trial, many untested. Some gave initial hope, others had little effect. All failed to stem the growing disease that engulfed her from within.

With no further avenues of treatment, he finally accepted the end was coming. He could now give in to the pleadings that he accept the inevitable and let her rest.

And now, she was in the best hospice he couldn't have afforded on his day job salary. At last, she was at peace, with gentle caring people around her, until the final day would come.

He still needed money for that top-quality care, for whatever months she had left.

There was another benefit to his second part-time career. The planning and preparation required, gave him a vehicle to put his darkest and saddest thoughts to one side; for a short time at least.

2. BROTHERS

Later that evening, from his burner phone, The Engineer called another burner phone, the one he'd issued to his client for communications. As usual, he muffled his voice.

"The contract was enacted one hour ago. All clear, no issues. As agreed, the balance is now due."

In Anthony Barker's view, contractors were lowlifes who charged extortionate fees and couldn't hold down a proper job. And The Engineer was no better than the rest. They all sat at the bottom of the pile of people he respected.

Anthony Barker was not a pleasant man. He hated his four foot, eleven-and-a-half-inch height, and especially anyone five foot or more. Apart from his half-brother, Joseph Morris, there were few people he liked; or even respected.

So, when a contractor reminded him of their agreement, it didn't please him at all. Actually, he was pissed off with the cheeky, arrogant lowlife!

"You'll get paid once I get proper confirmation, not just your word," came the gruff response. No one instructed Anthony 'Nailer' Barker to do anything, especially a contractor!

"Understood," said the lowlife contractor formally. "I shall expect payment tomorrow evening latest. I'm sure by then you'll have confirmation from your contact inside the house, as well as the morning and evening news. I believe you've also got an ear to the ground on what the police are up to."

"You don't assume anything about me, and you know nothing. Your job is to kill."

What particularly irked Barker was the price he'd paid for this contractor's services. It wasn't easy to get a judge killed. The repercussions would be so enormous that most were frightened off by the aftermath of such a kill.

This hitman was the only one of any quality, prepared to do the job.

The good side of this one was his secrecy, so no one would know who set the contract. The downside from Barker's perspective was not knowing with whom he was dealing. And he liked to be in control. Correction, he needed to be in control.

Barker was not a poor man. While the £100k advance and £100k on completion was not a lot to him, it was several times more than he'd pay when using his usual thugs. However, this kill was different. There could be no mistakes. His freedom rested on the judge's death, without any link to him.

"Once paid, I shall advise the location of the equipment used, and as agreed, that would conclude our contract."

The Engineer prided himself on never lying to clients. His reputation was built on his effectiveness, credibility, and honesty. He smiled at the thought of using the word 'honesty' in this business.

Bottom line, while it irked him that his client wouldn't trust his word, it was how Barker spoke to him that grated. However, business is business, and he chalked this up to experience.

He closed the call.

****

The first of many confirmations from multiple sources that the judge had been killed, came during the night.

"What a shame," the little man grinned over to his brother while sipping his favourite malt. "And he was just about to pronounce me innocent of the alleged murders."

"But, Tony, you did kill them, I was there. Don't you remember?" There was no sarcasm from his big, younger brother, just straight truth and fact.

"Of course I remember, you numbskull. I was joking!"

The big man burst out laughing since he now knew his brother was being funny.

The small man also laughed. Not at his joke, but more at his brother's response, and also through a feeling of relief.

The threat to his freedom was over, at least for the immediate future. He could relax. At last, he could now enjoy a good night's sleep.

Anthony Barker was born two weeks before his half-brother, Joseph. He took his father's surname since he was born in wedlock. Joseph Morris' mother was Mr Barker senior's girlfriend, so he was given her maiden name; hence the difference in their surnames.

The two half-siblings started off life in separate households, not knowing each other. Both children were badly bullied by those who didn't like anyone different; also because some were just mean.

Anthony was bullied because he was small for his age and unable to look after himself. Being brought up in a rough neighbourhood, when naturally good at school, made that target on his back even bigger.

Worse still, Anthony was a pretty child with sharp elfin-like features who always dressed smartly. Even at an early age, girls were naturally attracted to him. Some might say it was due to their mothering instincts because he was like a real-life doll. Their attention created jealousy, making him even more of a target for the bullies.

On the other hand, Joseph was bullied because he was, as people would say in pre-decimal times, 'eleven-pence-in-the-shilling', or, 'not-quite-the-full-shilling'.

(Ninety-five pence/cents in the pound/dollar doesn't sound quite right, does it?)

Even though he towered above those who victimised him, was twice as wide, and many times stronger, he never lashed out or defended himself. He was the ultimate big victim. Street and school bullies love beating up people weaker than them. What further stroked their egos was bullying someone far bigger and stronger.

Six years after giving birth, Mrs Barker died. Joseph and his mother almost immediately moved in with Anthony and his father. She treated and loved Anthony as her own right from the start. She was one of the few people he respected, even loved.

When the half-brothers were introduced, Anthony immediately realised that he, at last, had someone to bully. He was the elder, the legitimate sibling, and it was his house. Joseph accepted his fate, as he always did.

However, the half-brothers soon became inseparable friends. Anyway, there was no alternative; they had few friends. Joseph idolised his older brother.

Anthony capitalised on that adoration.

In school or on the street, their relationship was a marriage made in heaven. When Anthony was bullied, he explained to Joseph what he should do to the aggressor. Joseph enthusiastically followed his instructions. When Joseph was bullied, Anthony gave the required advice, with similar results.

The bullying quickly stopped.

The pendulum now swung in the other direction; the bullied became the bullies. Anthony enjoyed his newly found position of power. As well as a sharp mind, Anthony had no boundaries to revenge against those who'd earlier abused him.

Joseph was built like a buffalo. It was not long before Anthony's brains and cunning, and Joseph's brawn resulted in them ruling the playground. They were nicknamed the 'evil twins', but only behind their backs.

The parents were relieved their children were no longer victims and encouraged this arrangement. They no longer had to worry when their children were at school or just outside playing. The stress of making complaints about other children disappeared.

The complaints did an about-turn. They now started to come in their direction; from neighbours, the school, and later from the police. Since no one earlier listened to Anthony's and Joseph's parents' tales of woe, why should they now listen to them?

At last, all was good; their children were safe with each other.

As the siblings grew older, Barker learned that people could easily be scared into parting with whatever valuables he deemed appropriate. The pair soon became adept at extortion.

After leaving school as soon as he could, Barker's father managed to get him a job as a joiner's apprentice. He was lucky. At that time, apprenticeships were rare.

His father thought that honest work would be the making of him.

It was during that short-lived time of honest employment, apart from the stolen tools, supplies, and equipment, Barker junior picked up his hallmark torture and revenge tool; the nail gun.

He loved the sound of the thwack of the nail being released and fired, and the victim's scream of agony.

With age came maturity. Anthony Barker matured into a ruthless gangland boss whose empire had no boundaries to its criminal activities.

He had the perfect combination of intelligence and ruthlessness required to run a business involving drugs, prostitution, theft, money laundering, fencing stolen goods, and anything that offered a good profit. He had to be sharper and worse than the others around him, and he succeeded.

The more legal side of his business included pubs, pawn shops, and property. They were all perfect platforms to launder his ill-gotten gains. Others in the criminal fraternity also used him to launder theirs, for a small 60:40 share; in his favour.

Barker wasn't averse to killing to achieve his ends. Several unproven murders had been attributed to him.

Morris just became bigger and stronger. He still idolised Barker, following his every command without question, being ingrained from an early age.

Did that make him a bad person?

Perhaps the strong, big man was just weak?

More likely, he'd no one else and the smaller brother protected him, in his selfish way.

3. AFTERMATH

Joseph's phone rang while he and Anthony were enjoying a late breakfast; it had been a long night with many calls. Barker hated interruptions during his meals and was about to shout at him for taking the damned call when the big man said, "it's Miss Beverley."

Mrs Beverley Jones was what Barker termed his accountant. She wasn't really an accountant but more a highly conscientious and capable bookkeeper.

She knew how to navigate the tax laws for his taxable and legitimate businesses; and keep separate books for his non-taxable illegal income. Where they overlapped, she knew how to properly account for, and track any laundered monies.

"Hi, Mr Barker, your phone was off. Just checking when I need to make the second transfer for The Engineer's services just rendered?"

"My phone's off coz I'm having breakfast with my brother."

"And, no you fuckin' can't make the second transfer! That twat's got all he's goin' to get, and even that's too much!"

"Boss, he won't be happy, he's got a reputation, that one."

"And don't fuckin' I have an even bigger one!" he screamed down the phone.

The accountant backed down, then confirmed, "OK boss, sorry. Confirmed, no payment to The Engineer."

The boss cut the line.

****

Early evening, over dinner, Joseph's phone rang. It was his solicitor. "It's Fahmi," said the big man.

Fahmi had been Barker's solicitor for almost as long as he'd been practicing. He'd been introduced to Barker by a client, who also strayed over the thin

24

Characters do are as bad-tempered on occasion as we
would like to be, and rude.

blue line on many occasions.

Barker, then in his early 20s, was being interviewed by the police over a set of break-ins. Fahmi did a bit of wheeling and dealing behind the scenes and managed to extricate him from their clutches.

Barker took the phone from his brother and listened.

"Hi Tony, how're you doing?" was the rhetorical question he always used to open any discussion with his client. It was not uncommon for his client to fly off the handle at a moment's notice.

The solicitor always checked Barker's mood before imparting information, whether good or bad. It was safest to warm him up with good news first. And when the news was not particularly positive, he was pre-warned of the potential fall-out from the small man.

The solicitor continued. "Do you know your phone's off?"

"I switched the fuckin' thing off to have peace and quiet from twats like you interrupting my dinner!" he snapped. "Wha' d' ya want!"

"Such a sad and untimely demise of Judge Charles Anthony Davidson who was presiding over your case."

"Yeh, yeh, will you get to the point!"

Fahmi wasn't to be deviated from his flow. "Such a tragic loss to society and the justice system," he continued with more than a hint of sarcasm. To anyone else listening, it could almost sound like true concern.

What Barker liked about his solicitor was the way he could simply and innocently turn a blind eye and become suddenly deaf when the occasion required.

There were also times when Fahmi irritated him. Now was becoming one of those times.

"Get on with it," snapped Barker. "I hate it when you prattle on like an old fish-wife."

"Of course," said the solicitor, who now realised his client was in a foul mood.

"As we expected, the case against you has been dropped."

"Thank Christ."

"Not too fast, Tony, it's just for now. There'll be a new trial and a new judge; pretty much as expected."

"And you lot make even more money from the new one."

Fahmi ignored the comment that was made to warrant a response.

"This time, the new judge will have security. Would you believe it, there are those who suspect you might have been involved with his killing. I told them I was appalled they could besmirch your good character without cause."

"Cut the crap Fahmi and get to the point," snapped Barker.

"OK. OK," the solicitor responded.

After reassembling his thoughts for his impatient client, he said, "we assumed any re-trial would take time to schedule. However, the judge's murder has stirred a hornet's nest against us, or rather you."

"And the bottom line?" demanded Barker.

"The CPS is going to fast-track the new trial through the system. Our barrister and I have been trying to block it from happening so fast. We pulled in favours, but there's nothing we can do to delay it."

Barker let out a torrent of curses.

When Barker had finished, Fahmi continued. "No date yet, but more likely in the next few weeks, rather than months. They're running with the same evidence and witnesses, and obviously a new jury."

The solicitor paused.

Barker said nothing, which was most unusual for him. He knew his solicitor, and there was more to come.

Fahmi continued, "there's nothing we can do about the evidence since it's sound and secured away. We've already tried and failed to discredit any of it."

"And?" hissed Barker, impatiently waiting to hear what was coming next.

The solicitor added, without hinting at a suggested course of action but very much implied. "It's a pity Miss June Mitchell won't change her mind about testifying against you with those horrid lies."

"Fuck that bitch! The filth has her squirreled away and no bastard's sharing."

"With all your contacts and influence, don't you have anyone who can help you have a chat to persuade her to tell the truth?"

"Been there, tried that. No one's talking; so far anyway."

Then as a parting shot, the solicitor said, "as soon as I hear anything more about the case, I'll be in touch. If you get anything, let me know."

Barker knew what he had to do but couldn't yet see a way to make it happen.

He cursed and threw Joseph's mobile at the wall, where it broke apart; not the first time this had happened, and it wouldn't be the last.

The case brought against him was going badly. Killing the judge was the only option he had.

Joe Morris beat a hasty retreat.

Anthony Barker was not a man to be crossed and definitely to be avoided when he was in a foul mood, which he was now.

While others of his ilk had some sense of boundaries to their behaviour, Barker had none. He built his business on fear, and what scared people most was his unpredictability. One minute, he could be cold and calculating, the next minute violent. It was rare for him to be approaching pleasant, something he considered a weakness.

A few minutes later, Joe reappeared with a new phone and inserted the destroyed phone's SIM. With a sigh of relief, the new phone recognised the SIM and all worked.

4. TIDYING LOOSE ENDS

That evening, while sitting in his study with Morris, Barker called at the agreed time. He used the same untraceable burner phone The Engineer had supplied.

Barker immediately launched into what he assumed would be an unrefusable offer.

"Got another job for ya. And this time I want it at a discount. You'll be using the same gun since it's part of the same deal. If you sort this out, you never know, there'll be others. Might even put you on a retainer."

Barker thought his nicely, nicely approach, with the offer of more potential business, would be snapped up.

The response wasn't what he expected.

The killer's reply was measured, emotionless, and straight to the point.

"You're already late with the balance. My jobs are binary, and I don't confuse matters. Once our current deal is concluded, I'd be pleased to discuss any additional contracts."

"Listen you little shite, no one tells me what and when to pay. I've offered you more business; take it or leave it!" said the gangland boss.

He waited for this lowlife contractor to think about the mistake he was making by refusing his generous offer. Mind you, once he had this contractor by the proverbials, he'd screw him as he did everyone. All capitulate to him eventually, or they suffer the consequences.

After a pregnant pause, "I'll leave it," the killer calmly responded.

He matter-of-factly followed up with, "the balance is still overdue, and I look forward to immediate payment. Pleased to talk then. Have a nice day."

The killer hung up the phone.

Barker stared at the burner phone in disbelief.

"I'll kill the bastard!" was all he could think to scream out.

He made to launch the phone against the wall, destroying it like many others. Morris, surprisingly quick, grabbed his phone hand by the wrist. The big man gave him a knowing look, followed by a smile of apology.

Barker, brows furrowed in anger, stared at his brother. He then grinned at the big man, realising he was being even more irrational than usual. He needed to maintain contact with the killer.

It had been many years since anyone had stood their ground to Anthony 'Nailer' Barker.

The killer had him in a corner. He and his team could do the job he was thinking about. However, he and the people around him were on the police watch list. The job ideally needed to be done outside his organisation.

Barker then called his accountant and snapped, "Bev, transfer the fuckin' balance to that fuckin' contractor!"

"Are you sure?" the accountant immediately replied. Beverley should have known from her boss' tone that now was not the time to question this instruction, even though it overruled this morning's one.

This was a lot of money, and whatever happened, Beverley knew she was in the line of fire. So, she had a momentary lapse in judgement by checking if Barker was certain.

"Of course I'm fuckin' sure, you stupid bitch," he screamed down the phone. "Do what you're fuckin' told!"

"I'll message you when the transfer's gone and when received."

This reconfirmation of his instruction covered her in case the boss demanded to know why she'd sent the money when earlier, he'd explicitly stated that she hold fire.

Sometimes there was just no reasoning with the little-big man. Other times, he was merely nasty.

While the pay wasn't great, the perks for handling Barker's money made up for the abuse she received. The accountant was building up a sizable retirement income from the leaking money that drip-fed into her offshore account; tax-free, of course. The nastier he was to her, the more the tap opened into his accountant's account. Today, as a result of his outburst, it would be more of a pour.

Barker knew she was fiddling the books. As long as it wasn't excessive, he accepted the small losses. He'd have done exactly the same thing himself, so how could he blame her?

A message appeared on his phone advising the transfer was done. A short time later a second message arrived. It confirmed the contractor had received the balance.

Tony phoned the number again.

The Engineer immediately opened with, "Thank you. I can confirm receipt of the balance. If you are still happy to use my services for another contract, I'd be pleased to discuss the job now."

"You know the case that judge was about to screw me over?" Barker said rhetorically. The killer knew it all very well from the briefing information he'd earlier given him.

"That bitch, June Mitchell, grassed that I killed two people. Her evidence is what they're using to get to me. They'll not use her again coz she needs to be six feet under. That's the job."

"Happy to oblige," acknowledged the killer. "Forward all the information you have on June Mitchell and her whereabouts. Once I know what needs to be done and when, I'll advise a take-it-or-leave-it price."

He had to remind Barker about his contract red-lines to minimise later arguments. Yet there was no balk at the mention of a non-negotiable price via an expletive-riddled response. That surprised him.

Most of The Engineer's clients were thugs but were always civil leading up to the enactment. Some could be rude and ungrateful for his services when they had to pay his balance after the contract was concluded.

Rude behaviour always annoyed the killer, but as the saying goes, 'the customer is always right'. He never rose to their bait. He always kept calm and professional.

However, Barker was the exception. He'd been rude and difficult from the start. Dealing with Barker was a stretch, even to his patience.

The killer had a similar rule to the accountant, although more overt. Rudeness costs and the client always pays. He'd already inflated the cost to this client; if only Barker knew.

Barker surprised the killer by being calm as he said, "agreed. I'll get that information to you." It was his turn to hang up the phone.

Then to Joe Morris, he said, "I want that fuckin' bitch found, coz she's dead when I do."

"Bro?" responded Morris with uncertainty. Morris liked to use that nickname for his brother; it made him feel close to him.

"Anything wrong?"

The big man had a worried look on his face but said nothing.

"Spit it out, what's wrong!"

Barker took a deep breath, then sighed, as he always did when his brother was acting stupid; no, being stupid!

"But I like Beverley, she's always nice to me. I don't want you to hurt her," Morris pleaded.

"For fuck's sake, have you been standing in this room covering your fuckin' ears!" shouted an exasperated Barker. "Why the fuck would I want to kill our accountant, you imbecile?"

"You called Beverley a bitch, and you then said kill the bitch," replied Morris innocently.

"There's only the one fuckin' bitch, you arse!" scolded Barker to his brother, "and that's Mitchell. Our accountant's a stupid bitch."

"Ah, OK then," said Morris not fully understanding what his brother explained. But it was now clear that his friend Beverley would be OK.

"It still isn't nice speaking to her like that."

"For fuck's sake! Forget I called her that!"

He knew his brother had a soft spot for their accountant, so he retracted the 'bitch' reference to her. Life's sometimes easier if he pandered to the big man when he's confused.

He needed to keep things simple for him. "Let's be clear. I meant find and kill June fuckin' Mitchell! Only her."

Morris stared at his brother until he got his thoughts in order. "Ahhh, so it's June Mitchell, that's OK then." His face lit up with relief that they weren't

31

going to kill their nice accountant lady.

Morris added, "I never liked that Mitchell woman. She isn't nice to the other nice ladies who work for her."

"Glad you're on board," Barker said, with a hint of sarcasm that went over his brother's head. His younger sibling could really frustrate him.

He patted his brother's arm in affection. If there was one thing he knew for certain in this world, no matter what, the big man always had his back.

Barker spoke gently to his brother. "I need to know where Mitchell is. Let's find out who in the police knows, what's their price to tell us, and we'll then squeeze 'em."

The big man gave him a beaming smile in return.

"Let's chase up Bill 'n' Ben; especially Ben, She needs to screw her contacts in the fuzz who've given us warnings of raids and such-like. They now need to earn the bungs we've been giving 'em."

"Some porker will grass for the right price."

Bill 'n' Ben were brother and sister. Their dad liked a joke with the lads in the pub. With the surname of Potts, their father thought it would be a laugh to call his two boys William (Bill) and Benjamin (Ben). Their father loved the children's TV programme, the Flowerpot Men, when he was young.

Unfortunately, the second child was a girl, therefore had to be Benjamina. Their father now had an even funnier story to tell his drinking compatriots. The mother had no say in the matter.

Sadly, their father's pub humour backfired on his two children. They didn't have a good time in primary school due to the teasing they received about their names. Similarly to Barker and Morris, they were bullied. Being only one year apart, they became inseparable, doing their best to support each other.

The teasing ended in Ben's year three when they started to hang around with the 'evil twins'. Other pupils soon realised it was less painful to respectfully use their full names.

Barker had little respect for anyone and the siblings accepted his use of their nicknames. Eventually, the words just rolled off his tongue. Even then he was becoming their boss and they were part of his growing gang.

Benjamina was the sharp one of the two siblings. She was the go-to member of the gang when Barker needed someone with brains and cunning.

Barker would have also liked to use her intimately since she was slim, pretty, and in his view, available. Ben wasn't stupid and kept him at arm's length.

Many of Barker's relationships ended in disaster, and the team had a good thing going. There was also another issue. She wasn't going to spread her legs for someone she didn't find attractive; although many women did comply due to Barker's pretty-boy looks.

She could have relented, but the result would be them losing everything they had worked for. No one on the team ever tried their sexual luck with her. Being vicious in a scrap, the team treated Ben with respect.

William's passion was cars. From an early age, he tinkered with his father's and father's friends' cars.

As soon as he could see over the steering wheel, he had to drive.

He solved the problem of his young age stopping him from legally driving; he 'borrowed' them. From joyriding, he moved into street racing. Car theft was his parallel occupation.

Bill was Barker's preferred wheel-man. On several occasions, his driving skills saved their hides.

Morris called Ben on speakerphone so Barker could hear. He asked for any update from her informants in the police about June Mitchell's location.

"Since the judge's been topped, it's been impossible to get anyone in the police to give, no matter the pressure. They're all running scared and staying schtum."

"Fuck!" cursed Barker. "OK, put the word out. There's ten grand in it for information. Wha'd'ya' think?"

"That'd definitely work," responded Ben.

"Ben, another job for ya'. I want that contractor dead after that bitch's been topped. No one disrespects me. Find him and keep quiet about it. This contractor's connected but we dunno where and who. We'll do him ourselves, coz I'm goin' to fuckin' enjoy having a thwackin' good time with him."

"Will do boss."

5. SOLUTION

The following evening, Barker's solicitor visited.

Fahmi drove up the house's long driveway and parked his large, expensive German SUV in front of the house. He slid his lithe frame out of the car. Being a little below average height, the 2" heels of his boots gave him that extra height to get in and out of the relatively tall vehicle.

After putting on his light blue sports jacket which had been carefully hung in the back, he checked his appearance in the front driver's window.

He adjusted his brightly coloured cravat, carefully chosen to match the rest of his attire. The solicitor ran his fingers through his long, slicked-back dark hair. He was pleased with what looked back at him.

"You're looking Sic, man," he mumbled.

He bounded up the steps to the large porch and loudly rattled the door-knocker.

Joe Morris opened the door. Fahmi, sporting a wide grin, breezed past the big man.

"The little fella in his office? Anyone with him?"

"Nah, he's alone and expecting ya."

He opened the door without knocking and closed it behind him.

As the door to his brother's office closed, Morris wondered why his brother tolerated this man who could sometimes be so disrespectful.

"Yo, Tony." Fahmi sat in his favourite chair.

Barker came out from behind his desk. As usual, when his solicitor came around, he pored each of them a generous measure of his best malt. Few visitors got this treatment.

Barker handed over the drink. "OK, Fahmi, what's going down? You never come here unless you want to impart dodgy information you don't want to give over the telephone."

"Tony, I resemble that," said the solicitor, word-playing with 'resent'. "I'm an honest solicitor, just doing my best for my equally upstanding and sadly maligned client." He had a droll sense of sarcasm.

Fahmi often liked to word-play with Tony when he'd useful information to pass on, but he only did this in private. It was his way of dealing with his client's erratic client. He was one of the few people Barker would allow this behaviour.

Barker liked Fahmi, although he'd never admit it.

Knowing Barker's somewhat nationalistic tendencies, someone once asked him why he tolerated and even respected Fahmi.

"I don't give a fuck about his colour," he responded angrily to the implied racist question. "He's more fuckin' British than the rest of your lot put together!"

No one ever asked again.

Barker just sat and waited for what was coming next from his solicitor. They'd played this game for years, and he wasn't in such a bad mood as earlier.

Fahmi continued. "Just been called by someone who'd like to talk with you about where you can find an old girlfriend of yours. He knows you'd love to catch up again with her."

Barker was hooked. Now impatient for more information, he leaned forward and spat out, "will you stop being a waffley prat! This office gets checked for bugs every day. Give!"

"As I was saying," he continued. "Shortly after the call, a parcel was delivered to my office with this burner and note." He handed over the phone and a folded sheet of paper. "Have a read. I know you'll enjoy."

Barker unfolded the note containing typed wording:

'I know the whereabouts of an ex-girlfriend, June Mitchell. If Mr Barker would like more information, ask him to call the number plumbed into this phone. I'll be available at 7 pm this evening.'

Fahmi waited until Barker smirked, suggesting he'd finished reading and digesting the information.

35

"So, as suggested, I thought it better to bring this round directly, rather than have a telephone conversation."

The solicitor never liked to speak over the phone about sensitive, or even worse, incriminating information. Phones are so easily tapped. He didn't trust secure messaging either. In any case, he had the parcel to deliver.

Barker's eyes lit up at the news, and he was now grinning.

"Joe!" He shouted for his brother to come.

When Morris arrived, Barker chuckled, "looks like we've good news about where that fuckin' bitch, June Mitchell, is." He emphasised her name plus expletive, to ensure his brother wasn't confused.

"That's great bro."

Glancing at his watch, the solicitor said, "that's in thirty-two minutes, enjoy. Gotta go, have a date with a hot stud." He winked, made a suggestive sign, and then left, letting himself out.

Nodding in the direction of the departed solicitor, "I hate ponces, but I like him coz he's bent."

"Eh? You like him coz he's a poofter?" Morris knew his brother was the ultimate homophobe and was surprised to hear that he liked this solicitor because he was gay.

He gave his little brother a worried and confused look. "I thought you only liked women and didn't like men like that?"

For Christ's sake, you fuckin' arse-wipe! I'm not a fuckin' bender! I like him coz he's one of us. I meant 'bent' as in crooked and dodgy."

Morris blew out a sigh of relief and grinned.

Barker was pretty sure this lump of grizzle didn't fully understand much of what he'd just said. However, Morris seemed happier now, which was all Barker could ask for. He didn't need Morris to understand everything. Barker just needed his unwaveringly loyal brother to do whatever was asked, keep his gob shut, and hurt people when required.

So, he left it at that.

Barker then explained. "Looks like we've a friend who's goin' to tell us where to find June Mitchell. I've to call at 7 pm. Better you hang around. Also, get

Ben over. I expect we'll be needin' her to follow up."

Over the next thirty minutes, Barker paced up and down while downing another couple of large measures of his favourite malt. Morris thirstily looked on, but the expensive malt wasn't for the likes of him.

Before the silent thirty minutes expired, Ben arrived.

Barker made the call. "Hello?" he questioned.

An electronically shrouded voice said, "good evening Mr Barker. Let's cut to the chase. You want the address of June Mitchell, and I want three hundred thousand pounds."

"Three hundred grand, fuck me, she's not royalty!" screeched Barker.

"I think she's better than royalty. Here's how I see it. They've got you for two murders at fifteen years each; that's thirty years. And that equates to a mere ten grand per year. It's a bargain. Then you add in loss of earnings from being locked up, a collapsed empire, and maybe someone will even stick you while inside."

Barker fumed. He was lost for words.

Morris and Ben said nothing, waiting for Barker's eruption.

The informant filled the silence with, "seems to me it's a bargain." He had Barker over a barrel, and they all knew it.

Barker needed to find June Mitchell or leave the country.

The informant let Barker stew in silence and then said, "call me at 8 pm if you want the deal." He hung up. The conversation only took a few seconds.

Barker looked at the phone in his hand and screamed out a series of expletives as he stamped around the room. He then settled in his chair, just watching the fire glowing in the grate.

Morris and Ben still said nothing; it was safer that way.

It was a most uncomfortable hour for the other two as the little man sat, staring into the fire, fuming.

Just before 8 pm, Barker piped up, "OK, we're gonna do this, no choice."

Exactly on the hour Barker called again and said, "how can I trust you?"

The recipient simply said, "you can't."

"Then what am I doing talking with you? No way I'm goin' to hand over a penny to someone who admits to being a liar."

"You've got me all wrong. I never said I was a liar. It's all a matter of leverage," said the person on the phone. "If this conversation was passed to the police, I and my sources would be compromised. Same applies to you. It's a matter of knowing we're both in the frame."

"You could still be anyone."

"I know. However, here's a little credential check for you. Ms Mitchell visited The Steadings yesterday. If it checks out, then you know I at least have inside knowledge."

Barker grunted.

"When you've checked my credentials, deposit one hundred and fifty thousand pounds into the offshore account I'm going to send you. Once I've received the money, I'll message you how to find her. As soon as you've confirmed the target was at the location, send the balance." He again hung up.

A message appeared on the burner phone with an offshore bank account number.

He looked at Ben, "check out what he told us about yesterday."

"No problems."

She immediately called a number and put it on speakerphone. "Charlie, seen June recently?"

"Dunno if I can say. I hear your boss is after her. Don't like the bitch, but I don't want done as an accessory."

Barker made to grab the phone and explain in no uncertain terms what he'd do to this woman if she didn't answer. Ben turned away, keeping the phone out of his reach, and covered the speaker. She gave him the wait-a-minute sign.

"Listen, darling," continued Ben. "I just need to know when you saw her last. That's not going to hurt is it?"

"Dunno. It's risky."

"We can do that special thing you like."

Barker gawped at her. After all this time, he realised she was also a ponce. He wasn't annoyed, quite the contrary. It reassured him to know why she'd refused his charms all these years. What he didn't realise was when women who were initially attracted by his looks got to know him, they were soon repulsed by his behaviour and preferences.

"OK, OK, it's a deal," Charlie giggled. "She was here just after lunch yesterday. Call me, you promised. Gotta go, see ya." The line went dead.

Barker realised he'd no choice but to agree to the informant's request. He called his accountant. "Wire one hundred and fifty grand into the account I'm going to forward to you."

"I'll let you know when the money's been sent and received," his accountant replied.

Barker hung up and said to Ben and Morris, "once we've got everything we need, the bitch is toast."

He looked at the burner phone that was still in his hand. "And that tosser can sing for the rest of it. He's got more than enough! It's fuckin' extortion."

They all laughed at his joke; that is after he started laughing.

****

The informant knew there'd be no balance. One hundred and fifty thousand pounds would do just nicely for the information on June Mitchell.

"Thank you Mr Anthony Barker," mumbled the recipient at the phone after the call had ended.

A few minutes after the informant received the money, Barker received the information on June Mitchell he needed, her location, availability, travel plans, and security deployment details.

****

Tony Barker immediately forwarded the information to The Engineer. At the prescribed time that evening, he called him back.

"Thank you for the information. It'll be two hundred thousand pounds for the hit."

"Fuck off!" snapped Barker. "Fifty grand is more than enough for a hit."

"It is likely that this will require the killing of additional people. There are added risks to this hit, and the extra covers my exposure," explained the killer.

"Bollocks!" exclaimed Barker. "If you want to kill other people, that's your problem, not mine. I'm paying for one kill."

"This is a dangerous and complex hit. She has police and her own professional security. The information you've supplied means we, or rather I, don't have much time to prepare."

The Engineer added, "that makes me nervous. So the price is therefore reasonable."

"You ain't getting a penny more. If you don't like fifty, I'll find someone else."

"In that case, I thank you for the business. I look forward to working with you again in the future."

The Engineer never wanted this hit. There were too many issues and he didn't trust Barker. Better to walk away from a deal, than walk into prison. Saying that, if Barker did agree to the big bucks, the killer would have agreed; it was just too much money to walk away.

He was certain Barker would balk at the amount he'd proposed, so the question would never arise, he hoped. He was proven right.

The killer finished with, "as our current relations are at an end, I'll message you the pickup location for the equipment as per the contract." He then hung up.

Barker screamed out loud in anger. He was about to throw the phone at the wall close to his last strike, when Ben intervened. "Don't we want the gun?"

Barker grunted an OK. He walked over to his drinks cabinet and poured himself another large measure of malt, downing half in a single gulp. He could feel the warmth as the amber liquid slid down his throat into his stomach.

He stared at the fire, mesmerised by the flickering yellow, orange, and red light.

He recovered, cursed, then threw his glass and the remaining spirit into the fire. The flame momentarily turned blue.

Turning to face the other two, he said calmly, "we're going to do that bitch ourselves."

He knew this would be risky for them. However, they had to take it.

"No problem bro. We gonna go nailin' again?" the big man said, smiling, hoping to cheer up his brother.

"Nah, different this time. We're putting that contractor bastard in the frame."

Ben immediately realised what Barker was planning. She smirked and nodded enthusiastically.

Morris gave an uncertain look to his brother. He wasn't sure if he should ask, since Ben visibly got the plan. He didn't like to appear stupid to his brother.

Barker let him off the hook by explaining. "He's giving us the gun he used on the judge. What a twat! We're doin' Mitchell with that gun, same as he does. The police'll see his MO, as the yanks say. He'll be in the frame. And that means we're in the clear."

"Ben, call Bill over. We need to plan this kill. I need you to follow and research her movements. That bloke's given us less than two weeks of her whereabouts. I'm going to enjoy doin' her myself."

Barker received a message from the killer with the gun's location. He then sent Morris with Bill to retrieve the weapon.

6. LET BATTLE COMMENCE

Jennifer Graham arrived at Doctor Hardcastle's house just before 6 pm and rattled the knocker.

Robert Coleville, the doctor's receptionist-cum-aide, opened the door a few moments later. While she and Robert weren't close friends, they got on well; and the doctor, his boss, liked her.

"Hi Jennifer, by the looks of you, this is going to be a lively one."

Robert had known her for as long as he'd worked for the doctor, a shade over two years. He'd seen most of Jennifer's differing moods, not that he'd ever seen her in a bad mood. Today, her agitated demeanour suggested her evening with the doctor would be more fraught than usual.

"Has he finished with his last patient?"

As an afterthought, she remembered the pleasantries she sometimes overlooked when fixated on an issue. "Sorry, hi Bob, how are you doing? A bit preoccupied, you know."

"I know the feeling, and no problem, he's all done for today. So come in and go for it," he jokingly said. "He's waiting for you in his consulting room. I've already prepared some tea and biscuits for you both in there. If you're going to be long, there's stuff in the fridge to make sandwiches."

With a knowing grin, he followed up with, "and by the looks of you, I'll open a bottle of his usual Rioja Reserva; methinks he'll need it."

He knew Jennifer didn't drink, or rather, not regularly. She never drank when engaged with the old man; she needed her wits around her.

"Yeh, yeh, you know he looks forward to it," she responded. Her face lit up into a beaming smile as she followed up with, "well sometimes anyway." She breezed past him into the consulting room.

Jennifer was a crime buff. While many people fall into that category, her relationship with crime was far more personal. In particular, she hated inaccuracy. When the evidence in crime programmes didn't add up, it could severely wind her up. There were even times when she wrote to the scriptwriters and programme producers when their lines of thinking were, in her mind, all wrong. She was invariably correct.

She never got a reply. It could have been because of her directness. People don't take well to criticism, and she could be quite brutal when the case demanded it. Still, she found a level of catharsis in writing emails, posts, and even letters. So it didn't matter they never responded.

The other vehicle for her psychological relief was the sessions with the doctor.

She didn't knock when she entered the consulting room. The part open door was a sign that she could enter. It was a large room, a cross between a study and a consulting room.

The doctor was sitting in one of the wing chairs, facing her as she walked in.

He grinned as she flounced in and dumped herself into the armchair opposite him. He got up and poured tea for them both. This action was the ritual precursor to the commencement of the battle to come.

Jennifer was in her mid-twenties. The doctor, her best friend, was in his late sixties. Despite the great divide in years, they enjoyed their hobby and each other's company.

It was here that Doctor Hardcastle practiced as a clinical psychiatrist. He also consulted at the nearby St Judes NHS Trust twice a week.

They were in his favourite room, where he spent most of his working time; also a lot of his personal time. The kitchen where he mostly ate and his bedroom were the only other rooms he used.

His wife loved to entertain and cook for friends in the house. After his wife died ten years earlier, all that stopped. He stopped using the dining room or the living room. When he entered these rooms, a depressive cloud would descend and hang over him for the rest of the day.

After the shock of his wife's death, he was prescribed anti-depressants by his doctor. When he needed more, medical friends would help. It was an easy, slow decline into self-prescribing opioids.

When the addiction demanded more drugs he couldn't self-prescribe without being noticed, he bought heroin off the street. In his business, he knew people who knew suppliers.

The doctor had two children, a boy and a girl. Both had long since flown the nest and lived away from the city where he lived. They had children of their own.

His years of slow decline into addiction caused him to drift apart from them. His children were angry then. Now, their lives no longer included their father.

Now he was off drugs, they no longer had ill-feeling towards him; more of an apathy. They couldn't understand that his addiction was an illness. They blamed him for his weakness and lack of support after his wife's death. He was a psychiatrist after all!

His children probably still loved him in their own somewhat selfish and medically uneducated way. There was always an excuse when he wanted to visit them and see his grandchildren.

His daughter did keep a modicum of contact going, as daughters often do.

So, he was always pleased when he got a visit from Jennifer. She brought a breath of fresh air into his dull, yet mentally stressful life. Their relationship started as doctor-patient. Over the years, it migrated to more of a friend-guide one, perhaps even a father-daughter one. He hadn't had a close friend since his wife died.

Little did Jennifer know, her friendship and companionship helped support him kick his addiction. He'd been clean for the last four years.

Jennifer was like a whirlwind in his life. He didn't know from one day to the next where their chats would start, then end. He welcomed that lack of predictability.

Their discussions could be heated, even from his side. With Jennifer, he could let his physician role slide and have intellectual fun with her.

Fortunately, he'd been able to control the endings to date, always gently bringing her down to normality; or what was normal for her.

When he first met Jennifer, her condition was deteriorating, made worse by the recent death of her parents. He had first-hand experience of the pain that could be felt from the death of a loved one. He tried many ways to treat and help her manage her condition, eventually stumbling upon the use of crime as a focus.

Unexpected friendship between psychiatrist Heathcotte · his patient Jennifer – meeting · tally word _crime_ . Everyone is in to crime

in its back!

He enjoyed novels and TV and film programmes about crime. Once he'd found this platform for her to engage and share with him, she never looked back.

From his side, the focus she now had, gave her a reason to visit and spend time with him. He adored Jennifer and truly enjoyed her sometimes crazily pleasant company.

She loved having someone with intelligence with whom she could sensibly interact. He was always kind and mostly softly spoken. Jennifer loved her aunt, with whom she lived. However, the old woman couldn't match the intellectual stimulation the doctor supplied.

This evening was going to be one of their more vociferous ones. Jennifer had been watching what was purported to be a 'true-crime' programme.

"How stupid can these people be?" she started as she went through the video recording with the doctor. "The evidence base is all wrong."

"As I've said, not everyone can be like you," he gently countered. "You need to be patient with them."

"Well, if they don't understand crime and murder, why are they writing about it? They're taking people's money for rubbish. It's immoral. It's just damned wrong!" she said loudly, almost shouting.

"You have to understand people's failings; they're just trying to tell a story in their way. It's only a story." His voice was raised in competition.

"In that case, they should be writing magical stories or fantasy, where they can make up the rules as they go."

The doctor laughed. He reached for the opened wine bottle that Robert had sneaked in while Jennifer was in full flow. He poured himself a large glass.

Robert's intuition was correct; this would be one of their more heated sessions.

At that point, Robert popped his head around the door and said, "I'm off."

They never heard him. They were already doing battle.

"He's got the patience of a saint," mumbled Robert about the doctor as he walked to his car.

7. UNNATURAL DEATH

The following morning Robert Coleville let himself into the doctor's house. He never announced his presence since he knew Dr Hardcastle would be hard at work.

He was allowed to interrupt the doctor with a mug of tea though, as he did every weekday morning. Robert brought tea plus two slices of buttered toast to the doctor's study at 8:30 am. This timing allowed the doctor 30 minutes to prepare for his first patient.

Robert knocked on the door. No answer. Sometimes the doctor could be so engrossed in what he was doing that he shut out all sounds.

Since there was no, "I'm busy" coming from within, he quietly opened the door. He held the cup and saucer in his hand, while the side plate rested on his wrist, waiter-style. He carefully walked in.

Robert stood inside the open doorway and looked to see where the doctor was.

The doctor stared at him from behind his desk. His face was ashen, his open eyes lifeless.

Robert's hands went to his mouth, forgetting what he was carrying. He dropped the toast and spilled the tea on the carpet and his trousers.

He stood there stunned.

Recovering, he ran over to the doctor to check his pulse. No blood pumped under his cold skin.

He immediately called 999.

****

In response to Robert's call, the emergency services dispatched a patrol car to the doctor's house. The two officers confirmed this was indeed an unexplained death. Duty Sergeant Paul Hayward was called to attend the scene, accompanied by PC Evelyn Cameron.

Hayward and Cameron made preliminary enquiries, pending the arrival of their boss, Inspector Barrie Turnbull.

Normally, deaths are initially investigated by the uniformed police force. If they suspected murder, they'd immediately call in the Major Investigation Team.

This case was a suspected suicide. As such, it was the local uniform branch that would attend and investigate. They'd perform all enquiries, then submit their report to the coroner.

When Turnbull got there, he said, "OK Sergeant, gimmie."

In private, he'd have used his Christian name, Paul, since they'd known each other back when they were beat PCs. However, in this formal setting with other uniform officers present, they had to have a formal exchange.

Responding equally formally, the sergeant commenced his verbal report.

"The deceased, Doctor Peter Hardcastle, was found slumped over the right arm of his office chair. The left arm had a belt wrapped around the upper part, likely used as a tourniquet to help find a vein. In the upper forearm, there was a recent injection site. We found a needle and syringe on the desk where he was sitting. The duty doctor believes the contents to be heroin, or similar."

Turnbull nodded, and the sergeant continued.

"Doctor Hardcastle is a practicing psychiatrist, and this is his office-cum-study. He is the sole occupant of the house. The duty doctor said he's a highly respected clinician and has also published research."

"The on-duty doctor suggested that the likely cause of the death was a self-inflicted overdose of an illegal, or possibly prescribed, substance."

The inspector remained silent, knowing there was more to come from the sergeant.

"He has a receptionist-cum-assistant, Mr Robert Coleville, who works here during the day."

"A Mr Receptionist?" interrupted Turnbull.

47

"Equal opportunities and all that sir," replied the sergeant.

The inspector grinned and shrugged his shoulders. "Carry on sergeant."

"He found the doctor just after 8:30 am when he brought him some tea and toast. You can see the spilled tea stains in the doorway, where he dropped the tray."

"Doctor Hardcastle's diary didn't have any appointments after the receptionist left. He did have a visitor, a Miss Jennifer Graham, who arrived at 6 pm. This was his normal finish time, hence the reason he could be specific."

"Mr Colville told us Miss Graham has a strange relationship with the doctor. She used to be a patient, and now they're close friends."

"They both love crime stories and argue about them. Sometimes their discussions get quite animated. On numerous occasions, he could hear their loud voices arguing. Yesterday was warming up to be one of their more heated discussions."

"She was the last person to have seen him. Since this is obviously a suicide, and they are close friends, we believe his death is unrelated to her visit."

"Anyone know when she left?" asked the inspector.

"Not yet, sir. When I'm finished here, I'll check with her. She lives close by."

Since no further questions were forthcoming, he continued.

"There are no signs of forced entry. We checked outside this room's bay window, and around the house, but nothing obvious. The house has security, but not enabled."

"From our enquiries with neighbours and Mr Coleville, we now understand that the deceased had previously been a drug user, actually a heroin addict. It's therefore likely his death was either suicide or accidental death by drug overdose. Toxicology and the autopsy will confirm the cause in due course. We are awaiting the test results of the contents of the syringe."

He continued his summation. "From what we could gather, the doctor's been clean for several years. If I might suggest, it looks like he had a re-lapse into taking heroin and possibly misjudged the dosage."

He then made a seemingly self-contradicting observation. "Perhaps it had something dodgy cut into it."

Thinking about it again, "which is actually unlikely. In his game, he'd know the best sources of clean product."

The sergeant concluded with, "the coroner's been notified and we're waiting for the body to be picked up."

From the doorway, Turnbull looked around the large room, typical of the Victorian townhouses in this area.

To his left was a bay window. A settee, covered by a throw and matching cushions, had its back to the window. In front of the settee was a low wide coffee table. On each end were large winged chairs with small side tables.

To his right stood the doctor's desk and behind it was the chair in which the doctor still sat, open-eyed. Behind the dead doctor was a built-in bookcase, which fully extended across the wall. On the other side of the desk were two chairs.

Facing him and in the middle of the far wall was a large open (unlit) fire. It was full of ashes, probably from the evening before.

The room was clearly designed to make patients feel comfortable. It would have also given him a sense of ease had it not had a dead body still in the desk chair.

"Are you sure this was self-inflicted?" checked the inspector.

"Absolutely," confirmed the sergeant.

As the sergeant and inspector talked in the doorway, the doorbell rang. It was answered by PC Cameron. In front of her stood a young smartly, yet casually, dressed woman.

"Can I help you?" asked the constable.

"I live down the road and saw the two police cars parked outside Doctor Hardcastle's house," said the young woman standing outside the door. She had a concerned look on her face.

"It's usually Robert who opens the door. Is there anything wrong? Why are you here?"

The constable ignored the question but asked, "Do you know the doctor?"

"Yes, he's my friend." After a short pause. "And I suppose I'm also a patient."

49

Rethinking what she'd just said, she added, "or was a patient. Anyway, we're friends. But he still helps me," she rambled.

The PC could see was trying to stay calm, but becoming anxious.

"Can I see him? Is he in trouble?"

"I'm afraid you can't see him," said Cameron in a soft voice she always used when imparting bad news. "I regret to inform you he's passed away."

The PC almost immediately regretted telling this young woman about the death. She knew it should have been the sergeant, or at least she should have had permission.

The young woman's face drained. She placed her hand on the doorframe for support and stood there saying nothing for several moments. Her eyes reddened.

At that point, Robert Coleville, who heard the doorbell ring, came to the door.

Seeing the visitor, he said to the PC, "I know her. Her name is Jennifer Graham. She's a very close friend of the doctor. She lives down the road and is always popping in to see him. I can vouch for her. Can I take her into the kitchen for a cuppa and explain what happened?"

The PC nodded and stepped to one side for Robert to help the woman enter the house.

She and Robert walked down the hall, past the inspector and sergeant, to the kitchen at the back of the house.

The constable joined her two superiors, who were now in the living room.

Turnbull said, "nothing more we can do here until the coroner sends someone over."

"In the meantime, could you find out if the doctor has any next of kin? We need to notify them. I expect the secretary will have information on them."

The PC and sergeant left the inspector in the study with the deceased doctor. He wanted to look around the room to check for himself that this was indeed not a suspicious death.

Satisfied, he went into the living room across the hallway. He needed to make a few calls and answer what messages had come in. It didn't feel right talking on the phone with the dead doctor just sitting there; actually a bit rude.

The sergeant and PC headed back towards the kitchen to get the doctor's next-of-kin details from Robert Colville. They passed a red-eyed young woman entering the toilet off the corridor.

The PC explained to the sergeant, "that's Jennifer Graham. Mr Colville said she's a close friend of the dead doctor."

"She saw our cars outside and wanted to have a nosey." PC Cameron added with some disdain in her voice. She hated nosey parkers since they always got in the way of their work.

"Mr Colville knew and vouched for her. They went into the kitchen for," she hesitated, "I suppose solace, perhaps gossip over some tea."

"Ah, useful, saves me some time. I was planning to talk with her," responded the sergeant. "She was here last night and might have been the last person to see him alive. We'll give her time and wait in the kitchen."

****

Once he'd dealt with the calls and messages, the inspector exited the living room. He saw the young woman standing inside the study doorway, staring around the room.

Most people would either gawp at the dead man or not want to be there. Yet, she just stood there taking in all the surroundings. It was most strange to see this young woman looking about the room in that way. She repeated what he'd done some minutes earlier.

The young woman intrigued him. He watched and waited quietly to see what would come next.

The PC came down the hallway, interrupting the moment. She said to the inspector, nodding in the direction of the woman, "sorry sir, she wasn't feeling well and needed to use the toilet; we thought it would be OK."

The young woman, seemingly lost in her thoughts, paid no attention to them. She continued to stare around the room. The inspector said nothing but held up his hand to stop the PC from further interrupting the moment. He didn't know what to make of this strange woman's behaviour.

51

After waiting another few minutes, the inspector looked at the PC and shook his head toward Jennifer.

The PC walked up to the young woman and touched her forearm, "I was worried about you when you didn't come back from the toilet. You shouldn't be here. How's about we head back into the kitchen to finish our tea?"

Jennifer turned around and responded said matter-of-factly, "do you know who killed him yet?"

The PC looked at the inspector for approval to speak, who nodded in agreement. She then said to the woman, "I'm sorry to tell you that he died from a drug overdose. We think it might perhaps be suicide."

"No, he was killed," Jennifer simply and formally stated.

The inspector said, "I know it's hard to accept that your friend would want to kill himself. He could have done this by mistake. Perhaps the drugs he used were to blame? We're waiting for forensics to confirm what happened."

He was doing his best to reassure this woman that her friend perhaps did not mean to take his own life; more likely an accident.

She turned to face the inspector. "No, that's wrong. It's obvious. People killed him," she said, making the accusation again.

He didn't know what to say in response.

The sergeant joined them.

She stared at the inspector incredulously, almost accusatory. "You are police, surely it's perfectly obvious? I don't understand why you can't see it?"

"Can you explain?" asked the inspector, intrigued by her behaviour.

Staring lifelessly outwards, in full view, was her close friend. Yet, this young woman had turned from a grieving friend to a dispassionate onlooker. Even more disturbing was her somewhat over-confident way of speaking to the police about her friend's death.

The young woman looked at the two police officers in turn, to see if they agreed with the inspector. There was no contradiction from them. She then explained, as if she was a teacher explaining to school children.

"He's given up drugs and I'd have known if he was taking again. He was my best friend."

The PC interrupted, "we're not saying he was taking drugs again but exploring the possibility. Also, in my experience, even the closest of friends and family often don't catch the symptoms until it is too late."

"Yes, yes. I know most people overlook any change in their loved ones, often refusing to admit they've reverted. However, that hasn't happened in this case, for several reasons."

Jennifer paused to collect her thoughts before explaining.

"If he was injecting himself, he wouldn't do it in his office chair. It has no proper side support. He wouldn't want to risk falling in case he passed out. He'd have used one of his winged armchairs; as he did previously."

Jennifer paused again in case there were questions. She wanted to keep it simple for these three officers.

"One of the cushions and the throw," she pointed to the settee, "are out of alignment, which is wrong. He's fastidious about the appearance of this room. He had company at the time. I expect they killed him."

The young woman again paused for her small school class to take in this information.

"His killers needed space to work, the reason why the chair was at that angle away from the desk."

The PC interrupted with, "there are no appointments in his diary after Mr Colville left, and there are no signs of forced entry."

"He knew them and let them in," Jennifer retorted.

"Tell SOCO to check for stands from the throw on his shirt," said the young woman, who was surprisingly comfortable using that acronym.

"Also, get them to check if the syringe had no fingerprints on the shaft, and if the tourniquet belt had only a few fingerprints."

"I also noticed that there are two more cups on the drainer in the kitchen than I'd normally expect. I'll bet there are no fingerprints on them either."

"Why do you know all this about how the doctor died?" asked the sergeant.

"I saw it. It's obvious. I still don't understand why you can't?"

The inspector didn't know what to make of this woman as she calmly spoke about her friend's death. There was no emotion, just factual delivery. It worried him. All she said made sense now that she'd laid it out for them. The death might be suspicious after all. He made a decision.

"Sergeant, secure the scene, and I'll get CID out here to go through this. Keep the young lady here until they arrive and pick this all up."

The sergeant asked, "Sir?"

"This could be a murder. This lady has cast doubt on our initial findings. We need to double-check."

The sergeant sealed the room as requested while the Inspector left them to make a call.

"Hello, sir," the inspector opened the conversation with Detective Superintendent Christopher Merriman. DSU Merriman was the head of CID at the station servicing this part of the city. He would allocate an officer to investigate this case.

"Hi Barrie, you're lucky to catch me," responded the DSU. They had a long history, back to when they were officers on the beat together. First names always stuck when they chatted one-on-one.

"Anything urgent? I'm about to head back into the judge's briefing with the MIT and will be pretty much tied up the rest of this morning."

"Yes, it is. We've got a dead body here. Initially, we thought this was self-inflicted, but we're no longer sure. Could be a possible murder scene disguised as a suicide or accidental death. Anyone you can send down to check it all out and process if a murder?" said the inspector.

"OK." The DSU thought for a moment. "Dave Peterson is the least strapped of the team. He's not involved with the judge's case and this meeting I'm in. Call him and give him the details. I'll message him to expect to hear from you. OK?"

"Thanks, Chris."

8. IF IT LOOKS, SWIMS, AND QUACKS LIKE A DUCK

Detective Inspector David Peterson epitomised people's vision of an old-school detective.

Most of his peers tried to stay in some form of physical shape to help keep the encroaching years at bay. However, he and his body had long given up fighting the good fight, assuming it had ever started.

DI Peterson was just under average height. His tiny hips and the skinniest of legs made even the tightest of trousers flop around his bottom half. Together, they made his already significant beer belly, the result of many nights in the pub after the day's casework, protrude disproportionately.

He was at the station when he received a message from DSU Merriman and the follow-up call from Turnbull.

"Oi Bhatia, off yer bum, get yer stuff, we're off to a case," Peterson shouted through the thin glass to one of the sergeants sitting outside his office.

Detective Sergeant Audrey Bhatia was sharp, new-school, but quickly learned to know her place with this old-school detective.

It wasn't because DS Bhatia was female or of Indian origin that he addressed her in such an off-hand manner. He wasn't racist or misogynistic. It's just that he was an inspector, and she was a sergeant on his team. He saw it as a privilege of rank. It was how his bosses addressed him almost forty years ago when he first started. He saw no reason to change what the decades had imprinted.

People working under him needed to follow the line of command. Once they got to the rank of inspector, they could follow their own gut instinct. But, until then, his team needed to follow his gut; substantial as it was.

Working for Peterson, Bhatia soon learned to control her enthusiasm and keen attention to detail when around him. She was relatively new to his team. It wasn't her choice to join, but she was going to make the best of it.

55

Looking past his faults, she could see her guv had good detection skills and experience. There was a lot she could learn from him. So, she planned to use the time with her new boss to extract what useful knowledge and skills she could.

After this secondment with him, she'd hopefully move on to one who was more in tune with modern technology and thinking.

No matter what people thought of Peterson, he did have a strong instinct for criminals. "My gut never lets me down," he liked to tell everyone; he was usually proved right.

Peterson and Bhatia arrived at the doctor's house and were met by Inspector Turnbull and Sergeant Hayward. Turnbull let Hayward talk the two detectives through the facts as they currently knew them. This included what additional background information they had so far managed to gather.

They left out any reference to Jennifer Graham at this time.

As he listened to the evidence, Peterson responded with, "just wondering why we're here? Seems to be a clear-cut case of accidental death or suicide?"

Inspector Turnbull enthusiastically nodded. "We also initially thought this was an obvious suicide or accidental overdose."

Peterson held off responding to Turnbull since he could see more was to come. He merely nodded in agreement.

Turnbull now brought in Jennifer Graham and her involvement.

"Now, this is where it gets interesting. A female patient, or friend, or both, it's actually still not clear ..." He hesitated, internally struggling to explain or label Jennifer's and the doctor's relationship.

"Anyway, this woman, Jennifer Graham, came to the door asking for him. As I was trying to say, we've not been able to get a clear picture of her relationship with the doctor. The bottom line is this; I think the boundaries are blurred between them and that's interesting in itself."

"Are you thinking about sexual involvement?" asked DS Bhatia.

"Too early to say. Here's the thing. Her behaviour started as being sad and upset as we'd expect."

"Then, when she was looking at the crime scene, she seemed to absorb the doctor, staring open-eyed at everyone, as nothing more than part of the furniture. Something else seemed to take over. The sadness was replaced by what I'd say was," he thought about the right word, "dispassionate interest. It was like there were two sides to her character."

"Out of the blue, she asked us who killed him, as if it was a normal assumption we'd have made. It was such a strange statement for her to have made when we've already judged it was self-inflicted, one way or another. I think this was your view as well before we brought in her involvement."

Peterson nodded agreement to the suicide aspect. His eyebrows furrowed as he was getting drawn to Turnbull's line of thinking.

"Then there were things she was coming out with, about the death, that a lay person would not comprehend. She explained aspects of the case that she shouldn't be aware of if she was not there when it happened, or told after the fact."

Turnbull paused, letting it sink into the detectives. He continued. "That was all strange enough. Now, the most worrying part was when Miss Graham started talking about 'seeing' what had happened."

"What do you mean?" questioned the DI. He had a good idea where Turnbull was heading.

She was teasing them! It was like she was being the hero who solved the crime.

The inspector carried on. "She talks about the case as if she was physically there. She talked about aspects of the evidence that we never picked up on. No one, in my experience, would have been able to pull her conclusions from the current evidence. Not even the DCI."

The reference was to DCI Wills, Peterson's boss. The DCI was considered one of the best detectives in the area and admired by everyone for his closure record.

"And you're saying?" asked Peterson, hoping to get the conclusion from Turnbull, without being seen to lead him on too much.

The uniform inspector picked up the thread and continued.

"If everything she said was true, it could make her a likely suspect to murder, not a suicide. Or, at the very least, a witness, perhaps even an accessory."

57

"Also, when she arrived at the house yesterday evening, she was highly agitated. The assistant could hear raised voices from the room as he left. Both were too engrossed in their argument that they either ignored him or didn't hear him shouting goodbye."

Turnbull had now finished his line of thinking.

After listening to the explanation of what was going on here, he'd normally have questioned uniform's ability, even sanity. Worse still, he'd be worried they were dumping a case on him to reduce their workload. It had happened in the past, but never by Turnbull.

He'd known and respected Turnbull for more years than he could remember. Peterson agreed that this whole thing was too strange to be taken at face value and supported his colleague's implication or rather, accusation.

"OK, I suppose we'd better chat to the woman and hear what we can make of the whole situation."

"Hoped you'd say that," said Turnbull. "Got a domestic to deal with and see if I can cool down some hotheads. I expect you'll need female uniform help with the woman. We'll leave you in the safe hands of PC Cameron."

At that, Turnbull left the house with Hayward in tow.

PC Cameron was standing in the background. She came over when she heard she was to help the detectives.

The three of them joined Jennifer in the kitchen, who was chatting with Coleville. Robert left the four of them when the DI asked if they might talk alone with Jennifer.

She gave them the same story, repeating to them what she could see had happened, while adamant she wasn't there. As Turnbull said, she was identifying possible evidence that she couldn't possibly know, let alone interpret. She also shared her intimate friendship with the doctor. Theirs was a more personal relationship, definitely not doctor-patient.

Their suspicions were further raised when initial forensics analysis started coming back. They were confirming the evidence she'd identified.

DI Peterson decided he'd seen and heard enough. This woman needed to be properly interviewed at the station. He decided that a gently, gently approach, at least initially, would deliver the best results.

"Miss Graham, would you mind coming down to the station? From what you've told us, we could really do with your assistance with the death of your friend Doctor Hardcastle."

"That'd be wonderful. I'd love to help. When can we go?"

"How's about now? We can run you down to the station."

"Can we go by my house first? It's just down the road. I need to tell my aunt I'm helping you and I'll be and not be home for lunch."

"Of course," said the DI with a reassuring smile. "I'll arrange something for you to eat and drink at the station."

9. BRIEFING

On the same morning Doctor Hardcastle was found dead, a briefing was held at the same station to which DI Peterson was taking Jennifer. The briefing was to review the Major Investigation Team's progress on Judge Davidson's murder investigation.

It was 8 am on a beautifully sunny, crisp, early spring morning. The light from the low sun was doing its level best to stream into the southeast-facing row of windows covering the whole side of the room.

Even with the blinds fully closed in the large team meeting room, chinks of almost horizontal bright light managed to penetrate the gaps in the old blinds. They seemed to delight in catching the corner of Detective Superintendent Christopher Merriman's eyes as he paced to and fro in front of this MIT.

Behind his back, he was called 'Smilie'. His nickname derived from his surname and the rare occasions when he actually smiled or responded to any form of levity.

His lack of outwardly facing response to humour wasn't because he was grumpy or even bad-tempered. He just liked to keep things in his team formal, and in his mind, professional. He believed joviality and high spirits should be kept to the end of the shift.

He had friends (of sorts) in the force who used his first name in private. Otherwise, he expected to be referred to by his title, 'the Superintendent', or at least 'the Super' or the 'DSU'. To his face, 'Sir' was acceptable.

The DSU wasn't an imposing man. He was of average height, lean looking, with what many would call a gaunt face.

He liked to take the lead and encourage others to eat healthily, sleep sufficiently, and take alcohol in moderation to keep body and mind healthy. In his view, a healthy lifestyle meant minimising time out of work caused by health issues.

He looked around at the mass of bodies in front of him.

'Half you lot are in line for heart attacks, strokes, and the like.'

He kept those opinions to himself, being the practiced politician he was.

The briefing room was arranged with six rows of 8 chairs wide, with a passage up the middle.

Opposite the east-facing window was a half-height glazed partition wall; its blinds were closed for privacy. The entrance door to the room was at the far end of the partition wall to where the Superintendent stood.

There was a large open area between the back wall that faced him and the rear-most row of chairs.

The front quarter of the room was also empty, apart from a small table in the middle. On top of the table was an open laptop, connected to a roof-mounted projector. It wasn't planned to be used today, but just in case.

All the visible information on the case was on display across the front wall, now behind him, supported by two large free-standing whiteboards. All were covered with pictures, lines, arrows, and notes. Together, they laid out the case under review.

There was also the mandatory flip chart and marker pens should anyone feel the need to visually explain a point.

While trying to find a place in front of his team without being blinded, and as the Senior Investigating Officer in charge of this case, he felt obliged to open the meeting.

Usually, the SIO of a murder would be at chief inspector grade. However, they'd had a Senior High Court Judge professionally killed on their patch. Such a high-profile murder created a level of visibility from on high that necessitated the police be seen to be taking it with utmost priority, and to a rapid conclusion.

That meant having a higher-ranking officer own the case. In this case, Merriman, the policeman-politician, was the perfect candidate to take the lead and be the case SIO.

The annoying light was a minor irritation compared to his frustration about the lack of progress with the case, now seven days old. It wasn't helped by the chief super, his boss, demanding regular updates.

She, in turn, needed to appease the chain of command. Their role was the dispersal of relevant information to the parallel hangers-on, some with genuine needs and others with political agendas.

He'd not been able to offer them any progress during the past few days, which was becoming uncomfortable for everyone on the ladder of blame; and he was on the bottom rung.

He opened the meeting with a simple, "right, let's get started."

After giving the team a few further minutes to settle down and prepare themselves, he commenced.

"This meeting is for all of us to share the status of where we are with the investigation into Judge Charles Davidson's murder."

"Everyone needs to be on the same page, so listen up. Share your ideas and thoughts, no matter how daft they might seem. When we leave this meeting, we will have measurable and time-bound actions agreed and allocated to each of us."

He emphasised the word 'will'.

When he said 'us', he meant everyone sitting in front of him.

Little did these people in front of him realise that his job was the most complex. It was up to him to manage those above him, to keep his team free from interference.

"We're now on Day 7 of this case. This case is countrywide news. Everyone is looking at every single one of us to deliver results. We need to make better progress than we have to date."

It was actually Merriman who was in the firing line. However, it didn't hurt to ramp up the level of urgency he felt the team lacked.

"I want to show all of them we are the best of the best," he finished.

Merriman was not the best at rousing speeches, but he felt he needed to inspire them as best he could.

He then looked at Detective Chief Inspector Jonathan Wills to take over.

While DSU Merriman was the SIO for the case, everyone knew it was down to DCI Wills to ensure the investigation delivered results.

Jon, as most of his friends called him, Wills was Merriman's most experienced and best detective. He was a far better investigator and team leader than his boss. Everyone knew it, including Merriman, who happily acknowledged the fact.

Both senior officers were in their early 50s. Like many ex-military personnel, they found themselves in the police force. The difference in their rank was less to do with their detection skills but more about political manoeuvrings.

While Merriman was a good detective, he got to his elevated rank by excelling at politics. He knew how to say the right thing, at the right time, to the right people.

What frustrated him about this case was not being able to offer those right people any new information or insight, leading to the arrest of those involved.

He was adept at accepting full credit for successes. He also ensured full blame for failures was placed squarely where he deemed it needed to be; typically outside his team. For all his faults, he protected his own. Keeping his team clean never hurt him in any case.

Most importantly, he always strived to minimise embarrassment to the chain of command. He was focussed on the next promotion to chief superintendent. His bosses also knew that.

So far, they respected him for ensuring clean and effective investigations. Unfortunately, this one was straining their confidence in him.

As well as being a murder case, the killing of a senior judge had politics written all over it. The longer the case took to get resolved, the more time the press, lobbyists, and his promotion competitors could air their particular agendas.

Therefore, time was of the essence to close the case and for the DSU to have any chance of prompt further promotion.

He sat down in a chair in the front row as Wills took to the floor.

Where Wills excelled was simply being damned good at his job. He was an excellent detective by anyone's standards, with hardly an unsolved case to his name.

He was happiest when taking the lead in working cases. Wills also accepted that his current position would likely be the pinnacle of his career ladder. He was happy with that. Not being a politician like Smilie, he knew he'd most likely struggle in that role.

Like Merriman, he was one of the old-school coppers that kept abreast of the times. Unlike his junior, DI Peterson, Wills' focus was on understanding how the latest science, methods, and thinking could help him catch criminals.

Wills also knew how to get the best out of people and help them excel at what they did. He was friendly, but not overly so. He knew there had to be a balance of relationships. Everyone in the station respected him and most liked him.

The only people in the station who ever disliked him were the temporary visitors he confronted in the interview room.

The DCI addressed the twenty or so officers in front of him, most of which made up this Murder Investigation Team.

"OK, here are the facts as currently known, with some stretch extrapolations. I'll take questions as we go through. So, just fire away, and let's not lose any thoughts. OK?"

Most of the audience nodded.

"At approximately 2100, on 2nd March, witnesses heard two loud noises, in quick succession, coming from the residence of High Court Judge, Charles Anthony Davidson, at 22 St. Saviour Mews, Bishops Town. The report was called in at 2112."

"The noises, while loud, were not excessive. The missing minutes were due to the neighbours being unsure if they should call the police or bother such an important person. Most likely, they didn't want to disrupt their TV programme until the advertisements," he opined the latter.

"Since this address was a senior member of the judiciary, dispatch prioritised the shout. Fortunately, a patrol car with two PCs was in the vicinity and directed to attend. They arrived at 2124."

"The officers were unable to get a response to the front door. They then searched around the house. One officer found an open door at the rear of the house and a broken pane of glass in an opened side window. This suggested a forced entry."

"The duty sergeant immediately approved them to enter the house via the wide-open rear kitchen double door."

"They found the judge in his living room, slumped in a large winged armchair. He had a wound to the chest and another to the centre of his forehead. One police officer checked for signs of life while the other called the local duty doctor, ambulance, and paramedics. Death was confirmed at 2205 when the duty doctor arrived."

"While waiting for the medical services, the two officers checked the house for signs of an assailant still being on the premises but found none."

"Our lot was immediately called out. SOCO arrived soon after. The two constables stayed on site to ensure no contamination of the crime scene."

"Detective Sergeant Barrie Sykes was the first of the Major Investigation Team to arrive on the scene; at 2201. He ensured the site was sealed, performed a preliminary investigation, and kicked off necessary background checks. Detective Inspector Terry Hansen arrived some minutes later, as did I. I then took control of the investigation."

"Due to the potential sensitivities of the murder, DCI Wills contacted me. I arrived at 2240," interjected DSU Merriman.

Wills nodded an acknowledgment to his boss and then carried on.

"We notified the coroner, and the Home Office Registered Forensic Pathologist, Dr Ajith Buddhi, attended the crime scene at 2252."

"The elderly live-in housekeeper, Mrs Marjory Taylor, returned to the house at 2235hrs. She's a long-serving employee of more than thirty years and was out at bingo with her friends when the murder occurred. Her alibi was confirmed, actually twice, by different officers."

"She was in shock and had to be sedated by the attending doctor."

"Mrs Taylor later confirmed that the judge had an evening ritual of smoking a cigar while listening to classical music and catching up on the daily news. He always had a wee dram, as they say on the other side of the wall up there."

"It is reasonable to assume that any assailant, with the minimum of research, would know this," he added.

"The victim had a wound to his chest, just left of centre. There was a second wound to the centre of his forehead. It was later determined both wounds to his chest and head were 19mm calibre, fired from the same gun. The chest shot was through the centre of the heart."

"There was no gunshot residue on the victim, so the shots were made from several feet away. The accuracy of the shots, even from that range, suggests a professional kill; by an expert."

"The gun has so far not been recovered. It is reasonable to assume the killer removed the weapon from the crime scene and the surrounding area. In my opinion, another reason why this was a professional hit."

"The killer entered the locked house via the study at the south side of the property. And for those of you who were not in the Scouts, that's the left-hand side if looking at the building from the front."

There were scout jokes and a lot of 'dib-dibs' shouted out, accompanied by three-finger salutes from the audience at this sarcastic joke'ette.

Merriman stared poker-faced at the speaker.

These briefings were hard going for everyone. Wills knew the death of a judge, actually, any death, was serious business. He also knew from experience that keeping the team engaged in light-hearted banter helped keep their attention.

The DCI continued. "The killer broke a pane of glass to the right of the double casement window from his perspective. He then opened the window and made his entry."

"How do we know it was a man?" asked a female voice from the back.

"Ah, good question from our newbie to the team, and great to have new blood joining us. Everyone, please welcome PC Lesley Sherrard. Now you lot, be nice."

Wills waited a few moments for the hand-waving and chatter with the new member to subside. He raised his voice over the talking. "OK, OK, enough. Make your introductions later."

"Back to the question. We are working on the following assumptions. This was a contract kill due to the professionalism of the murder. And if that assumption is correct, it is more likely to be a male. Saying that, we need to keep our minds open to this being a female."

The policewoman smiled and nodded. At the back of the room, someone sang a few lines from an old song, "and the female of the species is deadlier than the male."

Wills ignored the song, originally from the Rudyard Kipling poem of the same name.

He continued. "Once in, the killer crossed the study and made his way into the hall via the study door, which he closed behind him."

"He then crossed the hall and entered the living room, where the judge was sitting. The living room door is directly opposite the study.

The killer shot the judge twice. The newspaper he was reading was still in his left hand, and the cigar was still in his right."

"The killer left the house via the kitchen at the rear of the house into the large garden. The kitchen door was unlocked from the inside. The housekeeper confirmed it's always kept locked. However, the key is always kept in the lock on the inside since it was always being lost."

"We believe the killer made his way over the back patio and walked down the gravel path down the side of the large rear lawn. He would have exited the property via the side gate, which can be readily opened from the inside."

"There's a road at the back and another on the north side of the property where the side gate is located. Apart from the front gate and drive, and entrance path, a six-foot wall runs around the property."

"The wall could easily have been scaled, but if that were me, I'd have gone for the gate. Jumping over a wall would attract attention. It would also have risked injury. Professionals don't do risk!" He emphasised the last sentence.

"Oh, and as an FYI, there's a double garage next to that locked side gate. There's no evidence to suggest the garage was used for entrance or exit."

"This is an expensive neighbourhood with low housing density. Neighbours were asked, and no one saw anything."

"Saying that, the front door camera of a neighbour a few houses away, picked up an image of a man with an umbrella. It wasn't a clear image and couldn't be enhanced."

"That's the key highlights. Any questions so far?"

"Any fingerprints or DNA," asked PC Sherrard.

"Another good question. You're on a roll Sherrard and embarrassing the rest of you lot sleeping at the back," he commented jovially to boos and hisses from the rest of the audience. It was all good-humoured banter with each other and which included the new PC; a great way to get her integrated.

Holding his hand up, the DCI waited for the team to settle. "In answer, no fingerprints from anyone other than those expected, same with DNA, so absolutely nothing. And again, that's also why we think this was a professional job."

"Now, from smudge marks, we believe the killer was wearing gloves. Where the killer touched anything, it was wiped clean. Most pedantic. Now that could give us a clue as to character. As an example, the handles on both windows were wiped clean of fingerprints."

"Any other questions, or is everyone apart from Sherrard still focussing on the forthcoming weekend's excesses?" It was said with a smile, to try and break up the monotony of these briefings.

He needed to keep people talking and interacting with other. The two questions he planted with the new PC succeeded in creating the buzz he always cherished during these meetings. In his experience, it was important to challenge each other; and him.

At last, one of the team raised an unprompted hand and asked, "if the glass was broken on the window, wouldn't a neighbour or even the judge have heard it? And what's about fragment spread?"

"SOCO checked and tested for noise. Unlikely this level of sound would have been heard inside or out. The thick carpet, curtains, and soft materials in the room would have further deadened any noise. Heavy shrubbery would also have gone some way in dampening the noise outside."

"It would appear the cause of the impact to the glass was by a sharp object, perhaps a fine pointed hammer, or similar device. That would have further reduced the noise."

"On the other point you raised. The full-length curtains were closed in front of the casement windows, as always in the evening. There was glass on the inside, so definitely an external strike. Most of the glass was between the curtains and the left-hand side window looking from the inside; that is, the window used as the entry point. There were also fragments of glass on the carpet of the right-hand window, again from the living room perspective. There was no glass outside on the paving, amongst the stone chips, or elsewhere in the room."

A DC at the back of the room shyly raised his hand.

Wills pointed in his direction.

"Sir, I've been wondering if anyone could have seen what was going on from the road. Looking at the layout of the house, it looks like there's a clear view from the road?"

"Yep, good one Philips. That got me as well until I went through the motions of the break-in at the same time in the evening," interjected DI Terry Hansen. "DS Sykes and I checked this out. While I was standing by the access window, he couldn't easily see me from the roadway due to the overhanging foliage casting shadows and blocking the view."

Hansen continued. "The left-hand side of the house has a one-foot-wide line of stone chips along the side of the house wall, more than likely for drainage. There's a paved path running alongside, then a ten-foot-wide bed of large established shrubs that could do with being trimmed. The boundary to the next house is a six-foot-high brick wall."

He concluded with, "and, there's no chance to identify footprints on those surfaces."

Another hand was raised. "The CCTV umbrella man? Why would anyone be using an umbrella that evening? It was damp and cold, but not raining."

"Now that's a cracker of a question from DC Simpson."

Simpson nodded, with a smidgen of a blush for being called out.

"Simmo's raised a great point." Wills used the DC's station nickname.

"This needs to be followed up. Let's see if we can track this man. Simmo, since this is your shout, arrange to have the neighbourhood canvassed for other sightings and CCTV footage. Let's get on this one fast, in case the recordings get overwritten. Also, if this could be our man, we'd at least know the direction he took to get away."

"I know we've canvassed the neighbours already, but this is a new question to trigger memories. Report to DI Hansen on this."

The DCs sitting around him nudged and patted acknowledgement of well done, as Simpson's blush deepened.

Then to DS Sykes, Wills asked, "any update on the weapon used?"

Sykes stood up and faced the audience. "It's been confirmed that the weapon used was a SIG P226. Sound tests were done with the neighbours who heard the shots. We've pretty much determined that the pistol was suppressed. Another tick in the box for a professional hit," he nodded in affirmation to his DCI.

"As the boss mentioned, we've not been able to find the gun. We have no evidence that this gun has been used in the past. So that's a dead-end for the moment."

"Also, I've gone through unsolved murders, paying particular attention to those that lent themselves to being professional hits.

"There was a double murder four years ago in Liverpool, using the same type of gun as this. A drug dealer who was preying on someone else's turf was murdered via chest-forehead double-tap.

"One week later, the other dealer had the same double-tap happen to him. The same weapon was used in both those kills. That weapon was also a SIG P226. Again we believe it was suppressed."

"That gun was used in a later attempted murder and recovered. It was part of a shipment of guns seized in Morocco, which then disappeared without a trace. There's no further history to that gun until those killings."

"Now, that hit could have been a third drugs group wanting to take over or some other spat. However, our mates at the Drugs Squad advised there were no further takeovers. So, all bets are on the second guy not paying up as agreed. The word on the street was that he was given a lesson in honesty and integrity."

There was a titter of laughter and comments about honest drug dealers and hit men.

Sykes waited until the team settled down again before continuing. "There's another one, two years ago in Manchester, with the same MO; a forehead and chest double-tap with the same make of gun, and suppressed. I'm in the process of following the money for both these."

"Word on the street and from our friends up north is that those two could be attributed to someone called The Engineer. I expect some of you have heard of him, or her," he looked and smiled at Sherrard in acknowledgement of her point of being a woman.

DSU Merriman interjected. "For you others who've not heard of him, and let's call him a 'him' for just now, read the briefings about this contract killer."

The DSU looked back to Sykes to continue.

"There are quite many others that could very likely be attributed to The Engineer, but we cannot be 100% sure. So, we agreed it's best I focus on a couple of certainties and not get led down a wrong route."

"And one last thing. The reason why he's called The Engineer is that he fixes people's problems. He's meticulous in his research and planning, and damned good at what he does."

He looked at Wills, signifying he'd finished.

"Good report, DS Sykes," replied Wills, again taking to his feet.

"Any questions for DS Sykes?"

Without any takers, he asked Sykes, "do you need any help tracking the money side?"

"Not at the mo', sir, but I'll shout if I do."

DCI Wills gave a questioning look to his DSU. After a pause to confirm what was being non-verbally said, Merriman also stood up then said, "I need a coffee. Let's resume in fifteen minutes. Then we can go through where we are with our suspects."

It was at this time that Merriman took the call from Inspector Turnbull from the scene of the doctor's death.

****

Detective Inspector Terry Hansen took over the next session of the briefing. His part was to lead the team through the suspects; their alibis, motives, and status.

He couldn't remember when anyone last used his christened name, Terence, apart from his mother. When he heard the word 'Terence' from her, he knew he was in trouble for something or other. Otherwise, he was Terry to her as well.

He was younger than both of his bosses, being in his late thirties. He also liked to keep fit. Having boxed and won some inter-station medals, he'd the personal respect of the people sitting in the room. He was also rated by all as a quality detective.

Being younger and less experienced, he wasn't as comfortable as his boss standing in front of this large group. He always admired Wills' natural of-the-cuff banter. Terry had to prepare, practice and practice since this could be a hard audience.

(If only he knew that Wills' of-the-cuff banter, was equally well-rehearsed)

So, armed with his script, Hansen stood up, faced the terrifying audience, and started.

"Top of the list is our dearest friend Mr Anthony Barker, better known as Tony. For some who'd fallen foul of him, he's got a daft nickname 'Nailer'.

Some of the most raucous of the team booed reference to the name.

The initial few minutes of any session he gave, always made him nervous. Starting with the reference to 'Nailer' Barker helped him get through that first part with the audience. Now, hopefully, he could settle into his stride.

Once they'd sufficiently calmed down, he carried on.

"Clearly, a lot of you know this man, at least by reputation. He's graced our humble station on many occasions."

 "Sadly, we've never been able to enjoy his company for more than a few hours. His brief's well versed at extracting his client from our little chat'ettes."

Hansen had warmed up. Now more relaxed, he talked without reading his script verbatim.

"Our Mr Barker is a major player in organised crime and has his itsy-bitsy fingers in almost everything illegal in the city."

"Or rather, allegedly," Merriman added, ensuring the correct process.

"Of course, sir."

Taking a breath after the big boss' point, he continued what he'd prepared.

"He was being tried on two counts of murder dating back almost three years. The killings were done using his favourite weapon, a nail gun, from when he worked as a 'chippie' in the building trade.

His then-girlfriend was a witness to the dual killing. She is key to the CPS' case against him."

"The deceased was presiding over that case, which has now collapsed. Great news for Barker, bad news for us good guys. The case against him was and still is, pretty much clear-cut. Whoever killed the judge did him a favour."

"Questions so far?" asked Hansen.

There were none, but a lot of chat around the room taking Barker's name in vain.

Once the audience settled, he continued. "The case was at the stage where all evidence had been presented and argued from both sides. Barring any last-minute additions, closing arguments would have already been delivered by now, with the jury going through their deliberations."

"No one expected those deliberations to last long. With our eye-witness to the murders, supported by strong forensics, the case was looking bad for Barker, and he knew it. He was about to be put away for a long time."

Wills stood up again and turned to address the team, to make a point, before Hansen continued.

"This means a re-trial with a new judge. The good news is that the CPS is expediting that re-trial. While this is going on, that slimy toad is walking the street with a big smile over his gob. Worse still, having heard the witness testify, he now knows her damming evidence. She's now in even more danger."

"She's still in protective custody and outside his grasp. She needs to stay that way. Given the chance, she'll be next."

Wills turned back to Hansen to carry on.

"Now," continued Hansen, "Barker has a solid alibi for the judge's murder. Some of you out there, working with Sergeant Evans, are going through all his known associates to see who might be a likely killer or know of one. We need names. Use your contacts on the street to support them."

There were groans from several of the audience.

"Yes it's tedious, but it's police work, so enjoy."

With a sneaky grin, he added, "I so miss doing that stuff, it made me the copper I am."

The groans changed to banter with the presenter that he should join them.

He was comfortably on a roll now.

Hansen carried on. "No one, so far, has come to light from that line of inquiry, but we still have to make sure. If we can identify the killer, and get to him, or her, we'll have the bugger."

"And as the boss and Sergeant Sykes said, it's looking more and more like a contract killing. That means outside his organisation. So, it'll be almost impossible for us to pin it on him unless someone squeals."

"Following the money is another avenue we have to follow. The problem is that since most of his money is stuffed into his various proverbial mattresses, it's gonna be tough. But again, if we could find something, or he made a mistake, we'll have 'im."

"Right! The next favourite in the frame is Alan Forrest. He's the nephew of his housekeeper and the judge's handy-man-cum-gardener. A carpenter by trade, Mr Forrest has worked part-time for the judge for many years. They both got on reasonably well. In case you're thinking if there is any link to Tony Barker from their common trade, there's nothing to link them at the mo."

"Forrest has minor form for drug dealing and a couple of counts of drink-related GBH. He is also known to like the gee-gees. He's a bookie's dream since he always picks the dobbins. He was initially a possible suspect since he had open access to the property."

"However, his alibi checked out. He'd been at his local pub, the George and Dragon on Pembroke Street, three miles from the crime scene. He was playing in a darts tournament that started at 2100hrs, which was when the murder took place. He arrived at the pub around 2000hrs, to warm up for the match. The 2-3 minutes comfort breaks he took, wouldn't have given him time to do anything. Even a one-mile run is not much less than four minutes.

So, he's in the clear."

"The housekeeper was eliminated as a suspect since she'd been out with friends from late afternoon until 2235hrs. Anyway, she's no motive and has been a close and loyal employee. While she's well looked after in his will, she was especially well looked after during his life."

"And for those of you looking at other old cases where guilty parties had threatened the judge, we still need to progress that line of investigation. Others are likely to come up since the judge has tried and put away many bad-uns."

"There'll be a lot of grudges out there and happy people now he's dead. One of them could even have worked with Barker to settle a grudge and get paid at the same time."

"Any further questions?"

Nothing came from the audience. Hansen then looked to his bosses, Wills and Merriman.

Merriman stood up, faced the audience, and said, "Meeting over, let's get to it."

10. LURED

That afternoon, DI David Peterson, DS Audrey Bhatia, and PC Evelyn Cameron brought Jennifer Graham to the police station. They planned to interview her as a prime suspect in the death of Doctor Peter Hardcastle.

From Jennifer Graham's perspective, this was an innocent visit to the station to help them. However, Jennifer was also experiencing mixed feelings.

There was great sadness and fear at the thought of going through the evidence of his murder.

On the other hand, she had to admit feelings of elation. She was revelling in being directly involved in helping the police solve a real crime! And be able to help the police find the killers of her friend.

All evidence related to Jennifer's observations and suggestions had been sent over to forensics. As the morning progressed, the results that had come back so far had all validated her comments.

Both detectives believed she knew too much about what happened to the doctor.

Peterson took Bhatia to one side, "these can't all be coincidences?" he said, with the intonation of a question.

"I know guv, but she looks like such a nice lady, polite, helpful. Can't imagine she'd be involved."

As an afterthought, she said, "Saying that, she could be playing us."

"Agreed, so let's see where this takes us. If she's what I think she is, you never know …" He left the unfinished sentence in the air, thinking there might be more to her than meets the eye. He wondered what else she might have been up to.

If she's playing us, what's her game?'

The interrogation of Miss Graham required a formal interview room.

Unfortunately, the duty sergeant advised that all the interview rooms were busy. They were all booked out immediately after the morning briefing on the Judge Davidson case, which was taking priority.

While it was almost certain, in everyone's minds, that Tony Barker was guilty as sin, they still had to go through due diligence. Another line of investigation might even open up.

In court, any decent barrister would ask about other lines of investigation. If there were none, that would look bad for the prosecution. The defence could argue the police were out to get Barker. Hence, all rooms were booked out, with interviews across multiple lines of enquiry.

Jennifer waited with PC Cameron in the police station reception area while DI Peterson and DS Bhatia went off to find their boss, DCI Wills.

They found Wills in his office where they explained the circumstances that led to them bringing this suspect down to the police station. They needed his help to free up an interview room or suggest an alternative.

"Guv, there's no interview room available, and I can't use an office in case this turns formal as I expect it will. Any ideas on what we can do with her in the meantime? She's playing a Miss Innocent game. I want to play along and keep her sweet."

"Stick her in a meeting room or empty office with a female PC until a room becomes available," suggested Wills. "In the meantime, get an expedited search warrant to release the professor's file on her. If she's what you think she is, we need to understand what makes her tick."

"Already in process. The request is being typed up as we speak. It'll be with you shortly. I'll get it walked up to the Super for his counter signature and over to the duty judge."

What Wills liked about Peterson was when focussed on a case, he was like a dog with a bone and wouldn't let go; until completed.

In this case, Wills' decades of experience helped him already see what was coming and take proactive steps in navigating the processes. Wills was a cautious officer and sometimes had to reign in the inspector's exuberance. Sometimes Peterson's instinct could get the better of him.

"Don't interview her before we see that file," cautioned the DCI. "Let's see what insight the dead doctor can give us. From what you've said, she sounds sharp, so we'll need every edge. Let's use that file to see how we blunt her. Perhaps there's something in that file that might give us an idea why she'd want to kill him."

"Also, what's her agenda with seemingly wanting to help us? And, you're right, it's too strange?"

"I'll bet you it's all about him abusing her, and this was her revenge," responded the DI.

"Not going to take you up on that bet," the DCI said, agreeing in principle.

"Even though that thought's going through our minds, let's keep them open, eh?" he cautioned the DI and DS.

The Peterson and Bhatia nodded in agreement.

At that moment, the request for the file on Miss Graham was brought in by an admin for his signature.

Wills signed the document and handed it over. The DI followed his sergeant out of the office. Before Peterson closed the door, Wills reminded him, "David, don't forget, when you get the warrant, first share the file with me. I want to know what she's all about before we interview her. Let's go through this together, eh?"

The DI turned round to face his DCI. "Of course, sir."

As they walked back to his office, Peterson said to his DS, "find a comfortable room and leave her there with a female PC. How's about the PC who came with us and now sitting with Miss Graham? Cameron, I seem to remember?"

"Right guv, I know her. She's a good'un. She'll keep an eye on Miss Graham. I'll ask the duty sergeant if we can have her help for a few hours."

"We need to keep that Graham girl on side until she spills," Peterson reminded the sergeant.

"Guv, she's not a girl, she's a woman, well into her twenties," the DS corrected her boss with a sigh. "If she was a girl, she'd be underage, and we'd need an appropriate adult."

Despite his foibles, the DI respected Bhatia, and they had a good relationship.

So she felt empowered to correct the old policeman.

"Bhatia, I'm not blind." He pointed to his grey hair. "At my age, she's a girl." He replied with a smile, not at all offended by her chastisement.

DS Bhatia glanced up at the ceiling and said nothing. Bhatia was fond of the old bugger but still wondered when this dinosaur was going to retire. Peterson sometimes still lived in the 80s and 90s.

"Give her anything, within reason, that she wants. Let's keep this 'girl' happy," said the DI to his sergeant. He grinned when emphasising the word 'girl'.

"To me, she's boasting about this. With any luck, we'll catch her out and close this case today."

He made the sign of a tick, meaning another one quickly closed. It would be excellent for his closure figures and help keep Smilie off his back.

"Right'o guv," said the DS. "Once an interview room frees up, I'll find you."

****

Behind reception, the duty sergeant advised DS Bhatia that only the large team meeting room was free.

"Sit her at the back away from the information on the judge's case."

He knew the PC would be sitting with her, so all would be OK. The information on the whiteboards could not be viewed from that distance.

Bhatia walked to the waiting area and said, "sorry to keep you so long."

Jennifer smiled an OK.

The sergeant shouted over to PC Cameron, who was still sitting with Miss Graham, "you're with DS Bhatia and DI Peterson this afternoon."

"Yes, sergeant."

Bhatia pushed open the un-clicked security door and held it open for PC Cameron and Jennifer to go through.

As they walked along the corridor to the lift, Bhatia said to Jennifer, "Hey, while the big bosses aren't around, please feel to call us by our first names. I'm Audrey, and the constable is Evelyn. We're all girls here."

After saying that, Bhatia inwardly smiled at her own use of the word 'girls', when she should have used women. Just a short time earlier, she was jokingly chastising her boss for the very same thing.

Bhatia was doing her best to keep Jennifer sweet and on side. Not that Jennifer gave any hint of not being supportive.

The DS continued the charm offensive. "It's been a horrible morning for you. We really appreciate you coming down to assist us with this case. My bosses, DCI Wills and DI Peterson, and I are so looking forward to your help."

The three of them took the lift to the third floor. En route, Audrey asked, "can we call you Jennifer, or do you prefer Miss Graham?"

"Jennifer is fine."

"Is there anything you need?"

"Water with fresh lemon would be nice," said Jennifer. She disliked the city's tap water. The lemon took the edge of the chemical taste.

"Aunt Doris is from Dorset. She hates the tap water here. Living with her, I've become used to filtered water for drinking and tea. I hope that's not too much of a problem?"

Jennifer hesitated, and finally asked, almost apologetically, "could I have a sandwich or something, I'm really hungry. I missed lunch to come down here and the nice inspector said he'd sort something out. I hope it's not a problem?"

"No probs, better still, how's about a burger and fries?"

"Oh no," replied Jennifer with a look of disgust. "Yuck. Do you know what goes in them?" she said rhetorically, screwing up her face in mock disgust.

"Any preferences?" asked the PC, knowing the job of getting food for Jennifer was about to come her way.

Jennifer replied, "just a simple chicken sandwich would be lovely, but please, not with reconstituted chicken."

"Breast or thigh is equally fine," she followed up, trying to be as flexible as possible.

She knew people thought she was a fussy eater. However, she knew what she liked; and she did not like fast food.

"Of course," put in Audrey Bhatia.

Then to the PC, she asked, "Evelyn, could you please arrange the drink and the sandwich?"

The PC inwardly sighed. She wondered where she could get fresh lemon juice in the station.

Even worse, the staff canteen didn't do real food. Her sympathies were with the suspect. She'd also have loved some decent food in the station.

However, most of her colleagues only ate food that came with chips, or fries and lashings of tomato sauce to offer some form of taste.

"Could you take her to the back of the team meeting room, while I sort out an interview room," said the DS to the PC. She smiled at Jennifer, then left.

PC Cameron took Jennifer into the meeting room and sat Jennifer at the back. She wondered if it was OK for this civilian to be in this room. There were still a lot of pictures and imagery at the far end of the room. However, from where they were, nothing could be read, viewed, or interpreted.

In any case, she was told to take her to this room. Despite her reservations, this was an instruction from two sergeants, so it was bound to be OK. The PC would only be leaving her for a few minutes anyway. The local delicatessen was just around the corner.

"Will you be OK while I sort out your drink and a spot to eat?"

Jennifer nodded enthusiastically.

The PC hurriedly left.

11. STUNNED

As she entered the team meeting room, Jennifer noticed all the information from the earlier meeting on the whiteboards. There were pictures, comments, bulleted actions, and flow diagrams of what looked to be an investigation.

A real live case? Surely not?

It intrigued her. Unfortunately, she couldn't make out the detail from where she sat. She was drawn to the front of the room. Her investigative mind overcame caution, and she felt compelled to go over there.

Standing in front of all the information, she immediately realised this was a real case on display. Jennifer stood there, awe-struck, while she absorbed all that detail.

She walked back and forward in front of all that information, thinking, *'this is too good to be true, it's so exciting!'*

This was so much better than the crime programmes she loved to watch on TV and read about. She revelled in this real and live murder investigation. It was all laid out and organised down to the tiniest detail. Jennifer's elation grew as the case unfolded before her eyes.

Then she started to get confused. She began to wonder why the direction of the investigation wasn't following the evidence; or at least in part. It started to frustrate and confuse her that it wasn't making sense.

It must be her. What was she doing wrong?

After all, this was the work of many experts, and she was a mere layperson. She started to question her interpretation of what she was seeing.

What was she missing?

She went through it again. It still didn't make sense. Then it occurred to her that perhaps she had to question whether the professionals were actually on the right track.

When she did, it started to make sense.

At that point, DS Sykes entered the meeting room to sanity-check some information from today's earlier meeting. He saw Jennifer with his back to him, pacing back and forth in front of the whiteboards. She was nodding and shaking her head while staring intently at the evidence.

He walked over and said to her in a friendly, colleague sort of tone, "hi, not seen you here before. I'm involved with this case. Can I help you?"

He was also validating if she was authorised to be in this room.

Jennifer turned around and gave him a wide smile that immediately disarmed any concern he might have. She gave the air of being perfectly natural there, which was confirmed by her reply.

"Hi, I'm Jennifer," she said looking up at him. She barely came up to his chin; her 5ft 4in, to his 6ft 1in.

"Audrey, sorry DS Bhatia brought me here. I'm assisting DCI Wills and DI Peterson on another case."

Realising she's in job, Sykes relaxed a little, although still cautious. Being more at ease, he saw her properly for the first time. He liked what he saw.

She wasn't actually film star pretty, but very pleasant on the eye nonetheless. However, it was her open, friendly expression that warmed him to her.

She wore no make-up that he could see, not that she needed any.

Skyes responded with, "Sergeant Barrie Sykes, how do you do."

They shook hands.

He wondered if he was being too formal.

She liked the look of this policeman and his guarded approach. She liked old-school. He had a kind face and an open smile that included his eyes, and she liked that.

'*This sergeant is definitely arresting*,' she inwardly smiled.

She didn't like pretty-boy, magazine-handsome men. Her experience with them wasn't good. They were more interested in themselves and what they could get out of any relationship, than contribute.

When she'd gone out with that kind, there was always that dancing around the topic of sex and the expectation of engaging in it. Why couldn't men just relax?

His sort of rugged'ish, comfortable appearance and relaxed demeanour, warmed her to him.

'Here is a gentleman," she mused.

She looked him straight in the eyes and very pleasantly said, as she pulled her long brown hair back, "what a coincidence that someone working this case would come in."

Seeing her welcoming manner, and from what she'd said, he was expecting a compliment on the investigation. Perhaps she might use that comment as a chat-up line, to which he wouldn't have objected.

However, what he got instead, took him aback.

"I don't understand your line of thinking."

"Pardon?" was all he could say.

Recovering, he followed up with, "I wasn't thinking anything, I just asked if I could help."

Looking at her, he was actually thinking a lot, but he wasn't going to tell her that.

"No, no, sorry. Not you personally," she half apologised.

"It's good you came along. I was struggling with this case here."

"Glad I could be of help," he jokingly responded.

"It's just that from what I can see from all this here, some of the conclusions are wrong. Also, at least one line of enquiry is missing." Her widened dark brown eyes with raised eyebrows also questioned the evidence as she spoke.

He'd started to take a shine to this young woman but was taken aback by her directness. As an active member of the team involved in this case, he'd a vested interest in the work that had gone into building the case.

All the evidence and conclusions in this investigation were the team's baby. Being part of that team, Sykes was naturally protective of their work. This woman was calling their baby ugly.

"What do you mean?" he said a bit too defensively, which he quickly regretted.

Sykes was becoming concerned about the real reason for her being there and questioning this case. This woman had challenged him and the team after only a short view of the evidence. Even though all the evidence was visibly laid out in front of them, she made these comments without explanation. That wasn't possible; unless she'd been briefed in advance.

It was starting to smell of Smilie or someone further up the command chain circumventing the team.

The realisation struck; she was one of those know-it-all 'consultants'. He and the team had previously worked with various members of this breed.

In his mind, some of these types were useful, such as profilers. Others, at best, added little value. At worst, they were a time-wasting distraction. They'd ask questions and make suggestions that took them down ratholes, creating added work.

The thought of this woman being in the latter somewhat cooled his ardour. He did, however, stay polite and professional, definitely more formal, and now very cautious.

If Wills had been informed, why hadn't he told the team at this morning's meeting?

What was even more worrying was the thought that this woman had been brought in by someone even higher.

Surely not!

However, they all knew that Smilie was getting it in the ear from the Chief Super.

Even worse, was the mention of that old codger, Peterson. Hansen would go ballistic if he thought Peterson, via, or along with this woman started interfering with their case. He'd have to give Hansen the nod about what was going on.

She interrupted his thought process with a response to his earlier question.

"Since it's obviously an inside job, I was just wondering why you aren't following up on that line of investigation. Shouldn't you be questioning employees or family about who helped the killer and why?"

"What are you talking about!"

Sykes couldn't keep up his anger as she innocently looked at him. He again regretted his terse, over-defensive response.

"Ah, that's why I was confused. So, you really missed the whole point. Now all of this makes more sense. Thanks for clarifying."

He was having difficulty coming to terms with what she was saying. There was no hint of gloating as she politely advised him the whole team had made a mistake. He couldn't identify any hint of deceit that she might be playing some sort of game with him.

He was even wondering if this was one of those spy-in-the-camera things, and shortly someone would pop out and shout, "gotcha." He had to look around, just in case. He then felt a bit stupid thinking that.

Whatever was going on with her, he was hooked. "I'm sorry Miss, you're going to have to explain yourself," he said, trying to be as calm as possible.

"Yes, yes, of course," she replied. "I was looking at the information you have here. Now, while it's all there, I think you've misinterpreted some of the data. You've missed that this was an inside job, or perhaps someone inside was working with the killer."

Now he was no longer warm to her. She wasn't even questioning if any of the information might be wrong or missing. She was challenging over a hundred years of combined murder policing experience, and some of the best detective brains in the country!

"And what did we miss, that you so quickly identified?" he said tersely, arms folded, looking down at her.

And she did as requested, without any emotion, just formally and professionally, as they did in the crime scene investigation programmes she so loved.

"The full-length curtains were closed and there were glass fragments between the broken window and the curtain. However, if someone came in, surely some fragments would have been walked in? There were none."

When she was going through crimes with Peter, he hated going into such detail. It was the detail that so many of the programmes and books overlooked, which needed to be explored.

However, with this policeman, she could see he was interested in the detail. So, she was happy to describe the finer points. And, she felt she could talk 'crime' with him. He was interested in hearing what she was going to say.

Unfortunately, in her enthusiasm to explain, she didn't catch his defensive demeanour.

Then she highlighted another point of evidence interpretation.

"There is glass on the room side of the unbroken window; that is the window on the right side looking from inside the house. The full-length curtains are very close to both windows. None of the glass should have strayed there. That could only have happened if someone from inside the house pulled the right-hand curtain to one side and opened the right-hand window."

"That person then leaned outside and broke the window; to imply the breakage was from the outside."

Sykes stared at her, open-mouthed.

Without any response from Sykes, she continued.

"Also, why was the room door closed after the killer walked through? If no one was in the house, why would the killer take time closing the door and risk making unnecessary noise?"

Jennifer was on a roll now. "Looking around the room with the broken window, clearly the housekeeper was fastidious. Almost, but not everything is perfectly in place. Look at this photograph. That brass elephant ornament is out of alignment on the mantel place; I think that's something worth checking out."

"Oh, and by the way, don't forget to check the cleaning of each of those elephants. For example, if the elephant that is out of position was cleaner than the other one, it's an important sign. Similarly, if one elephant was wiped for fingerprints and not the other, could it have been used to break the window?"

Jennifer was enjoying herself as she could see the realisation building on Sykes' face as she went through her points.

"If I'd break into a room, I wouldn't clean the other window catch. In any case, as you've all confirmed, the killer was wearing gloves. So, why clean the window handles of fingerprints, and not any of the other handles?"

He was now leaning in and watching her intently as she talked through the evidence. His arms were no longer crossed.

She still hadn't finished. "Look here," she said pointing to the pictures of the kitchen.

"The end kitchen chair was nudged towards the doorway to the hallway. All the other chairs are up against the table. Could the killer have nudged it on the way into the house? It sort of suggests that the killer came in from the back door, perhaps in poor light?"

And as a final note, she said, "all the points I've highlighted are not conclusive individually, as I'm sure you're aware. It's just that if you put them all together, they put a different and more sensible slant to the story. And that's what was confusing me when you arrived."

Earlier she was hesitant about her statement to Sykes. On one side, she was sure of her analysis. However, going up against all those professionals and their experience cast doubts on her thinking.

Going through all this evidence again with Sykes and verbally sounding it out as she spoke, supported by her visual interpretation, she was certain she was right.

"Yes, it is definitely an inside job," she said half to herself and Sykes. "Not the actual killing though, but someone from within the household, or with regular access, helped the killer."

"I think they wanted this to appear to be from someone breaking in. They wanted you to look away from this murder being helped by an inside person."

"The killer didn't want to take chances of being caught during the break-in or having the authorities notified. That would have reduced the time available to make the kill. So, he needed easy access in and out."

"How do you know all this? Has someone briefed you on this case?" He was keen to know who'd engaged her.

"Not at all, just professional interest you might say. Just thought I'd nosey around while I was waiting at the back for Audrey," she answered matter-of-factly.

Sykes stood there gob-smacked. He now realised that she was not only good but brilliant.

As she went through and explained her justification for this different interpretation of the evidence, it all fell into place. While all of the MIT was aware of these points, they hadn't put them together in such a holistic flow. Basically, they had missed this crucial line of thinking.

How could this woman draw those conclusions purely from the information on the boards?

It amazed him. No, it stunned him!

"You beauty!" exclaimed Sykes. Almost forgetting himself, he grabbed the woman's head in his hands and was about to kiss her forehead before he stopped himself. "Oops, sorry, I got carried away."

She gave him an embarrassed 'it's OK' laugh. She liked him and was pleased he was happy with what she'd said. Sometimes people found her frankness disarming, even rude. He was so receptive to her ideas, even more so than poor old Peter.

"How on earth did you pick out your conclusions from just that?" he asked, pointing to the images around the room.

"It's so easy. I just enter the crime scene. Using evidence, I walk through the crime as it makes sense."

Peter explained that for people to understand how her brain works to solve crimes, she should take the video game analogy.

So, she explained as Peter suggested. "Imagine you're in a 3D video game, not just looking at the screen, but actually in it. When all the evidence and its interpretation are right, I can walk through how things have happened and see it all in my mind's eye."

"Now, if something is wrong, nothing works until I get more evidence or data. Often I walk through it and take a different doorway, so to speak."

"OK so far?" she asked Sykes.

He nodded yes.

"The mistake I initially made with the case was starting with the wrong conclusions your team had made. Think of it this way, I entered the video, halfway through, without a clear path to where I was. It confused the whole video. There were gaps, and it didn't make any sense."

"This happened before. The way to fix the video game, let's keep to the same analogy, is to force myself to think afresh. So, I had to go back and re-visualise everything from the very beginning. Going through my rationale again with you, helped me. Thank you."

He couldn't believe that she thanked him! This woman opened the whole case up again, and she thanked him!

"Jennifer, could you please come with me? I need you to meet my guv, sorry, my superior."

"Sorry, but I'm supposed to be waiting here for Evelyn Cameron and Audrey Bhatia. Do you know them? I really should wait, Evelyn went off to get me some lunch and I'm expecting her back any minute."

"OK," said Sykes. "In that case, please don't move an inch. I'll be right back with my guv. He needs to hear this!"

She nodded in assent.

Sykes needed to find Hansen before Peterson got his nose in with the woman and took all the credit for this new line of inquiry. At that, he dashed out.

Jennifer watched him rush away, hoping he'd be back soon. She'd like to spend more time with him; not only talking about crime.

There was nothing more to see at the front of the room, so she went back to her original seat. She sat there with a big grin.

It was a wonderful experience to have been able to immerse herself in a real crime!

12. IN THE LION'S DEN

PC Cameron had been longer than expected. The few minutes she thought the search for food and drink would take, turned into twenty. She was worried about the woman being alone in the meeting room for so long, so was in a hurry.

Cameron thanked Sykes for holding the corridor fire door open for her to rush through. She was armed with lemons and water plus a chunky, expensive, freshly made sandwich. With her hands full, she appreciated his help.

Sykes had just left the meeting room as Cameron was heading there. From what Jennifer had said about Cameron being involved, he thought about asking the PC for some background information but decided against it. He was in a hurry and could see she was too. And anyway, he suspected the constable wouldn't know too much about this consultant.

Jennifer, now satiated from her exciting crime rush with Sykes, was sitting at the back where Cameron had left her.

"Sorry for being late," she apologised to Jennifer. "There's nothing remotely resembling 'fresh' in this station, let alone food. Had to go to the delicatessen down the road. What a piggin' queue!"

"You must think I'm a fuss-pot."

"Nope, I think this station needs real food in its canteen," Cameron grinned.

She was relieved that Jennifer was still in good spirits.

"I was fine here. Detective Sergeant Sykes came in here a little while ago and kept me company. He's such a nice guy. Do you know him?"

"The PC replied, "yes, sort of, but only nodding terms, but I'd love to know him better," she winked.

"Me too." They both shared a conspiratorial laugh.

The PC mentioned that Sykes was a career officer in the degree fast-track programme. "The word around here is that he keeps his relationships outside the station. There's no station gossip about him being involved with anyone here, otherwise, I'd have known. We girls like to chat about them, a lot. And he's straight, so go for it girl. He's a good catch."

She regretted saying the last bit since Jennifer was a suspect in the doctor's case. But she was warming to the woman and beginning to believe that she was not a killing type; if there was a type.

The two women made further idle chitchat while Jennifer ate her sandwich.

Bhatia called Cameron on her mobile, "interview room two's free now. Could you please escort Miss Graham there? We're already here waiting and not letting anyone else in, in case we lose it."

After closing her call and now that Jennifer had finished eating, Cameron said to Jennifer, "we've now got a proper room for a chat. Let's head over."

"But I was asked to stay here?" said Jennifer referring to the request from Sykes.

"Don't worry, we'll all catch up in the room." She assumed that it was DS Bhatia to whom the woman was referring.

"That's OK then." Jennifer was relieved she wasn't letting Sykes down.

She followed the PC down the corridor to the interview room.

While they waited for PC Cameron and Jennifer to join them in the interview room, Bhatia asked Peterson, "any chance of a quick read of her file?"

"Not arrived yet."

"Guv, shouldn't we wait for her file as the boss said?"

"He's up to here." He held his level hand to his forehead. "With the judge's murder. He'll be glad we didn't interrupt him once we close this one quickly."

"Are you sure? The DCI was quite adamant."

"Bhatia, we're good," he insisted. "Get with the plan." In his mind, following the chain of command didn't apply to seasoned senior officers like him when they were right.

And he was right!

However, to assuage any further concerns from Bhatia, he followed up.

"Listen, Bhatia, she's been waiting for a while now, we need to catch her while she's ready to talk."

"Anyway, it's just a chat, isn't it, sergeant." Peterson said the last few words emphasising the discussion was closed.

When Jennifer and Cameron entered the interview room, PC Cameron took up her station at the back of the room by the door. DI Peterson was seated at the only table with DS Bhatia. He stood up, smiled, and warmly beckoned Jennifer to sit in one of the two chairs opposite them.

The twelve by fourteen feet, sparsely furnished interview room was one of the larger ones. It had a table in the middle with two chairs on each of the longer sides. On the table were two microphones on each of the longer sides. The recording system sat on a shelf on the opposite wall to the door.

Behind where the DS and DI sat, was a large mirror. Behind the mirror was a small viewing room, invisible to those in the interview room. The viewing room had a large shelf for taking notes and three chairs behind it. Audio from the interview room was fed into the viewing room via two speakers.

Jennifer was surprised and disappointed not to see the nice, tall policeman, Sykes, in the room. Cameron said he'd be there, and he was so easy to talk to.

DCI Peterson was nice enough but not as friendly. Jennifer could tell he was cool toward her.

She wondered what had changed his mind that he wasn't there. Then he'd been so keen for her to meet his boss. Maybe he was still coming?

Before she could ask where Sykes was, the DI said, "let's talk about the death of your friend." He slid over another glass of iced water with two halves of a lemon on a plate, "this OK?"

PC Cameron had the presence of mind to get a couple of lemons while she was out and handed the pieces of the second one over when she came in.

"Thank you."

Jennifer was worried about going through this again, so was keen to get this over with quickly. It was devastating to think about Peter being killed. No matter what, she was determined to go through this.

Those people needed to be arrested!

Peterson went through the usual pre-interview formalities. Jennifer declined representation.

'Why would I need representation?' she wondered.

It seemed a strange question to ask her when she was there to help them identify the perpetrators. She was surprised at the formalities. Perhaps it was just this old policeman's way.

DI Peterson opened the interview.

"Now, according to the housekeeper, you and the doctor often had heated discussions. You say he was your friend, so could you explain what these arguments were all about?"

She thought this question was also strange but answered directly and briefly so they could get back on track.

"I often get wound up when things don't make sense, and he helps me see why people can sometimes be stupid. Well, not exactly stupid, but when crimes are investigated, it's important to get the evidence right. Don't you agree?"

The DI responded, "absolutely, and that's why we're here."

Jennifer wanted the old policeman to get back on track. "Good, can we talk about the killers now?"

"Of course. You were correct, we checked the evidence as you suggested, and yes, we now believe, and agree with you, this was murder."

Jennifer gave him a relieved smile, "thank goodness, that's super to hear."

"So," said Peterson, "tell me how you know all this?"

It seemed a strange question to her. After all, the evidence was straightforward. So, she answered. "Same as you. I saw it as clearly as I'm sure you now can; it's just evidence after all."

The DI leaned forward, "so what was it that you saw?"

"I could see how at least two people held him and killed him. At least one was a strong person, most probably a man. He used the cushion to silence and hold him in place. The other secured the doctor, possibly knotting the throw at the back of the chair. Once secured, they simply injected him and waited for him to die."

94

Jennifer's face became sad and her eyes reddened. "His eyes were open. I saw a look of fear on Peter's face. I don't think he had a nice death."

As Jennifer thought more about what happened, she started to get visibly upset; tears grew and rolled down her face.

"Were you there when he was being murdered?"

"Of course not! They'd have killed me as well."

Jennifer started to cry. She was becoming confused with their questions which weren't making sense. It was almost like they were accusing her?

"Mr Robert Coleville told us that you both argued a lot. Did one of those arguments get out of hand?"

Then the realisation hit; they did think she was involved!

'It's actually me who's stupid!'

Jennifer wondered why she didn't see how this was playing out. With the approach the DI took and her knowledge of police procedures, she should have seen where this was going. However, she was so focussed on her agenda of going after the culprits, she missed the signs.

What was previously the nice DS, also started. "You know too much detail about what happened. There's no way you could know all this without being there. We think you are playing a game, teasing us with evidence, but it backfired. We know you were involved with the murder of Doctor Hardcastle."

Jennifer looked aghast at this woman, who, less than one hour before, was so pleasant and understanding. She didn't know what to say. She couldn't find the words to respond to the allegation.

Bhatia continued. "You said Dr Hardcastle was your friend. If he was, could you explain why you did this?"

Jennifer was shocked at her accusation. She sat there, not knowing how to defend herself, even if she could. Her mind had gone blank. She withdrew from the situation. It was like she was watching the proceedings from outside her body. She hadn't felt as bad as this for such a long time.

Peter explained what she was now experiencing was her body's coping mechanism for dealing with stressful situations like this. He could help her come out of herself when she felt oppressed like this. But he wasn't here now, and she couldn't go to him. She couldn't go to him ever again!

Panic hit her. She withdrew further from the situation.

Her friend had coached her to manage stress like this. He taught her techniques to extract herself from situations like this. By learning how to view stressful situations dispassionately, she could manage the emotions that often locked her down.

This was how she dealt with Peter's death and being in the room with him. Putting all her focus on examining the crime scene was how she could manage the intense pain and sadness she felt. And it worked; then.

But now, with both of them badgering her, question after question, she couldn't concentrate on managing her condition.

There was no way out.

"Or perhaps he wasn't your friend. Was he abusing you? Were you always arguing because you wanted him to stop?"

Jennifer could say nothing. Her sobbing became worse.

The DS continued in a more sympathetic tone. "It's OK, you can tell me. I understand. Men can be such shits. I know you got someone to help you stop him. The doctor, your doctor, and your friend, he abused your trust."

"He helped me," she managed to force out a barely audible whisper, almost choking through her crying spasms and tears.

The sympathy had left Bhatia's tone. She snapped the response, "who helped you?"

"Peter," she sniffed.

"Peter who?" Bhatia thought the mention of Peter, was her accomplice's name.

It was over for Jennifer. She could no longer speak as she just stared at her lap. Her vision blurred from the tears in her eyes.

As her mind was locking down, the voices faded into the background.

"You had help, who was it?" Peterson said loudly. "Who is this Peter?"

Jennifer continued to sob. She stared at her lap, avoiding eye contact.

She didn't handle confrontation well at the best of times. Now, with these people badgering her, it was awful. She hadn't felt like this since college; at least then she could walk out at any time.

They had her trapped there!

PC Cameron, who stood behind her during the interview, stepped forward and leaned down. She felt for the woman and put her arm around her shoulders. She tried to help Jennifer take a sip of water.

However, DI Peterson leaned forward and irritably waved the constable away.

Cameron looked disbelieving back at the DI, wondering why he couldn't see the state this woman was in. She looked back at the DI. She was angry and wanted to challenge him. Her career was on the line if she did.

"Sir…" She didn't know what she could or should say next.

"Constable! Your station now!" he ordered her.

Cameron hesitated.

She reluctantly stepped back.

The DI turned his attention back to Jennifer. "If you tell us who helped, it will go easier on you. So, who helped, and what was your part? Then we can finish all this."

Jennifer heard his voice, but no longer the words. She wanted to talk, to explain, but couldn't think straight. It was like her brain had closed down.

Seeing her reaction to facing the truth about her murdering the doctor, the DI knew they'd broken her down. And now, with his suspect in a weakened state, he could close in.

At that point, the door swung open, hitting the doorstop with a bang. DCI Wills stomped into the room and strode to the recording machine. He spoke into the mic while staring directly at Peterson. "DCI Wills entered the room at 1505. The interview is now terminated."

He stopped the recording machine.

Wills said to the PC, "please stay and comfort Miss Graham. The inspector and the sergeant are leaving the room. We are heading back to my office."

He turned to Peterson and Bhatia. "With me, now." He walked to the door, expecting them to follow him.

Bhatia went through the door and waited for her boss outside the doorway.

Peterson didn't move. He sat there, glaring at Wills, visibly fuming.

Bhatia didn't know what to do next.

"Now!" said Wills firmly to Peterson as he stood by the door. The DCI stared at Peterson, daring him not to follow him through.

Peterson said nothing, looked away, got up, and walked into the corridor.

Once outside, and barely able to control his anger, Peterson quietly said to his boss, "we had her. I was on the verge of closing the case. She was going to cop for this, and I'd have had her accomplice."

"Not here, my office. Now!" said Wills angrily.

Peterson backed down, biding his time until they were in private. He'd never seen Wills as angry as he was now.

The three of them walked briskly and silently to Wills' office.

Wills opened the door, "Bhatia, the DI and I are about to have a private discussion. Make yourself scarce."

Bhatia looked at her guv, who was staring at Wills and ignoring her. She then said to her boss' boss, "yes sir." She quickly left the scene.

Once in Wills' office with the door and blinds closed and in a tone of frustration and anger, Peterson verbally launched into an accusatory, "I told you, we had her! And now we've lost the momentum. You stopped that!"

He was overly aggressive to be respectful, but he was so livid with his boss that he didn't care.

"She'll now probably lawyer-up and that'll be the end of that!"

Wills said firmly in response, "you're right, I stopped it, thank god. Your clumsy cack-handed approach has potentially compromised this, and also the judge's case!"

Now it was his turn to show his anger. "I said, or rather gave you an explicit order. Before you interviewed Miss Graham, we needed to review the doctor's file on her. You ignored my request. No, my order!" he exclaimed at his subordinate.

Peterson made to respond, but Wills firmly raised his palm towards him as a sign to stop. "Now, before you do, or say anything further that you might regret, read this." He thrust Peterson a document with the other hand. It was the doctor's file on Jennifer. "And make sure Bhatia reads it as well."

"Once you've both read this, you'll realise why your line of questioning was a waste of everyone's time. Come back into my office with Bhatia in 30 minutes. Only then will I listen to anything you have to say."

"In the meantime, I've arranged for a car to take Miss Graham home."

"Thank you, Detective Inspector Peterson. You may now leave."

Peterson didn't know what to say. By the looks of Wills, he thought that right now, discretion was the better part of valour.

However, he'd read that damned file and show his boss that he was right after all.

****

Thirty minutes later, DI Peterson and DS Bhatia knocked on DCI Will's door. Wills waved them in and pointed to the two chairs on the opposite side of his desk.

They came in but didn't sit down. The two officers were not expecting to be there long.

Wills asked, "your conclusion after reading the file?"

A sheepish Peterson responded. "Sorry, sir. Agreed, she's not good for it."

Wills gestured to the DS that she should leave. He said to her back, "sergeant, close the door on your way out."

Wills waited until the DS left, and they were alone.

"Sit down Dave."

Peterson sat in front of his boss' desk. He then tried to justify his actions. "I could see this one getting away if I didn't close it. And how'd I know she'd have that condition?"

"There's following orders, and if you'd have done that, we'd not have the potential of being sued by an innocent woman. She was here thinking she was helping us, not a piggin' suspect!"

"Sorry, guv. I was following my gut."

The DCI snapped, "that wasn't gut instinct or even initiative. You blatantly ignored my orders! And to make matters worse, you put Bhatia in the firing line of any action against us."

Wills took a breath and calmed down. He knew Peterson of old and tried a more rational approach, even though he didn't feel like doing so. "Dave, please listen good. Could you imagine the field day the anti-police brigades would have on hearing about what happened here this afternoon?"

"Won't happen again, boss."

"Assuming you ride this one out, yep, it won't."

The DI said nothing further as the DCI grunted disapproval and nodded that he should leave.

As the DI stood up, Wills said, "have you thought of retiring? This is not the same police force you joined over thirty years ago. It's modern, tech-led, and even worse, it's in the public eye. If you haven't, then maybe you should."

At that, the DI walked out.

13. DAWNING REALISATION

After leaving Jennifer in the large team meeting room to await Bhatia's return, an excited Sykes rushed off to find his boss. He found DI Hansen giving instructions to one of the admin staff outside his office.

"Guv!" said Sykes excitedly as he hurried towards him. "Gotta' talk with you; urgently. It's about the judge's case."

"Gimmie a minute while I sort this out," as he explained what he wanted to the admin.

In the corner of his eye, Hansen could see Sykes desperately trying not to look impatient.

He teased the over-exuberant 'lad'. Again, he slowly explained the report to the admin. The admin was somewhat baffled by the extra effort Hansen was making.

"Guv!" exclaimed Sykes in frustration, knowing what the blighter was up to. "We don't have time."

Hansen looked up and acknowledged his readiness with, "you look like you've won the lottery lad."

"Even better, we've got a new angle to the judge's case," the sergeant blurted out. "And when you hear what I'm going to tell you, it's going to blow your mind. It did me."

Hansen was intrigued. He now regretted the time-wasting teasing of his sergeant. "OK, Sykes, I'm all ears, shoot."

"As discussed for the interview later today, I went up to the team meeting room to check some of the pictures of the judge's crime scene; where we had the briefing today."

"I know this. Take a breath and calm down. You're acting like a dog sniffing a bitch in heat."

He looked around, embarrassed at what he said. Good news, there were no women around who might take offence; today's political correctness sensitivities and all that.

The admin grinned at the DI's comparison of Sykes.

"Sorry." Sykes paused for a few seconds.

He continued. "There's one of those consultanty, criminology types in the team meeting room that the DCI or the Super have engaged; maybe even higher up the food chain."

"And?"

"She's working with Peterson, and when I went into the meeting room, she was going through our case. Cheeky sod, I thought. I was initially pissed off when I found her noseying around. It got even worse when she said we'd misinterpreted some of the evidence."

"Hope you put her in her place."

"No guv, couldn't do that. She was too nice to have a pop at."

"Let me guess, young, attractive?" he gave the eavesdropping admin a knowing wink.

"Guv!" exclaimed the exasperated sergeant. "OK yes, I liked her, but so will you when you meet her."

He paused to get himself back on track after Hansen's distraction. "Anyway, since she said the DCI's involved, I couldn't have had a go at her in any case. You never know, it could be the Super her who brought her in."

The DI nodded, encouraging his DS to continue.

"But then she explained it, and it all made sense. She's good, she's really good. No, no, she's piggin' brilliant. We need to get back there before Peterson comes along, finds out what she knows, and tries to take the credit."

"Why are you so worried about Peterson?"

"If she tells him what she told me and he goes up to Wills, or even Merriman, he'll not only take all the glory, he'll gloat that we didn't see it. You know what he's like."

"He's not as bad as all that, or at least sometimes anyway," Hansen commented with a grin.

Then back to the topic, Hansen asked, "what can she conclude from a load of pictures, diagrams, arrows, and notes? She's pulling your leg sergeant."

The DI was not convinced. He normally trusted Sykes' judgement implicitly, but what he said was a bit far-fetched.

"Honest guv, you need to meet and listen to her. She picked through all the evidence and proved it was an inside job. Someone with access to the house helped the killer get in. That means we've a new angle to get closer to who arranged the kill or put out the contract."

Hansen thought for a moment. If Sykes was right and this was a break, there's no way he'd wear Peterson taking the credit.

Even worse, if someone senior brought in this consultant, and her analysis was correct, politics would kick in. Then there was Peterson who might muddy the waters if he went to the higher-ups with the new information.

This all assumed what Sykes was saying turned out to be true.

DCI Wills was operationally running the show, but it was DI Hansen's team who were doing the bulk of the leg-work on the case evidence.

This was his baby!

"Go and bring what's 'er name to the DCI. In the meantime, I'll head over there and ask him what's going on."

Then thinking about the issue further, Hansen began to get annoyed. "He should have told me."

"Her name's Jennifer."

"Jennifer who?"

"That's all I got," responded his now more subdued sergeant. Sykes realised he'd dashed off blind to find his DI without thinking, barely even taking a breath. It wasn't a very professional image to make in front of his guv.

Hansen looked up to the ceiling in mock frustration, then laughingly said, "OK, off you go now, and no running in the corridors."

As he watched Sykes disappear down the corridor, he thought to himself that this fast-tracked sergeant might be his boss in a few years.

'*Heaven help us all,*' he inwardly grinned.

He liked the lad. Sykes was one of the good ones. The sergeant was the new breed of policemen and policewomen who would soon be the face of policing in this country.

Sykes arrived back at the team meeting room and found it empty. He phoned the desk sergeant and asked if there were any consultants in the building called Jennifer.

"Nope, none in today, let alone with that name."

Remembering that the consultant was working with Peterson and Bhatia and that Wills was involved, he went to Peterson's office. It was empty.

The admin outside told him that Peterson and Bhatia were interviewing a suspect in the doctor's case. She also said that Peterson had given explicit instructions not to be disturbed. What that meant was someone of his seniority or below.

Sykes was relieved that Peterson was tied up. He had time to find this consultant, whom he only knew as Jennifer. He wouldn't have interrupted the interview in any case. He didn't want to give Peterson a heads-up on the latest with the judge's case.

He concluded that the chances were the DCI also knew of her presence. In that case, he'd also know of her whereabouts. Perhaps she was even with him. So he thought it best he head over there and catch up with his boss and the DCI.

Hopefully, by then, Hansen would have already vented his frustration to Wills about using contractors on his case without telling him. Sykes could relax and avoid any fallout from being in the vicinity.

Wills and Hansen had both worked together for many years. Sometimes they had heated disagreements in private; this was acceptable. They never openly argued in public. Hansen respected Wills too much.

Sykes thought it unusual for Wills not to include the team in these procedural things, so he suspected Smilie's hand in this. But he'd keep that opinion to himself.

****

104

One of the admin staff knocked on Wills' door, then walked in after the DCI waived for him to come. The civilian staff member was holding several files that needed his attention.

Wills was on the phone, so he mouthed some words and pointed to the in-tray. The doctor's file on Jennifer was among those that now awaited the DCI's attention.

Once he'd finished his update call to Smiley, and before he could start on those files, he'd need to deal with DI Hansen who'd been waiting impatiently outside.

On his way over to the DCI's office and while awaiting his boss' approval to come in, his anger had been bubbling up.

Wills waived at Hansen to come in. His subordinate entered but didn't sit down. He could see the DI was fuming about something.

Wills knew Hansen could be a bit volatile, and seeing the DI's expression, his immediate thought was, '*who's wound him up this time?*'

He assumed he'd have to try and arbitrate another spat between his staff. It didn't take the DCI long to realise the direction where Hansen's anger was pointing this time, and that was himself.

Hansen's tirade started with, "why wasn't I told you and the Super hired one of those consultants on the judge's case? What's she doing? Is she working with Peterson on it?" He then finished with an exasperated, "and when were you going to tell me?"

Wills was rarely lost for words, and this was one of those occasions. So, he sat there saying nothing.

Hansen took his boss' silence as embarrassment for forgetting to tell him. Or even worse, Wills had been avoiding the issue. Come to think of it, that worried Hansen even more since his boss rarely behaved in that way.

Hansen continued, "and she's already gotten some strange ideas into her head about the case."

Wills recovered.

"What on earth are you blabbering on about? Have you been in the evidence room smoking ganja with the drugs team? It must be a good batch, coz you're talking bollocks."

The DCI then said jokingly, trying to calm the person standing in front of him, hands on hips, "if it's that good, hope you kept some for me?"

Wills added, "What consultant are you talking about?"

"Are you trying to tell me that you didn't hire a consultant for the judge's, or even the doctor's case?"

"Yep. I mean no. I did not hire a consultant for any cases."

"Then who hired her, and what's she doing here?"

"Let's start again," said the DCI. He held both hands up in a gesture for the DI to slow down and take stock of the situation.

Then grinning, Wills continued, "good afternoon, Mr Nice Calm DI Hansen, what can I do for you today?"

Wills quickly followed up with, "please, this time, take it from the beginning."

Now the wind had been taken out of his sails, Hansen relaxed. He sat down in the chair his boss pointed him to.

Hansen explained to Wills that Sykes had met the consultant in the team meeting room where earlier today they'd had their briefing on the judge's case.

Hansen started. "This consultant seemed to know everything about the judge's case. From the evidence we've got to date, she'd extracted some seriously contrasting conclusions compared to us."

"Here's the thing, if she is right, what does she know that I don't? And she had to have been briefed. Worse still, if it wasn't you who briefed her, who did? There's no way she'd have picked up on all her ideas without any background."

Hansen took a few breaths after that speech.

"And who was going to tell us that we might have to re-think our strategy. What's even worse, who else is involved? If not you, it must have been Smilie."

"Don't you mean Superintendent Merriman?" corrected Wills.

"Oops, sorry, yes. That just came out."

"Make sure it doesn't come out in different company, eh?" Wills warned.

Hansen then followed up with, "if she is talking shite," he emphasised the 'is', "what on earth is she doing here?"

"Now it's starting to make sense, it's not you," interrupted Wills, pointing to the approaching Sykes. He also showed signs of extreme agitation as he strode, almost running, toward Wills' office.

Sykes knocked on the door.

"Aha, so it's Sykes who's been smoking that pot downstairs."

They both looked at Sykes outside the door and laughed, easing the tension between them. A bewildered Sykes looked into the room.

Wills waved Sykes in, and he sat down next to Hansen.

"Right, Hansen's given me the heads-up on the consultant, so just hold on while I talk with the Super."

With his other hand held up for them to hold fire, he called DSU Merriman and asked if he knew about anyone hiring a consultant.

Merriman was intrigued and asked who the consultant was, where she was from and where she is now. Wills evasively said he'd get back to him once he tracked her down.

"Well, we now know it's not the Super. OK, Sykes, what do you know about her?"

"Just got her first name," said a sheepish Sykes. "Don't have anything else."

"Don't tell me, you fancied this woman and your hormones got the better of you," said Wills to a reddening-faced sergeant.

"That's what I said," interjected Hansen.

Wills said to Hansen in a joking conspiratorial sort of way, "I remember those days when I used to have hormones. Just used to bugger my thinking."

The two laughed, to Sykes' further embarrassment. There was no retort he could give back to them; without being rude anyway. And they were probably right in any case.

"So, that's it. Our top-performing, fast-track sergeant, has been knocked out of his stride by a woman," said Hansen to Wills.

Sykes' senior management was enjoying his discomfort. If only Sykes knew it, by winding him up, the earlier tension in the room between Hansen and Wills was being released; as was Hansen's initial anger.

"OK, OK, interjected Wills. Think the lad's had enough of us. We're senior policemen. So let's investigate where she is."

Then to Sykes, he asked, "what do we know?"

"Her name is Jennifer, and she's been working with Peterson and Bhatia on the doctor's recent death."

"So, let's start with finding out where those two are hiding," suggested Hansen.

"They're interviewing a suspect in the Doctor Hardcastle case sir," responded Sykes.

The DCI had a worrying thought and immediately called the front desk, put on the speakerphone, and asked, "who is DI Peterson interviewing, and where?"

"A suspect in the doctor's death, or rather now murder, called Jennifer Graham. She was waiting in reception. Then they took her to the team meeting room until an interview room became available."

The three of them looked at each other, and the realisation dawned. Not a consultant. Just someone off the street. And in their briefing room; alone!

Into the phone, he said, "so, a suspect in a murder case was left in a room full of delicate information on another case? Lovely," said Wills sarcastically.

He wasn't hiding his sarcasm aimed at those who thought it was a good idea to leave her, unattended, in the meeting room.

From the silence on the other end of the phone, they sensed the realisation hitting the desk sergeant.

Wills closed the line, leaned over, and knocked on the window to attract his admin.

The planners said his new office would be compact, and efficiently operational. Actually, it was just small. But at least he could knock on the window without getting up. So perhaps it was efficient after all.

The admin entered the room.

Wills challenged, "I asked that I'd be first to get Jennifer Graham's case notes from the doctor's filing system. Seems DI Peterson already has it and is currently interviewing her as a suspect."

"No sir. It's on your desk, as instructed," said the admin who quickly identified and picked it out of the files recently put in his in-tray. He handed it to the DCI. "Sir, this is the only copy and DI Peterson hasn't seen it unless you've shown it to him."

"Thanks, and I didn't, sorry, all fine."

The admin got the message and left.

As Wills scan-read through it, he soon realised that if Peterson was interviewing her as a suspect, there'd be deep trouble. And those involved, including him, could, as a minimum, be highly visibly embarrassed. This was serious!

After reviewing the file for about five minutes, Wills announced, "OK, here's the gist of what's in here. Basically, Jennifer Graham has a condition called Hyperphantasia. She's right at the top of what they call the spectrum. To make matters worse for her, she's also on the autistic spectrum."

"Never heard of Hyper Fantasy boss. Do you know anything, or is there some blurb in the file?" asked Hansen.

"It's pronounced hyper-fan-taz-ia," replied the DCI, pronouncing the syllables slowly. "It says here, 'people with the condition Hyperphantasia can imagine, picture-clear and highly detailed images in their mind. They're able to manipulate the imagery as if they were actually inside that picture.'"

"It gives an example of a house. 'They can imagine themselves walking through it. They can see, in their mind's eye, every part in detail, as they virtually look around inside. They have a spherical view of whatever they are picturing.'"

"So when Jennifer, oops Miss Graham, was seeing the pictures and diagrams on the boards in the meeting room, and she was saying that it was as if she was walking through it like in a video game, does that mean in her mind, she really was living it?"

"Yep, and there's more," said Wills. "When individuals high up in the spectrum of this condition describe some horrible incident, the imagery can be so strong, that to them it's happening there and then. It can be traumatic."

He continued, "So in Miss Graham's case, if she's made to re-live the death of her friend, Doctor Hardcastle, and without the right support, it could, at best, be traumatising."

"My god, is that what DI Peterson is up to?"

"Seems so," said the DCI.

"So, if anyone is going through the death of her friend with her, they'd have to be very gentle," interjected a concerned Sykes.

"Absolutely."

Wills continued. "Now, to add to her troubles, as I said, she's on the autistic spectrum. As you'll remember from the course last year, any discussion with her has to be sensitive to that condition."

"So, doubly hard for the interviewers. They'll need to proceed with extreme caution and be delicate. Ideally, it should be done in conjunction with a professional who understands this condition and works with autistic people. I really can't remember anything else from that course. I'll have to re-check my notes."

Sykes piped up, "Sir, I remember some of the key takeaways?" He said it question-like, checking if he was allowed to impart what he remembered.

Wills said, "shoot."

"So, as I remember, people with autism can have issues with communication, making eye contact, expressing themselves, sensitivity to sounds, touches, and smells, looking at or listening to people, and strange groups. It all stayed with me since it seemed such a tough place for people with that condition to be."

Hansen said to Wills, "this is why we love them university types on the force; he's like my personal walking encyclopaedia."

Then to his DS, he said, "Seriously, nice one Sykes."

"So if we go through any sensitive stuff with her, especially about her friend, the doctor, we'll need a shrink or some form of specialist present," summarised the DCI.

Wills then mused out loud, "if all this pans out, she's got the potential to be of some use to us in both cases."

110

Another thought hit the DCI. "What's about Malanga?" he asked referring to the criminal profiler they sometimes employed. "I seem to remember that she's a psychologist and might be able to help. Or at least she'd be able to point us in the right direction."

Wills pulled himself back to the urgent matter at hand. "Right, at least we know who and where she is and a little inkling of what she's about. However, we don't have time; the poor girl could be in trouble!

Wills stood up. "Let's head into the observation room and see what's going on before we jump to conclusions."

As the three entered the observation room, it was at the point of the interview when the constable was trying to help the woman while the DS and DI were in full flow.

As far as the interviewers were concerned, they were closing in on the suspect. They were looking for conspiracy to murder at least, as well as the naming of the co-conspirator.

To the three in the observation room, having briefly read the file and now with some understanding of its content, it was obvious to them that Peterson and Bhatia were trying to get a confession where none existed.

Their victim was an innocent. She was a harmless woman who was gullible enough to think she was helping them.

Conversely, it was very likely that she'd be a great asset in identifying the actual killer or killers. This assumed she was handled with care.

Wills said to Sykes, "from what you said, I take it you got on well with Miss Graham?"

"I think so," said Sykes.

"In that case, I'm going to close this abortion of an interview. After I take the DI and DS away, could you please escort the young lady home? Take the PC who is in there with you. I can see she's getting what's happening to that young woman."

"Of course sir."

"And Sykes, once Miss Graham's calmed down, "can you ask her if it would be OK for you to visit again? I think she could be a great asset in both these cases. I'd like her on-side if that's possible after all this."

As an afterthought, he said to Sykes, "also, anything you could do to appease Miss Graham, after the shit that's been shovelled over her, that'd be great."

Wills then offered, "I'll pick up on the idea about Malanga with the DSU. Let's see how, or if she could help us."

"OK, let's meet in the morning to discuss how we might get Miss Graham to help."

Sykes and Hansen acknowledged with a nod.

The DCI stamped out of the viewing room, barged into the interview room, strode over to the recording device, and terminated what was effectively an interrogation.

14. THE SEARCH

After Peterson and Bhatia left the interview room with Wills, Sykes quietly entered. PC Cameron was sitting next to Jennifer, doing her best to comfort her.

He sat opposite, reached over, and passed her the white cotton handkerchief he always carried for these occasions. It was such a simple thing, yet so handy. It never failed to warm the recipient to him, and when necessary, his questions.

Jennifer looked up and realised it was that nice policeman. He'd come back. Smiling at him through her tears, she forced out a, "thank you."

Once she'd recovered sufficiently, Sykes asked, "can PC Cameron and I take you home? It's been a trying day for you."

"Oh, yes please, thank you."

An unmarked police car was waiting for them in the police car park. Wills had authorised it to be available for the remainder of that day.

The driver opened the rear passenger door for Jennifer to sit in the back of the police car with PC Cameron. Sykes, sitting in the passenger seat, turned round and asked Jennifer, "could you please tell the driver where you'd like to be taken?"

"Fifteen Primrose Avenue."

"I understand you live with your aunt. Do you think I might be able to come in and explain to her what happened?"

"Yes, that would help. When I called, she was concerned since she'd not heard from me for a while. My aunt likes to know where I am, even though I told her earlier where I was. She's such a worrier."

****

It wasn't a long drive to their destination. Primrose Avenue was a tree-lined road with Georgian houses all set back from the road.

After the three exited the car, Sykes asked the driver to wait.

They walked up the stone path, down the centre of the front garden. Well-tended flowerbeds lined each side of the path. Lawns on both sides ended at neatly trimmed bushes that lined the boundaries.

Sykes looked around and admired the garden; simple but immaculate. Someone who lived here enjoyed gardening.

An elderly woman stood on the front porch watching their arrival. She'd obviously seen the car arrive with Jennifer and three strangers inside. Knowing Jennifer was at the station, it was an obvious deduction that the new people accompanying her were police officers.

Jennifer introduced her great aunt, Miss Doris Price. She was the sister of Jennifer's grandmother. The old woman was tall, with a pronounced stoop which Sykes assumed was age-related; she could well be in her 80s.

She had an imposing presence, made more so by her booming voice that took him by surprise. He didn't expect that from an old, apparently frail lady.

She rattled off to Jennifer, "I was worried about you. Why didn't you call me when you were going to be late? You said you were popping down to the police station to help them. And that was over three hours ago. Did you know that our friend, the doctor is dead? They said he committed suicide."

Jennifer said nothing but just gave her aunt a hug, which she eagerly reciprocated. It also had the effect of halting the torrent of questions and statements.

Then she introduced her companions. "This is Detective Sergeant Sykes and PC Cameron. I've had such an interesting time with them at the police station."

"You never said why you were going. You just rushed off, all excited. So what were you doing there anyway? Are you in trouble?"

"Definitely not," interjected Sykes, "she's been wonderfully helpful. You have a truly amazing niece."

"I already knew that," she replied with suspicion.

She stared at him intently as if trying to read his mind. If those eyes had the intention of disconcerting him, they succeeded. She eventually seemed to conclude that all was good, or at least he was acceptable company for her niece.

The PC was saved from the piercing eyes ordeal. In the aunt's opinion, she wasn't to be wary of.

"Why don't you all come into the kitchen, and I'll make some tea.

To Sykes, she aimed, "then you can explain why you've been keeping my niece for so long."

Over a pot of tea (this household didn't do teabags) and a slice of homemade sponge cake, Jennifer explained to her aunt what had happened that day. She skipped over the DI Peterson interview debacle.

"Aunt Doris, Peter was murdered."

The aunt put a hand to her mouth and gasped. "Oh my god, so awful. Who could do that? He was so nice."

Now seeing her properly, Jennifer could see her aunt had been crying. She gave the old woman another long hug.

"So, tell me, how do you know Doctor Hardcastle?" Sykes asked Jennifer.

"It's a long story and goes back to Aunt Doris." She then looked at her aunt. "Better she fills in the background, especially earlier."

"We're all ears," said Sykes on behalf of himself and the PC. "I'll just munch along." He eagerly took another proffered slice.

The aunt started the explanation.

"Peter Hardcastle's mother, Elsie, and I were friends. I used to babysit him some evenings while I was at university. I often spent time with them and grew very fond of him; he was a lovely child."

"Some years later, he became one of my pupils at his secondary school; I taught science there, mostly chemistry."

She thought for a moment, and a smile crossed her face as she thought about him.

"He was a bit of a favourite of mine at school, and I think it was reciprocated.

115

I watched him grow up, turning into such a nice young man, a lot like his mother. "

Then with a sigh and water-filling reddening eyes, she added, "so sad."

No one said anything; they waited for her to continue when she was ready.

Jennifer picked up her aunt's hand and held it tightly.

Sykes took yet another slice of cake.

Recovering her composure, the old lady continued. "I sort of lost touch with him and his mother when I moved away to Dorset teaching. I had a dalliance with a man and just needed to leave here. Not a pregnancy or anything like that."

"I loved him dearly and lost all sense of proportion. He lived locally, and I seemed to see him every day, almost everywhere I went. He wasn't stalking or anything. It was just the way I was feeling."

She took a sip of tea. "And being still young and rejected, I felt I had to get away. Looking back, I think I was in a bad way mentally."

Jennifer said, "He hurt her, and Aunt Doris never did marry."

"Anyway," she boomed. Her voice recovered with a start, clearing away old and sad thoughts.

"Jennifer's mother, my niece, and her husband died in a car crash when Jennifer was only sixteen. I was long retired by then, and she had her school to finish. She wouldn't have fitted in the local school where I lived. I don't know if you are aware but, Jennifer needs a certain level of understanding."

"I'm aware she has a condition that can give her certain abilities. Saying that, I cannot say I fully understand. I believe she's a form of quite extreme hyperphantasia."

Jennifer looked at him in surprise, wondering how he might be aware of her condition. She liked to keep that part of her life private. People were often put off getting involved once they realised she wasn't like most people. Looking at Sykes' uncomfortable reference to her condition, she suspected that any hope of a friendship with him could well be short-lived.

Ms Price continued. "So, I put my cottage in hibernation and moved back here with Jennifer. I'd always promised my niece I'd look after Jennifer if anything happened."

Jennifer interrupted the aunt's flow, teasing her with a comment, "and that was over nine years ago, and she's still not gone back home. Just can't seem to get rid of her."

"She's right," said the aunt. "Initially, Jennifer did need help."

She immediately corrected herself, "actually that's not completely correct. She also needed support and understanding then. But latterly," she paused, "well I just like being with her. Anyone who gets to know her will understand why."

Jennifer blushed.

"It wasn't long after I moved back here that I got reacquainted with Peter, sorry, Doctor Peter Hardcastle, who lives, no lived," she again corrected herself, "just down the road. Just so sad."

She dabbed her eyes with a handkerchief.

"Who could do that to him?"

She blew her nose on the handkerchief, then continued.

"He likes to pop over; oops, he loved to pop over at least once a week those days for tea, cake, and a chat. Sorry, I can't think of him in the past. His wife died, and he's very lonely. Such a nice man."

She looked at Jennifer, questioning if it was OK to now talk about her.

Jennifer nodded and kindly smiled in the affirmative.

"Jennifer is special. As well as being the most wonderful niece in the world, she has that condition. Initially, when I moved here, I could see she had challenges coping with everyday life. I was worried about her."

"There'd been all sorts of medical appointments, so-called professionals that she saw, tests and more tests. And, there was the most awful medication!"

"Nothing worked, and I think some of the treatments made her even worse."

"However, Peter realised her issues weren't being addressed. He did what little he could to help, but he wasn't officially her doctor."

"Eventually, we managed to get Jennifer to see Peter professionally. He never charged us money. He said the deal was what he used to call my lovely dri 'ᵔ cakes and tea when he came over."

"He soon became fascinated with her condition. Peter explained to us that hers is a very unique and extreme case. How did he say it? That's right, 'she's right at the top of the hyperphantasia spectrum'."

"This condition had made life difficult, sometimes impossible, for Jennifer. However, now with Peter's guidance, she was starting to manage it. She soon started to respond under his care."

"Peter also helped Jennifer manage and control its potentially life-threatening side effects. We knew of its dangers. We both did a lot of reading on the topic, although there's comparatively little research out there."

"In a nutshell, people with severe forms of her condition could easily live their life outside the present. Daydreaming can become a serious problem if not managed. Some can lose themselves in their visualisations so much that they have difficulty identifying what is real or not. It has led to other severe medical conditions such as schizophrenia."

"So you had to tread carefully with her and any interactions," interjected the PC. "My daughter's on the autistic spectrum. While I know it's not the same as this condition, I do understand the worries that family and carers have to cope with."

Miss Price responded to the PC, smiling, "so you'll appreciate when I tell you that she's also on the autistic spectrum, albeit not high. It's still a double whammy for Jennifer though."

The PC gave a sympathetic look.

"So, Peter had been helping Jennifer not only accept her hyperphantasia condition but channel it into positive ways. Unlike the others, his focus was to challenge her to use it constructively."

"Between you and me, I think he was using her as part of some research into that condition. It was fine for us. Whatever his agenda, it was helping her."

As the aunt spoke, she again looked at Jennifer for approval on what she was about to say next.

Jennifer said nothing, so Miss Price continued. "So it's important for those with extreme cases such as Jennifer to be grounded in reality.

Peter tried many ways to channel her condition into ways that could be of advantage. He wanted to help Jennifer build on the positives. They even tried the likes of chess. Building pictures of possible moves could be useful in that type of game."

"God, that got so boring," interrupted Jennifer. "Once I learned the rules, it was just a matter of comparing what strategies could give the right outcome."

"But he cheated and started using gambits." After a pause, "yes I know, using gambits isn't cheating, I was just joking."

"I broke a few of them, but others were really good. I'm not a great reader of text or technical books. Chess is not only about looking at the next combination of moves but also researching and remembering standard plays. It got so tedious and, eventually frustrating. It just wasn't my bag."

The aunt took over again.

"One afternoon, several months into Peter's working with Jennifer, he came over for his 'tea and yummy cake fix', as he called it.

He caught Jennifer in full flow about the failures of a crime programme plot, the evidence, and the like. Can't even remember which one. Anyway, she was failing badly trying to get me to understand what she was on about."

"She was wound up about the plot. She apparently could see all the incorrect assumptions that the scriptwriters had made up, for the characters to follow. She tried to explain why they were wrong. But, I simply wasn't getting it. It all seemed perfectly reasonable to me."

Jennifer thought back to that day and laughed. "We were having a real ding-dong that day, all light-hearted of course."

"Then Peter walked in on us. He immediately got it. That is, he understood the inconsistencies of the plot. We both tried explaining to Aunt Doris but she still couldn't appreciate why it was an issue. He also loves reading and watching crime stories. That's why it all made sense to him."

Her aunt continued again. "Jennifer loves those true crime programmes. All a nonsense, but she loves them."

"And it was that day he came up with the idea to have Jennifer focus her condition on crime. She's always been interested in crime. As he said, 'if she has a passion for something that can work for her, that's where we can focus our attention'."

"We did have some great times arguing about these cases," Jennifer reminisced, with a sad face, yet a smile at the same time.

"Then she used to go round to his house and explain to him why such-n-such a crime programme was just a load of rubbish, and why. She used to go into real detail and then they'd get into it. They both loved the banter."

Jennifer interrupted again. "Occasionally, the creators of those TV crime shows get them so wrong, and nothing made sense. Other times, it was just simple nuances. It's so frustrating. Why don't other people complain?"

The aunt regained control. "Those sessions became the platform on which he could coach her. Crime was the release from the potentially serious effects of her condition. He helped her enter and walk through the crime stories, living the investigations, then support her extraction from them. He guided and helped her manage her condition."

"They became the closest of friends, even though there was more than a thirty-year age gap. Their common interest meant that Jennifer was sometimes never out of his house in the evenings. He was a lonely man. He needed and enjoyed her company. It was a win-win."

Then Sykes entered the conversation. "I saw her in action in the police station. She is amazing. I'd love to get to know her better. No, no. I, I mean …" Sykes stuttered, then reddened a little, "I'd really like to know how she does what she does. She's already helped us with one case. I think she can also help us with the possible murder of the doctor."

"So, when Jennifer said it was murder, she was right?" the aunt confirmed.

"Someone killed him," Jennifer sternly interrupted. There was anger in her voice. It wasn't aimed at the people around her but toward the perpetrators of her friend's death.

Then to Sykes, she said, "I'd love to help. I need to help catch his killers, it's the least I can do for him. When can we start?"

"Do you mind if a friend possibly joins us? She's a criminal profiler. I think the two of you would be amazing together."

"Wow, yes, absolutely. That'd be fantastic," Jennifer retorted enthusiastically. She'd watched profilers in action, but she'd never met one. And now she'd be working with one, on a real case, albeit her friend's.

She again felt the conflict of mixed emotions.

Sykes picked up on those signs. "The lady we use is almost as amazing as you. I know you'll both hit it off. I promise, it'll be fine. Anyway, I'll be there as well."

He could see her tension ease. "How's about the day after tomorrow?"

"I'm free."

"Cool, I'll pick you up from here. How's 9 am sound?"

"Perfect."

They idly chatted while Sykes helped himself to yet another slice of cake.

Satiated on cake, Sykes apologised that they had to leave. As Jennifer walked them to the front door, Sykes stopped. He asked PC Cameron to carry on and wait for him in the car. He and Jennifer slowly walked behind.

Sykes had to raise the question about Peterson. Normally, he'd play a safe game. Some people loved admissions of guilt as a precursor to complaints or even litigation. With this lady, he felt it best to work on the principle of honesty. Hopefully, that'd close the matter.

"Are you feeling better after that interview with DI Peterson and DS Bhatia? They made an error in judgement, you know."

If she now said anything, he could well be in trouble for implying a superior officer and colleague made a mistake; which they did, and a bad one.

"Sergeant Sykes, if I'd a penny for every person I meet who doesn't understand where I'm coming from when trying to explain myself, I'd be rich. So, of course, I'm fine now, thank you."

With a smirk, she followed up. "I saw the look on your boss' face when he stormed in and stopped the interview. The shock on Detective Inspector Peterson's face was priceless. And if I was vindictive, that would have been revenge enough."

Then with a conspiratorial grin, she said, "I think DI Peterson might be in a little trouble?"

"Oh, and please tell your DCI Wills, thank you. His intervention saved me a lot of angst."

Sykes was relieved she was good with what happened, and she was OK. He then gave a questioning look, but no words came.

"I can see from your look, that you're still a bit uncertain about my response. I expect your boss asked the question which has put you in a dilemma. So, to be clear, I've no plans to make a complaint against DI Peterson."

Ah, Em," he stuttered, trying to find the right words. "Frankly, that's not what I was thinking. It looks like we might be working together, so I was wondering if I might call you by your first name; Miss Graham seems so formal. I'm Barrie."

As she walked alongside him down the path to the waiting car, she replied, "well, Barrie, whether or not we'd be working together, Jennifer definitely works for me."

He didn't know where this was going. She was so different from anyone else he'd met; even a bit scary.

But, he really, really liked her.

15. THE PLAN

Sykes was instructed to go to DSU Merriman's office on his return to the station. He was immediately waved in and sat next to DCI Wills, who was already there.

Merriman immediately came out with the question to address the elephant in the room.

"Right then, Sykes, have you worked your charm on the young lady? Is this station going to get a complaint?"

Sykes realised that Wills had updated the Super on the Peterson interview. Smiley was always keen to keep things in order and to ensure there were no political repercussions.

"I asked her, and the answer is no," replied the sergeant. "She was particularly happy about DCI Wills' intervention."

Sykes added, "she's such a sweet thing; I don't think she'd complain about anything."

"Well done, Sykes,"

"Thank you, sir."

Then to Wills, Sykes added, "I think you're her hero, sir. And she asked me to say thank you."

The DCI jokingly said, "ah, shucks."

Merriman's tension visibly relaxed. "Now that's out of the way, do you think she might agree to help us with both the judge's and the doctor's cases? DCI Wills has already made me aware of her background. We've also gone through the doctor's file on her."

"Absolutely, sir. She's heavily into crime, particularly murders. She's excited about coming back here and helping us with both of them."

"The doctor used crime-solving as a sort of therapy to help focus and manage her condition. They used to have a great time arguing about cases. I believe that working with us might help her in return. However, I'm no psychiatrist."

"If I might mention something else sir?" asked the sergeant looking to Wills and then Merriman, not sure to whom he should be aiming his question.

Both responded simultaneously with the same query, "yes?"

Sykes leaned forward a little as if to say something. There was an awkward silence. They could see that Sykes wanted to continue but felt uncomfortable.

Wills released the tension from the DS. "You've got something on your chest Sykes, spit it out."

"I honestly don't know how to say this. I hope I'm not talking out of place, but I think she might be uncomfortable working with DI Peterson and DS Bhatia."

Sykes felt very awkward saying this to the big bosses.

It was Wills who responded. "Don't worry sergeant. We've also discussed this issue, and neither of them will be directly involved with her."

Sykes gave a visible look of relief. "The aunt gave me some further insight into Miss Graham's conditions. As well as avoiding any upset or trauma, treading carefully would help us get the most out of her. I'm not sure of the right expression, but she is very vulnerable. Or is it sensitive? Anyway, if we're careful, we can get the most value from her; and vice versa."

"I was wondering if there is an update on our using professional help when working with her?"

It was Merriman's turn to respond. "I spoke with Mrs Tabitha Malanga this morning, and she's very keen to help us with Miss Graham. Mrs Malanga advised me she has experience with the conditions around neurodiversity, whatever that is. The upshot is that she is able to help us work with Miss Graham's autism."

"On the main issue, Mrs Malanga is aware of hyperphantasia. She'll do some research and consult with professionals in this area before they meet. Mrs Malanga's confident she'd be able to manage without additional help. She doesn't want too many people around, saying it would hamper the process."

"It's great to hear that Tabi's confirmed, she's brilliant."

"Is she indeed? And she's Tabi? Aha! The rumours are true," teased Wills.

Sykes ignored the wind-up and offered, "I've already suggested to Miss Graham about working with a criminal profiler from what you said earlier. She's mega excited about the prospect. With your permission, I've already provisionally arranged for her to come down at 0930, the day after tomorrow."

"Works for me," acknowledged the DSU. Then to Wills, "thoughts?"

"All good from my side, sir."

Wills then proposed, "Sykes, arrange things with both of them. We're all aware you and Miss Malanga were both good friends at one time. So, I'm assuming you still have her number? That is unless she's blocked you."

He had to have a final joking dig at the young sergeant.

Sykes was unfazed. "Yes sir, and no sir. All amicable."

"So that's confirmed. Any thoughts on the arrangements?" asked the DSU of Wills.

"For the judge's case, how's about we let the three of them rabbit together at the front of the meeting room? From what Sykes had said, she was on a roll with that information. I'll sit in the back, might even learn something from the youngsters. Hansen might also want to join me there."

"Perfect. In that case, I'll be joining the judge's session too," said the DSU. "I've heard a lot about Miss Graham so far. I'd like to see her in action. Good to know what all the fuss is about."

Wills continued, "for the doctor's case, can I suggest we use the other interview room, which also has an adjoining viewing room? DI Peterson and perhaps Sergeant Bhatia can look on from there. I'll be in the room with PC Cameron and Sykes."

"And I'll also be in the viewing room. We have a plan. Thank you, gentlemen" said Merriman as he picked up a file and started reading.

The two sitting opposite the DSU knew they were dismissed.

16. INTO THE MIND'S EYE

At 9 am prompt, Sykes pulled up at the entrance gate to Fifteen Primrose Avenue. Jennifer was out of the gate and into the car before he'd barely had a chance to think about getting out and opening the door for her. Being brought up with an aged aunt suggested that hers was a somewhat old-fashioned upbringing. So, he thought it would have been a nice touch. She beat him to it.

"OK?" said Sykes, looking over to check how she was.

"Definitely!"

In truth, Jennifer had mixed emotions about today and hardly slept the night before. She was excited about today's agenda, yet worried about being able to cope with the situation and these new people.

She tried to remember what Peter said, 'focus on the process and the positives, and the issues will deal with themselves'. She knew that wasn't exactly scientifically true, but focussing like this did help.

"Oh, I've something for you," as she handed back his handkerchief. It was cleaned and ironed.

She grinned as she spoke, "you might need this for some other damsel in distress."

He laughed quietly.

When they arrived at the station, her only formality was signing in. There were smiles and nods of welcome from police officers and civilians alike. It seems everyone knew why she was there. Jennifer's anxiety levels began to rise, knowing they were watching her expectantly.

The profiler, Mrs Tabitha Malanga, noticed Jennifer enter the meeting room. Her face lit up into a beaming smile as she walked over to introduce herself.

"I'm Tabi, lovely to meet you." She enthusiastically reached out and vigorously yet gently, shook Jennifer's hand. "I've heard so much about you and am so excited to see how you work."

Jennifer was normally uncomfortable with strangers, but this woman's pleasant and exuberant welcome disarmed and relaxed her.

"I've been so looking forward to meeting a criminal profiler, and now I'm supposed to be working with one. I'm scared and excited. Oh, sorry, and I'm Jennifer."

Mrs Malanga was tall, blond, and very pretty. She wasn't model slim, more what one might say as curvaceously sexy. Both men's and women's eyes tended to follow her everywhere, some lustfully, some enviously. They were all drawn to the bubbly personality that oozed from her every pore.

Tabitha turned to Sykes, and still with that wide smile said, "been a while, lost your phone?"

Sykes was now very uncomfortable. He knew she was teasing him, not nastily, but in her usual jovial manner. She had a wicked sense of humour, but people could never be offended by it.

Leading up to this meeting, he knew he'd struggle as he always had with her. And he didn't want to appear rude, uncomfortable, or anything less than professional in front of those around.

Sykes and Tabitha had known each other professionally for several years. Just over a year ago, when she announced that she and her husband were splitting up, she asked him out. She wasn't one to stand on ceremony, and as the expression goes, 'she's not backward in coming forward'.

They had several months of fun. Tabi was what he'd call a live wire. She was always joking and laughing. She loved to party, drink to excess, and enjoy enthusiastic sex. Worst of all, in the morning, she was right as rain. No hangover, no tired eyes, and sharp as a tack for what the day would bring.

Sykes suffered from alcohol-induced hangovers and needed his nightly seven hours of sleep. He liked quiet dinners, pleasant conversation, and nice wine; not so much a connoisseur, but he knew what he liked.

She called Sykes her 'fuddy-duddy old man' although he was two years younger.

While they were very fond of each other, perhaps even in love, she overwhelmed him. He often felt he was holding her back from the things she

127

enjoyed. He was never comfortable with the wild life.

And that's where the rot set in. Both knew they had to move on without each other but didn't know how to put it into words. The end of their relationship wasn't so much a parting of ways, just a slow drifting apart.

"Ah, hem," was as much a response that he could muster at that point.

Jennifer quickly picked up on the dynamics of their intimate relationship. She watched as Tabitha emotionally manhandled her favourite policeman. Seeing his increasingly uncomfortable demeanour and reddening face, Jennifer came to his rescue by changing the subject.

"Tabi, I'd love to hear about the cases you've been involved with."

Tabi had already recognised Sykes' interest in Jennifer by how he looked at her as they entered; one reason for the wind-up. Now he was on the ropes, it was time to let him off.

"Can't go into any detail, but we should grab a coffee sometime, and I'll tell you what I can."

Then conspiratorially, but not so quietly that Sykes couldn't hear, said, "I can also give you the inside track on his lordship." She meant Sykes.

They both grinned.

Sykes looked on and said nothing. He could see that Tabi had moved on; he hoped she had. Or did he?

Tabi's behaviour had two agendas.

The reality was that seeing him again, she still missed him.

Secondly, and most importantly, she'd made a point of diverting Jennifer away from anything that might be going on elsewhere in the room that might add to Jennifer's nervousness.

While winding up Sykes was fun, it also served the purpose of compelling Jennifer into his defence. That also took her mind away from the back of the room.

Now the virtual barriers were up. They were a team of three at the front of the room amongst the judge's case information, isolated from all around.

'Poor Sykes, you'll survive,' she inwardly laughed.

As they talked and bonded at the front of the room, Sykes began to relax with the situation.

While the three were participating in their banter, Merriman, Wills, and Hansen walked into the meeting room and sat quietly at the back.

Jennifer once tried to look to the back. Tabi put her arm around Jennifer's shoulders and gently wheeled her around to face the whiteboards. "Ignore 'em, c'mon, we've got a job to do."

Then she whispered loudly for all to hear, including the three at the back of the room. "Sykes'd also like to ignore them as I do; often. But he can't, coz he's a copper. I can, coz I'm a civilian."

The two women giggled. The ice was fully broken.

Sykes cringed and frowned in embarrassment.

Hansen and Wills grinned.

Merriman stared blank-faced, as usual. His reputation for not being good with humour remained untarnished.

"OK then, let's have some fun, shall we? Sykes here has extolled your observational skills," Tabi started, beaming a bright smile at Jennifer.

"Can I call you Jenny or Jen?"

"Jennifer please, it's the name my parents gave me."

"Gotcha Jennifer, I hate Tabitha, and everyone calls me Tabi. Each to their own."

Jennifer could hardly contain her excitement. "So, what do you want me to do?"

Sykes replied. "Tabi will be running this session. I know you explained to me, but for her benefit, we're all here to understand how and why you came to the inside-person line of thinking regarding Judge Davidson's murder."

"Then, with Tabi's help, we might be able to interpret some of your conclusions toward identifying the perpetrators."

Both women nodded in agreement.

"OK, you've already got a head start on me, so how's about you give me the gist of your conclusions and how you visualise what happened?" asked Tabi.

Jennifer then opened with, "I've concluded that it's an inside job. I suspect it would be an employee, family, or someone else with ready access to the house; someone who was there that evening, perhaps afternoon."

"The evidence was presented like this to hide it from being recognised as an inside job. As I see it, the accomplice broke the window from the inside. He/she opened the right-hand window, leaned out, then using one of the brass elephant's sharp edges, broke the window, unlocked, and opened it."

"OK that's the outcome, so the reasons behind your thinking?" asked Tabi.

"Many reasons. If someone climbed in from the broken window side, wouldn't there be some fragments walked in? No glass should be on the room side of the unbroken window, yet there was. This suggests the curtain was pulled back on that side, and the fragments bounced over."

"Also, why would a killer, who was wearing gloves, clean the broken window hatch? Even crazier, why waste time cleaning the catch on the unbroken side?"

"Then there's the study room door being closed after the killer walked through. Why would he-she take the time to close it, if no one else was in the house? This was a professional job. The killer would have done his or her, research."

"Look at the pictures of the room," she pointed to them.

"The room is pristine. So why would a brass elephant ornament be out of its proper place? It's slightly out of alignment."

"And look at this." She pointed to the pictures of the kitchen. "The end kitchen chair is nudged towards the doorway to the hall. It suggests someone in the dark, who wasn't familiar with the room, brushed into it on the way in."

The two women talked through the further details Jennifer had earlier explained to Sykes. The three at the back were now convinced Jennifer had made a good case for an inside job. And if she was right, they'd now have a potential link to the killer.

Sykes entered the discussion. "The only people who could have helped the killer would have been the housekeeper or her nephew. Both were there that day. The nephew was there until about 1930, washed then went off to the pub. Mrs Taylor left about 1500."

Jennifer followed up. "I can't be certain, but if I were the accomplice, I'd break the window when it was dark. If the patio door was unlocked earlier, it would likely be noticed, even locked again. The nephew was the only one around. I'd be looking to chat with him." Jennifer stood there staring at the whiteboards.

"Assuming Jennifer is correct, and it sounds like she's made a strong case for her argument, let's now have a look at Alan Forrest's motivation and relationships," said Tabi.

Tabitha asked Sykes, "does he have any form?

"Forest is a bit of a wild boy, not particularly bright, and easily led. From his reports and the support he's had, I think he's been spoiled by his mother, and later in life, by his aunt. He's got minor drug and drink-related GBH convictions."

"He also gambles on horses. The word is he's not successful because he doesn't understand the game."

Sykes shrugged, signifying to Tabi he'd finished.

Tabitha continued. "This was a very professional hit, and from what Sykes has told me, there are similarities to other very professional cases. From the interview reports, it's clear that his relationship with the judge was good, but not close. What I'm about to suggest is not conclusive. I don't think his profile fits someone that would knowingly be involved with a murder."

"Also, the accomplice made some basic mistakes. This makes me think he wasn't directly involved with this very pedantic killer. If he was directly working with the killer, he'd have been better briefed."

"Being involved in a robbery is more likely up Forrest's street. He'd justify to himself that the judge would be well insured, so not out of pocket and no one hurt; financially or physically."

"So, I think the approach you would take," she said to Sykes, ignoring those at the back of the room, "would be to suggest to him that you know he was hired by someone who wanted to rob the house. There is a lot of antique stuff there, and I expect some of it expensive."

"Let's assume he cops to the robbery idea, which is most likely. While not my place, I'd suggest offering the nephew a reduced sentence based on the robbery premise, assuming he talks about who set this up."

"Obviously, if he stays quiet, he's then an accomplice to murder."

Then she finished with, "as I said, how you approach him is only a suggestion. I'm a mere consultant after all. Let's not forget that this might well go differently in the interview. Anyway, that's how I'd at least start."

"Thanks, Mrs Malanga," said Sykes a little too formally.

Then Tabi realised why when she sneaked a look behind them. As well as the three senior offices at the back, she noticed many others had also sneaked in to listen.

"And these are the decision-makers, who will decide anyway." Tabi put her arm around Jennifer's shoulders and turned her around.

Tabi bowed to the now large audience at the back of the room.

Jennifer looked aghast. With a reddening face, she looked down. She'd never spoken to such a crowd before.

They all clapped. This time the DSU even had a smile on his face.

After a few moments, Jennifer shyly looked up at their appreciative audience and smiled.

"Right you lot," said Wills to the officers who had joined them at the back of the room. "We've got a new line of investigation and have a suspect in the frame as the inside man; Mr Alan Forrest."

"Let's get to it."

Hansen and Wills immediately set the Alan Forrest interview in motion.

****

"Seen the Super?" asked Hansen of Wills, who shrugged his shoulders unknowingly.

"He's taken Sykes and the two women out to lunch. He never does that unless it's with the top brass. Methinks he's taken a shine to our Miss Graham."

"Or he's making sure there's no come-back from Peterson's balls-up," mumbled Hansen to Wills.

"Nah, that's sorted. He wants to ensure the doctor's interview goes well this time. There'll be a lot of conflicting emotions flying about during that meeting. He's doing the right thing in checking. I suspect lunch was Tabi's suggestion."

17. PAINFUL ANALYSIS

On their return from lunch, Sykes, Jennifer, and Tabitha settled themselves into the second interview room. This next session was about the death of Jennifer's friend and erstwhile doctor, Peter Hardcastle, now confirmed as a murder.

Again, they would be going through Jennifer's view of the murder while taking Tabitha's perspective about possible assailants.

Despite Peterson's protests as the case owner, he wasn't permitted in the room with Jennifer. He was only to watch proceedings from the adjoining viewing room; without interaction. He was a most unhappy DI.

Tabitha advised they needed to avoid any unnecessary linkage to the previous interview by Peterson. This discussion wasn't recorded. The only officer present would be Sykes, and then only in a backup role to Mrs Malanga.

The two women sat at the table facing the mirror-cum-one-way window. Sykes had his back to the window and sat to one side, ensuring the women were in full view.

Those in the viewing area could only listen in and take notes as necessary.

The DSU entered the viewing room, soon followed by Peterson, Bhatia, and Wills. Bhatia, as the junior member of staff, stood at the back. Rank took precedence over the gentlemanly 'ladies first'.

Tabi checked with Jennifer. "Are you OK?"

"Definitely," she replied, although not too sure. This session was going to be about her friend after all.

Sykes started the conversation with, "OK Jennifer, how's about you start with what you explained a couple of days ago to the uniformed officers?" He didn't feel comfortable saying, 'the day when Dr Hardcastle was found dead'.

Jennifer wasn't one for fluffy speech at the best of times. Even worse, since this case was so close to her, she immediately launched in. She needed this part over with as soon as possible.

"It's not suicide, people killed him." She needed to get that statement made right from the off.

Then she launched in to get it all off her chest.

"He's my closest friend."

"I knew all about his drug use before he stopped."

"I'd have known if Peter was using again."

"And I know what you might be thinking. Those close to drug addicts don't' see what's going on, or if they do, they pretend it's not happening."

"I'm not blind. I knew the person he was before he stopped taking heroin."

"I knew how things changed for him after rehab and ongoing. I saw the different signs."

She paused.

Jennifer then emphasised, "I know the person he is now."

"Or rather, I knew the man he was; until he was murdered. I can assure you, he was not, taking drugs again!" The 'not' was said with almost anger.

Jennifer sat back and relaxed a little now all that was out.

Tabitha had to ask, "are you OK?"

"Yes, thanks, now I've gotten that lot off my chest."

She looked at Tabi and Sykes intently in case they wanted to question her reasoning. Tabi merely nodded in acceptance for her to continue.

Jennifer took several breaths, as Peter had suggested when she felt overwhelmed.

Jennifer swung both arms apart, palms down, as if she was conducting an orchestra. "Right, now my personal bias is out of the way, let's focus on what the evidence shows."

It was Sykes' turn to offer a supportive smile as he nodded encouragement.

"If he injected himself, it would be in the safety of his armchair for support in case he passed out. This was how he used to do it; never in that chair."

"Then there's the cushion and the throw. I expect you already know he's a bit OCD. But, it's not just that. He insisted his room was always consistent and ordered for his patients. So, everything should have been in place."

"If someone sat there, he'd have immediately tidied the settee after they left. He's like that, sorry, was like that," she corrected herself.

Tabi noticed that Jennifer was still dropping into the present tense about her friend, but said nothing. She was hurting.

"So, with the somewhat crumpled throw and the cushion out of place, he definitely wasn't alone when he died. He wasn't able to tidy after they left."

"As I said earlier, he'd have to be restrained in a way that there'd be no marks on him. If it was me, I'd have placed that cushion over his face to muffle any sounds. The other restrained him with the throw, perhaps tying it around the back. As a result, there would be negligible marking to his body."

This is one reason why I believe there were at least two people involved; who probably killed him."

"The other reason is there were two more cups on the sink drainer."

"Now, sitting in that chair suggests this was more of a formal meeting. It was with people he knew professionally, but this was not a consultation. If informal, he'd have been in his armchair."

Jennifer didn't stop to take questions. She had to get through this before she could relax enough for their comment.

"You'll have noticed that the chair was at that angle away from the desk. Its position was necessary, so they'd have space to work."

Jennifer finished. "Anyway, that's how I see it happened."

She breathed a sigh of relief. She was through it, and was OK.

Sykes responded. "SOCO and forensics checked to see if there were strands from the throw on his chest. You were right. They also checked and found his saliva on the cushion."

"I never suggested doing that?" queried Jennifer.

"Can't all be as perfect as me," he grinned.

Jennifer leaned forward and punched him on the shoulder in mock anger; her spirits were clearly lifting.

"Anyway," he said, trying to get the conversation back on track. "They confirmed you're also right about the syringe having no fingerprints on the shaft. Also, the belt used as the tourniquet had only a couple of his fingerprints. As you suggested, we'd normally expect fingerprints all over it."

Jennifer said nothing, just nodded with a twinge of a smile.

"And again, your image of how things would have happened was bang on. As you mentioned to uniform earlier, the cups already on the drainer from the evening before had no fingerprints."

"You do know that if it wasn't for you, we wouldn't have picked up on all this. The killers would have walked away."

Sykes had to get that statement in, for all to hear, especially Peterson. She needed to hear that vindication, and he felt all the better for saying it.

Now it was Tabi's turn to speak. "So we have at least two people he knew very well, possibly even trusted, who came into the house. Otherwise, no tea would have been drunk. Also, since the discussion took place in his office, it would be safe to presume that the doctor knew these people in a professional capacity that was not doctor-patient."

Peterson, in the interview room, visibly leaned forward with growing interest. He nodded in understanding to his DCI.

The profiler continued. "If the lead person was a male and they wanted to kill him, it would most likely have been done violently, perhaps knifing, or strangling? I can't be 100% certain though."

Tabi then thought further and followed up with, "using a drug overdose that simulated a suicide is an interesting one. It implies pertinent history. Perhaps this would have been someone with knowledge of his previous addiction."

"There are other and easier ways of simulating suicide. Choosing a drug-related death is more complex. It smacks of history and anger and very likely related to drugs. A bit of a stretch, but there are strong emotions at play here."

Jennifer asked, "what do you think about the lead person being a woman with a grudge? That's more a woman sort of murder weapon."

"Aren't you being sexist, or stereotypical?" asked Sykes jokingly.

"Not if she says it ma boy," responded Tabi light-heartedly.

The two women grinned at each other conspiratorially.

"OK. Back to the process," said Tabi, and then to Jennifer, "yes, you're ahead of me girl," she smiled at Jennifer. "I was thinking exactly that."

Now Peterson was intently staring at the interview on the other side of the window.

Without emotion, his Superintendent half-looked at Peterson. "A lesson for us all about jumping to conclusions. It's not always about gut instinct."

Wills had taken the wind out of Merriman's sails, by having already informally disciplined Peterson. The DSU was a bit miffed he couldn't then reprimand Peterson himself; formally. However, he accepted the DCI's handling of the matter.

Still, Merriman couldn't resist that comment as a way of emphasising his displeasure.

He turned back to the viewing window. He was enjoying the Jennifer-Tabi show in the next room.

Tabi continued, "I'd also suggest that to hold down the doctor, there was a high probability the other person was either an extremely strong woman or a man. I'd go with the man."

Now it was Sykes' turn. He formally summarised the conclusions from the discussion.

"So we have two perpetrators, a likely link to an ex-client, one a woman, and the other a man. They're angry and have known him while he was a user, and there is a drugs link. Wow!"

Now the process was over, Wills looked at DI Peterson. "They did the same for the judge's case. I'm assuming you've enough to go on?"

"Yes guv," said his DI with enthusiasm, albeit tempered with a lot of lingering embarrassment from his earlier encounter with Miss Graham.

"By the way, Hansen's young lad Sykes is good. He handled that perfectly," pronounced DI Peterson.

****

After the interview, and with the Super's blessing, Peterson caught up with Jennifer.

"I'm sorry I handled our first meeting like the cumbersome oaf I am. I was watching you in the viewing room. What I saw between you both was truly amazing. If only a part of that was accurate, you've helped enormously."

He held out his hand, and she happily accepted.

****

Back in his office, Peterson and Bhatia had already done some preliminary work based on what Jennifer had said earlier. They had a long list of potential suspects lined up should anything be useful coming out of this morning's meeting with Jennifer.

It wasn't long before a couple found itself on the top of their pile.

18. TESTING THE WEAKEST LINK

The day after the Jennifer and Tabi show, Alan Forrest arrived at the station just before noon. He'd agreed to come in first thing in the morning. As far as he was concerned, getting up at 11 am to reach the police station before noon was definitely first thing for him.

He knew exactly what the police meant when they agreed that time. They were going to dance to his tune and he'd enjoy playing with them.

'The fuckin' pigs could sweat and wait.'

The police were happy for Forrest to believe he was coming to the police station as a favour, to discuss a few points regarding the judge's murder. He was relaxed, self-assured, and very full of himself as he swanned into the police station. So, Alan Forrest never felt the need to be legally represented.

When he finally arrived, PC Joshua Barclay, who'd been waiting for him, was summoned. He rushed down to reception and escorted Forrest to the allotted interview room. There was going to be an audience, so they used the same room where Peterson interviewed Jennifer.

Barclay took up his position at the back of the room.

They had enough to charge Forrest, but they were happy to have him unaware of their plans until they dropped the bombshell for maximum effect.

There were a couple of reasons to hold off charging him. They needed time to close all the evidence's loose ends. Also, they didn't want to prewarn him so he'd want a solicitor present, which could interfere with their plans.

There was an unofficial reason; Forrest wasn't liked at the station. A bit devious, but what the hell.

The game now began to play out.

After thirty minutes, with no one coming, Alan Forrest started niggling at the PC behind him, who said nothing. Normally, the PC would have told Forrest to shut up, but he was in on the plan.

Forrest was getting the silent, 'stress-him-out' treatment. It was also payback for the little 'toad' for not coming down as agreed.

Wills joined Hansen and Sykes in the viewing room, "how's our little friend doing?" asked Wills of Hansen.

"Getting tetchy and agitated."

They watched him fidget through the one-way mirror. He furtively looked around, drummed his fingers, tapped his feet, and got up to walk around. He did his best to engage and taunt the PC, who completely ignored him. The officers watched his anger and stress levels rise.

When he was mentally where they wanted him to be, it was time to start the interview. DCI Wills and Sergeant Sykes were going to conduct the interview. Hansen had other matters to sort out. The senior officers felt Sykes deserved to be there and could get some good experience from being in this interview.

By the time Wills and Sykes walked into the interview room, their victim was beside himself with anger. He verbally attacked them with, "we agreed first thing; it's now almost one!"

Even worse, Forrest was starting to feel a bit strung out; he'd not had a hit since late last night. Normally, he'd be OK, but the stress from waiting had aggravated his need.

Wills and Sykes took their seats and said nothing in response. Their only words were in going through the interview formalities.

Wills opened the interview with, "sorry to have kept you waiting. As you just now said, we expected you first thing. Silly us, we assumed 8 am, latest, 9 am. Unfortunately, we had other interviews between then and now. Anyway, you are here now, and thanks for coming."

Forrest cockily replied, "my first thing is when I get up. And I get up at twelve. I'm early."

"Ah, that's the misunderstanding," said Wills, feigning apology.

Forrest wasn't intellectually equipped to pick up on the DCI's sarcastic nuance; it simply went over his head.

Wills continued, "we'd just like to clarify a few points in your statement. Since you've been waiting, we'll make this quick."

Forrest, seated opposite them, shook his head impatiently back and forth for them to get started.

"So, if you could please walk us through what you were doing before you left for the pub, that'd be great?"

"Again! Fuck me! How many times do I have to go through this? It's all in my statement. Can't you bizzies read?"

"Mr Forest, please bear with us. We have to go through the process of double-checking everyone and everything. Sometimes people forget things or get things wrong with the stress of any major event, in this case, Judge Davidson's murder. After all, he was your friend, as you stated earlier. I'm sure you want to help as much as you can."

Forrest stared up at the ceiling impatiently.

"Please be assured, it's not just you. We're going through a similar process with other witnesses as well," lied Wills. "We need to make sure our timeline of everything that happened is accurate, and everyone's movements are consistent."

"OK, OK. Let's get on with it then!" Forrest impatiently responded. He then rattled off his speech.

"I was workin' in the judge's garden till it got dark, about five. There was a leakin' tap in the utility room, wot I fixed. Maybe finished that about six, maybe six-thirty? Then cleaned up my tools 'n' stuff.

I washed in the shower next to the utility room. Had a change of clothes with me, got dressed, and about half seven, I left for the pub."

"And you were the only person in the house?"

"Until the bloke what dun the judge came, yep."

"Everything locked up? Nothing out of the ordinary."

"Yes of course. Aunt Marjory gives me a bollockin' if I forget, an' sometimes a smack around the head. She's a fuckin' stickler for security and having everything spick 'n' span. She can be a pain in the arse; or a pain in the head," he grinned.

Wills smiled in acknowledgement and support of Forrest's feeble attempt at humour. He continued with his line of questioning toward the forthcoming bombshell.

"If, as you say, everything was locked, how come the kitchen door was unlocked when you left?"

"Bollocks, I locked it myself!"

"OK. Here's another query we have. Could you explain how the window was broken from inside the house before you left?"

The bomb doors opened.

"One of the brass elephants was used."

The bombshell had dropped!

Wills awaited the fallout.

Forrest looked at the DCI aghast. He was now speechless.

The police officers sitting opposite him said nothing. They waited while their victim digested his predicament from the fallout.

"Dunno' anyfin' about anyfin'. I want my lawyer."

Wills expected this response if Forrest was indeed guilty. 'I-want-my-lawyer' was a common phrase used when the guilty had nowhere else to go.

They were right. Forrest was involved.

"Of course. We'll arrange a phone for you right now."

Wills nodded to the PC at the back of the room to leave and get it. The police officer was in on the plan and was going to wait outside.

"While we're waiting for your phone, you do know that if your lawyer comes, the offer I was about to make you is off the table. Lawyering-up means it all becomes formal, and you then become an accessory to murder."

He let that churn around Forrest's brain for a few moments.

"Not sayin' anyfin'."

Wills ignored the words and continued. "We know you didn't want the judge hurt. We know you even liked him, and he liked you. Mind you, it was gullible of him to have you around, knowing what you're like."

"I didn't do nothin'," was Forrest's only response.

143

So, Wills pressed a little further. "And I'm assuming you got a cut from what you thought was a quick in-and-out robbery."

He let the statement sit in the air for a few moments, then followed up. "That doesn't make you a bad man. To me, you're a victim. They set you up. You've been shafted good and proper."

"Lawyer!"

"I just want to give you a chance. You're an innocent who's going to take the fall for murder. The real killer goes scot-free. We know this was a planned hit, not a burglary that went bad. The person who set up that hit will let you rot in jail. For what, eh? How much did they pay you?"

"Lawyer now!"

"Understood Mr Forrest, of course. Sergeant Sykes, I'm off to see where the PC is with that telephone. While I'm away, please book him as an accessory to murder."

Wills stood up and walked to the door, then with his hand on the handle, he turned to Forrest and said, "and here's me about to offer you protection, a new identity, and a pussy sentence. You'd be out of their clutches and can start again."

"Wait! Wait! Are you offering protection and a new start?" Forrest was now interested and a lot less arrogant.

"If what you say can help put our Mr Anthony Barker in the frame, everything's on the table."

"Dunno' about Tony Barker. He's been good to me. Tony, dun me a favour a couple of days before. He bought my paper from the bookie who'd been after me. The bookie had already given me a smack for not paying up. They promised broken bones next time."

"Tony's bruvver, Joe Morris, told me there was a burglary team in town looking to do some rich folks' houses. They only wanted antiques. And did I know anyone who could afford to lose a few bits? He'd bung me a hundred quid for any info."

"I said, wot if I can get you into a house wot's got a loada antique stuff? He said they'd give me five hundred quid and ten percent of what they can fence. I was in trouble and needed the money. It was a good deal. What else could I do?"

"Joe then bought my debt to keep the bookie off my back. He reminded me that Tony wouldn't wait long for the money. Nicking the judge's stuff would pay him off, and I'd walk away wiff cash in my pocket."

"All I had to do was explain what the judge did most evenings and when would be a good time when no one was around. I wanted to make sure Aunt Marjory was out of the way. So, I told 'em when I knew she'd be out most of the day, and the best time to do his house."

"The old bugger's half deaf, and with all that shit music he blares out, he wouldn't hear 'em comin' and goin'."

"All I needed to do on the day was unlock the back door and break that window, so people would think they came in that way."

"How'd you find out? It was a good plan."

"We're detectives, and detecting is what we do," said Sykes vaguely.

Wills said to Sykes, "help him with his statement and terminate the interview."

Then to Forrest, he said, "I believe you, and as promised, I'll have a word with the CPS."

****

Thirty minutes after the interview with Forrest, Wills, Hansen, and Sykes were sitting with DSU Merriman in his office.

Wills summarised what they got from the interview.

"So, Morris was the in-between man. We've got Forrest's statement, but it's his word against Morris. That's not going to be enough to charge the big guy. It's all circumstantial. Morris could tell us their discussions were about the weather forecast, betting form, or the like. While we can't prove anything, at least we now know we're on the right track."

"This is where sergeants come to the rescue," said Hansen to Sykes. "Here's where the real police work starts; sifting the evidence to link Joe Morris to Alan Forrest for the conspiracy to murder."

Sykes sighed, knowing what was coming. This was the boring part of the job,

145

handled by the real workers.

"Even more problematic is linking that shit Barker to the case," said a frustrated Merriman. He didn't often use bad language, but this was a reflection of his mood. He looked at Wills.

Wills responded, but in a more positive way. "It's not all doom and gloom. We now know who was involved in what part of the murder. That means we are not working in the dark like we were two days ago. The way I see it is we've made massive strides."

And for the Super's benefit. "Sir, that'll keep the Chief, the ACC, and every Tom Dick and Harry off our backs for the moment." He meant off Merriman's back but used the royal 'we'.

Merriman was already, in his head, planning his briefing with the upper echelons.

"So, with your approval," Wills said to Merriman, "Let's see what we can get from Morris. He's Barker's weakest link. He's not bright but 100% loyal. I don't expect to succeed. But if he bottles up, we'll know 100% he was involved with Barker, and Forrest was right."

The DSU agreed without question. "In the meantime let's get more information from Forrest on where he and Morris met, telephone calls, and other witnesses. Without anything concrete, the CPS won't take it further."

Every link in the case was a step in the right direction.

They discussed the finer points, and the meeting ended to prepare for the interviews the following day.

19. GO-BETWEEN?

At the agreed time of 10 am the following day, Joseph Morris and Fahmi waited in one of the police station's interview rooms.

Fifteen minutes later, Wills arrived with Hansen.

"Mr Morris, Wills opened, "thank you for coming along this morning."

He looked to Hansen to commence the formal part of the proceedings.

The solicitor interrupted.

"Gentlemen, we did you the courtesy of being on time. I'm a busy man and on the clock. Your delay has already cost my client money. So let's get on with it."

He sat back in his chair, rocking it on its two back legs, and linked his fingers behind his head. He displayed his well-practiced supercilious grin, designed to annoy his opponents.

Wills ignored the solicitor and addressed Morris directly. "Mr Morris, or do you prefer Joseph, even Joe?"

No response from Morris.

Fahmi's smug look remained as he responded on behalf of Morris. "I have advised my client to say nothing until you explain why we are here."

"Mr Morris, as we told you, we are investigating the murder of High Court Judge Charles Anthony Davidson."

"And what does the poor judge's sad demise have to do with my upstanding client?"

The DCI ignored Fahmi and continued to direct his questions to Morris. "Do you know an Alan Forrest?"

No response.

Wills continued to address Morris. "We've gone through the phone records of everyone involved with the judge. Lo-and-behold, there are numerous telephone conversations between you and a Mr Alan Forrest, who worked for the judge."

Morris and Fahmi merely stared at Wills. It wasn't a question in any case.

Wills, however, just wanted that seed to settle before he asked the real question.

"Could you please explain what was discussed on those calls?"

No response.

The solicitor then brought the front two previously airborne legs down with a loud clunk. He leaned forward and looked Wills straight in the eyes. He smirked. "We are here as a courtesy to His Majesty's Police Force, whom we both respect enormously. We do not know why you are talking to my client about the judge's murder."

Wills kept his cool against the solicitor's obfuscation and smug body-language. "It just seems coincidental that there are calls between a member of the deceased's household and the brother of the man being tried by the judge."

"Are you implying involvement by my client?"

"We are just trying to build a picture of the people around the judge. Since your client is involved with one of them, we are trying to understand why."

Fahmi then turned his attention to his client. "Anything you want to say about their scurrilous insinuations?"

Morris whispered in his solicitor's ear, "what's scurrilous mean?"

The solicitor ignored his client's question. He then said to Wills, "my client just explained he has no idea what you are talking about and has nothing to say."

Further questions were all met with the same lack of response.

Wills carried on nonetheless. "Your continued refusal to answer my questions reinforces our thinking."

After he let that settle in, Wills said to Morris, "thank you for confirming what we believed. Your help and implied confirmation of guilt are much appreciated. We now believe you were party to the judge's murder. As such we can focus our efforts on finding the evidence on you. You've saved us so

148

much time."

Morris gave a concerned look to his solicitor.

Wills continued. "Had you been straight with us and responded to our questions, as any innocent man would, our assumptions might have been different."

Morris failed miserably to hide his look of extreme consternation.

Fahmi put a hand on the big man's shoulder to reassure him.

He stared at Wills, his smug grin still affixed on his face. "As I expected, you brought my client down here on a fishing exercise. You then accused him of being involved with the judge's murder and, I might add, without any evidence. What you've said confirms that."

Fahmi again leaned toward Wills "For the record, this badgering and unfound accusations are the very reasons my innocent client stayed quiet."

Wills ignored the solicitor's rhetoric and continued with the game, again addressing Morris. "And it's just a matter of time before we link you and Mr Barker to the judge's murder. Then it's game over for you both."

Before he could say anything further, the solicitor interrupted. "My client kindly agreed to come and help you eliminate him from your inquiries. We have not come to listen to your fictional statements and unwarranted threats. If you want to charge him, do so. If not, we are finished here."

Morris grabbed Fahmi's arm and gave him a terrified look at the reference to being charged. With his other hand, the solicitor patted the hand clasped around his arm. He conspiratorially winked at the big man.

Both policemen said nothing; they waited for the next move in the game, which was now Fahmi's.

Fahmi played the silent game to perfection.

For several moments there was a three-way stare-down; Morris didn't know where to look.

Fahmi eventually said, "it seems you have nothing further to say on this subject."

"As always, it was a pleasure for you to meet the both of us," he said, sarcastically misusing the expression.

"And have a nice day." As far as Fahmi was concerned, the interview had concluded.

The solicitor stood up and beckoned Morris to do the same. With no challenge from the two seated policemen, they made for the door.

Wills gestured to the PC sitting behind to escort them out of the room and building.

After Fahmi and Morris left the room, Hansen couldn't help but comment, "even when that solicitor talks normally, it sounds like he's sneering at us."

"He is," said Wills. He hated the solicitor's nasally, whiney way of talking. That man knows how to get under everyone's skin.

At least now they knew about Morris' involvement, and by implication, Barker's.

****

Sitting with Barker and Morris back at the Barker residence, Fahmi extolled the big man's wonderful job of saying nothing.

"He followed my advice to the letter. He never rose to Wills' bait."

The solicitor then started his post-interview briefing to Barker.

"From their questioning, they believe Joe was involved in setting up the hit on the judge. Crazy idea, but what would make them think this? If it were true, who would tell them?"

Fahmi let that hang with Barker for a moment before continuing.

"In the interview, they mentioned telephone records between Joe and an Alan Forrest, who worked for the judge. There was no reference to Mr Forrest saying anything; at this time."

He let that information linger with Barker. "Yep, crazy indeed to believe our bumbling, gentle giant could organise anything, let alone hurt a fly."

The big man didn't take offence at what he said. Fahmi was insulting him, as he so often did, in his disparaging way. However, these types of remarks invariably went over Morris' head.

Morris responded, "Fahmi, they did think I was involved. They said I was."

"Saying and proving are two different things in law, my big gorilla friend," the solicitor replied. "Don't worry, you did brill', and they have nothing on you."

At that, Fahmi stood up. "I'll leave you both to chew over this morning's interview."

Barker, deep in thought about what he was told, automatically nodded in agreement.

The solicitor then let himself out of the villa and drove off.

"I'll bet that fucker Forrest's been squealing! Or if not already, he'll eventually bring up what he knows. Bet they'll offer him a deal," grumbled Barker to Morris after the solicitor had left.

Barker agitatedly paced up and down the room. "Nothing we can do about this now. If they had more on you, especially leading to me, they'd have questioned you further."

"But Tony, they know about everything. They know about the contractor, how Forrest set everything up, and my involvement. They've even got times and dates of our calls. They said my not talking confirms everything."

Morris was starting to feel worried. "Fahmi's screwed me by telling me not to say nothin'."

And in a panicked voice, he followed up, "I can't go to prison! What'll I do without you to look after me?"

"Listen bro', Fahmi told you right, and you did right. It's all a fuckin' game to see who breaks. As Fahmi said, they've got nothin' they can pin on you, so relax."

He patted Morris's back as he walked past the seated man. "They were just chucking in bits of bait to see if you'd bite. You didn't, so well done."

"I'm so proud of you." He rarely said anything complimentary to his brother. These words had the effect of swiftly calming the big man's worries.

Morris looked at his boss-cum-brother, like a doting dog having just had its belly rubbed.

Half to himself and half to Morris, Barker mumbled, "Forrest needs silenced."

"However, there are more important matters requiring our immediate attention; June fuckin' Mitchell."

151

20. REST IN PEACE

Sykes visited Jennifer a couple of days after the two sessions with Tabitha Malanga at the police station. He was on the way home from the station and wanted to deliver some good news to Jennifer.

The aunt opened the door and offered him a welcoming, "hello. Sergeant. I expect you want to talk with Jennifer?"

"Yes, please, if it's not inconvenient. I know it's a bit late in the day."

"She's in the living room, let me show you in."

Entering the living room, he found, unsurprisingly, Jennifer reading a crime novel. She looked up and beamed him a warm smile. "Good evening Barrie. Please sit." She patted a space on the settee next to her.

"I'll make us all a cuppa," said the aunt as she left the room.

"Nice to see you again," said Sykes to Jennifer, then to Jennifer's aunt, "yes please."

"I hope you don't mind my calling around. I wanted to tell you that DI Peterson's team had a break in the murder of Doctor Hardcastle. I thought you'd want to hear about it."

Jennifer clenched her fists and shouted, "yes!" with joy.

"With the crime and personnel profiles from you and Mrs Malanga during that session in the station, DI Peterson made two arrests. I cannot go into detail, but the arrests were almost a perfect match to your explanation what happened; not forgetting Tabi's part in it."

"However, this is what I can tell you," said Sykes.

"While Dr Hardcastle was taking drugs himself, he was trying to help others deal with the self-same condition. In his drug addict, 'cognitive dissonant mind', a Tabi phrase," he added, "your friend rationalised that it made him better equipped to deal with drug addictive patients."

"However, the death of one of his drug addict patients, let's call him Patient A, from an overdose, made him rethink his behaviour and treatment of others. It prompted him to seek help for his own addiction."

"Written in the doctor's file on Patient A, was a soul-searching note. The doctor, looking back at his handling of that case, wondered if perhaps he could have been less biased in dealing with the man's condition. Perhaps he could have been more prescriptive in trying to help the young man?"

"The patient's mother never realised the doctor was an addict until later. After her son's death, it came out about Dr Hardcastle hiding his addiction during her son's treatment. Her anger was inconsolable. That anger seethed and boiled in her over. It also overflowed into and infected Patient A's brother."

"They later learned the doctor had treatment and was clean. In their minds they reasoned he should have referred her son to the same place where the doctor sought help. Because he didn't, they believed he just played with the son's life, while taking the mother's money."

"It was eventually too much, and they decided to teach him a lesson by getting him hooked again. They thought an injection of heroin would get him to relapse. They planned to create that relapse and watch him become an addict again, destroying his life and career."

"They didn't set out to kill or hurt him, so the cushion and throw idea made sense. Their plan backfired. Not knowing how much should be in a hit, they overdosed and killed him. They didn't panic as most would; for them it was fate taking matters out of their hands."

Jennifer's eyes filled up as Sykes explained the story. All she could say was, "so many wasted lives."

Sykes continued. "So, they cleaned up the room, put everything back in its place, and removed any evidence of them being there. If they got away with it, fate decreed the doctor's death was justified. If caught, they'd just explain it was an accident that got out of hand."

"As it turned out, the mother was actually quite pleased with herself for what she did. She's taking the whole blame for setting all this up, trying to protect her son. So, pretty much a 'slam-dunk' to use a common Americanism."

Aunt Doris walked in with the tea and cakes as he was finishing.

"All this was down to you," he said to Jennifer.

Then to the aunt. "You should be so proud of her."

"You don't know how happy I am to have been of help," responded Jennifer.

"Peter was such a nice man. He didn't deserve to die, even worse, like that. How could anyone want another to live through that hell again? Darkening his reputation was insignificant in comparison. Now his drug-taking is out there, everywhere; they succeeded in that part, at least. It's just not fair," she said sadly.

Trying to lighten her mood, Sykes added, "DI Peterson's ecstatic, and fair play to the guy, he's acknowledged the crucial part you played finding the killers."

"I must admit, I've been so worried and even doubting myself that I may have been wrong. When it's fiction or even reconstructions I'm seeing, there's no impact on anyone, no matter what I think. So, I can get all heated up and as emotional as I like."

"But when it's real, there's such a responsibility. Even worse, when close to home, it's terrifying. I didn't want to let poor Peter down."

Sykes could see Jennifer's face grow sad as she said, "I'm so going to miss Peter. We had such good times together. Those times are all gone now."

"I also know he helped me so much. There's no one to replace him."

"Tabi told me yesterday that I shouldn't worry about the future without him. From my files, she said that Peter was no longer treating me or even counselling me. While there's no cure, he wrote that I now have the tools to manage my condition. He wrote that I'm going to be OK."

"But I desperately miss him. He was my best friend." Her eyes welled up, and the tears rolled down her face.

Sykes' handkerchief came out again. When she'd sufficiently recovered, he made an offer. "In that case, can I make a deal with you? If you have a burning need to chat about a case, I'd love to help. And if I have another case that might benefit from a set of fresh eyes, could I ask you?"

"Wow, that'd be great," responded Jennifer excitedly. Her mood lightened somewhat as she thought about spending time with Barrie and on more real cases.

She immediately took him at his word and launched into her issues about a crime programme she'd been watching yesterday.

Two hours later, and not all a crime discussion, it was time for Sykes to leave. By then, Jennifer had pretty much recovered from her earlier sadness.

They both said their reluctant goodbyes.

After Jennifer went back in the house, Aunt Price came out and quietly called after him as he climbed into his car.

He came back and they met halfway down the path.

"She's very delicate you know. Please don't hurt her."

Sykes looked at the aunt for a few moments. He'd allowed himself to believe his visit was professional. This young lady could help the team with their cases and, in so doing, help herself. And yes, working with her could even help his career.

The aunt's comments forced a certain reality on him. As Sykes thought about Jennifer, the realisation hit that he truly liked the young woman and enjoyed her company.

"I'm honestly fond of her, but if you are thinking about us in a romantic relationship, that's furthest from my mind. To be honest, it scares me to be in a relationship with her that's anything more than friendship. Right now, can't we just value our friendship? Is that OK for the moment?"

"We'll have to see, won't we," responded Jennifer's ever-so-protective aunt.

****

The mother and son plead insanity at their eventual trial for the death of Doctor Hardcastle. Their lawyer and supporting experts explained their state of mind resulted from the anguish they felt from the death of Arthur Dunbar.

The jury took a different view, seeing the killing as pre-meditated murder.

In advance of sentencing, the judge asked for a psychiatric report, which was inconclusive.

They were both jailed for pre-meditated murder. However, for their own safety, they were placed on the watch list.

21. WITNESS TO MURDER

June Mitchell, the CPS' key witness to the murder of the MP and ACC by Anthony Barker, was a highly successful prostitute and madam.

Even now, in her early 40s, when many of her peers had already hung up their thongs and nurse's outfits, she was still servicing a select few long 'standing' (forgive the pun) clients.

While she was a beautiful woman, even when younger, there were always more attractive, younger, and sexier-looking women competing with her on the street. However, she had an edge that set her above her competition.

What differentiated June Mitchell from the rest was her ability to read her clients' needs. She listened and read clients' body language, preceding, and during any acts. Then she could turn on whatever enthusiasm, athleticism, or even a sympathetic ear to satisfy the client.

Few had that same empathetic skill.

Hence, she was highly sought after. And that demand came with a financial premium; to her clients, of course.

They had to be rich to afford June Mitchell. With their wealth, came her influence. When the chips were down, as they often were in the prostitution racket, she was well supported, albeit behind the scenes.

Nowadays, her main business was as a 'Madam' running a couple of brothels, plus numerous mobile 'hostesses'.

In the role of madam, her girls and boys (as she called them) were also in great demand. Few possessed that same innate empathy, but she used her years of experience to coach them, to give their best. She then tightly controlled them during their short careers with her.

Once they were less in demand, they were free to ply their trade elsewhere but never on her patch or with her clients. Some had tried but soon saw the error of their ways. June could be brutal in the education of her 'wayward' ex-staff.

Many of her clients preferred their girls and boys young; the younger, the better. June didn't officially use underage girls and boys. However, when their age couldn't be proven, as in the case of some imported staff, she was happy to accept whatever age they gave.

She drew the line at blatant paedophilia. She did have a daughter after all. She doted on April Mitchell. It seemed a good idea at the time, to also name her after one of the months.

****

June Mitchell met Anthony Barker ten years earlier when she was at the top of her game. It wasn't long before he became a regular 'punter'.

She never really liked him, but business was business. At times, it was very useful to have someone who didn't mind giving a competitor or a difficult client a 'gentle slap'.

Barker liked his extras, and he paid well for them. However, unlike buying an ice cream cone that could come with harmless and tasty add-ons like 'hundreds and thousands' or 'chocolate sauce', in her business, some expensive extra services could be challenging, if not outright dangerous.

For example, she wasn't really into sadomasochism. June's early dabbling into that form of gratification not only disgusted her but was also extremely risky. As an activity between consenting and loving adults, it was bad enough. However, for a sex worker, when there was no emotional attachment, things could go too far, and sometimes did.

So, for a preferred client, she would comply under tightly controlled circumstances.

And Barker was a preferred client. Unfortunately, Barker often wanted to go there. However, those controls and limits she insisted upon, were regularly exceeded, even blatantly ignored by Barker.

On the other hand, under Barker's patronage, her business blossomed.

It was also a perfect arrangement from his perspective. While he enjoyed June's services, he also loved her girls' fresh young flesh. For him, she was a one-stop shop for sexual gratification.

As an out-and-out racist, he always outwardly complained about her imported staff. However, that didn't stop him from sampling those delicate-looking Asian ones; a preference of his.

Over time, he demanded her exclusivity. As far as he was concerned, with him on her side, business was good, so she didn't need to do tricks. Once he had her as his own, he insisted on unprotected sex. His safety meant keeping June out of the game.

Also, from an early age, he hated people playing with his toys, or in her case, soiling his property.

June had different ideas. She continued to service her own clients but made sure she was more discreet than before.

Prostitution is a bitchy business. One of her boys found out that his best-tipping regular client wanted to try out a girl instead of him. Naturally, June supported the client's choice of a female this time round. After all, 'the customer's always right'.

In a fit of pique, the young man grassed June up to Barker; anonymously of course. He knew the repercussions if she found out. That's assuming she survived Barker's anger, which he hoped not.

Over the phone, a muffled voice called one of Barker's people. "Last night, June Mitchell was shagging Assistant Chief Constable Deacon. And two nights ago, she was at it again with that MP, Geoffrey Towsend-Smythe. Both at the Park Hotel. It's her usual place. You can check. See if I'm not right."

Barker knew there was always tittle-tattle surrounding June and her business. As usual, he had the accusation checked out. This time the tip was right.

****

"Got a surprise for ya." He kissed her on the cheek and smiled when she came to his door in response to his call.

She looked at him questioningly. Barker rarely smiled like that when something innocent was afoot. His eyes were bright and excited. Her first thoughts were this was the precursor to a session of 'aggressive' sex, to use a euphemism.

"C'mon, the car's outside and running."

"Where are we going?"

"Told ya, it's a surprise." He was still smiling, but a sinister undercurrent surfaced in his look.

She hesitated, uncertain of what to do.

June's minder read her caution, stepped forward, and made to reach inside his jacket. Morris, standing next to Barker, expected the move. He grabbed the arm with one hand, the other clasped around the man's throat.

"Tch. Tch. Your man should know better."

June scowled at Barker then Morris.

"It's fine." Barker waved Morris away from the man.

"Don't you trust me darlin'? Come on."

She could see he was unusually animated.

"Just a couple of hours, I promise, and I'll personally drop you back here afterward."

"Listen. Met some new friends and we're out together this evening. You'll love 'em, honest."

June knew she had no choice but to go with the flow. She was also intrigued. There might even be business out of this.

Barker snapped at her minder. "You're not invited, disappear!"

June moved her head to signify that her minder should comply. He departed without a second thought. In any case, his boss and Barker were close friends, of sorts.

The car, driven by William Potts, pulled up in front of one of his many storage facilities. They went inside via a side entrance. The inside was dark, and it took time for her eyes to acclimatise.

Barker kissed her hand gently. Then leading her by the hand, he slowly and carefully guided her into the facility.

She heard soft rustling noises. Rats? She hated rats.

"So who am I meeting? Why are we here?"

159

Suddenly, bright floodlights illuminated the centre of the empty warehouse where they now stood. Her eyes, previously acclimatised to the dark, were now blinded. As they recovered, she could make out two tables positioned side-by-side.

Barker beckoned her to come closer.

She screamed!

"What the fuck are you up to?"

The ACC and MP were naked, gagged, and tightly tied down to two wooden tables. Both tables had their legs cut to lower their height and be tilted side-on toward each other.

From where the small man stood in between, he could easily lean over and reach the far side of his victims. There was enough space between the tables for their boss to move around.

Both victims could view each other and Barker.

"Joe, make June comfortable."

Morris tied June to a chair, which he then perched on a raised platform.

"Look at you. You have a grandstand view of proceedings."

He looked at June sadistically while he spoke to his brother. "Joe, make sure she doesn't miss anything. It would be such a shame."

The two victims were in their early 60s. They shivered, but it wasn't cold. They watched Barker open a plastic case.

With an eager glint in his eye, he picked up and waved around his toy. It was a powerful electric framing nail gun. He demonstrated loading the long magazine of 4" nails. "Don't worry, we won't run out, I've extra."

At over 10lbs weight, Barker needed two hands to control it as he waved it in front of their faces. It could fire nails deep into timber without the head protruding.

Barker looked at June and pointed to the bound men. "These are what you've been shaggin' as well as me? They're old, scrawny, and wrinkly."

"They're more men than you ever were, with your tiny, itsy bitsy cock!"

Barker's face reddened. "Not anymore!"

He nodded to Ben, who removed their gags.

He pulled the ACC's penis down to the wood of the table. There was a firing sound, immediately followed by a thwack as a nail was fired into the wood of the table.

The ACC screamed in anticipation.

June screamed at him to stop.

Barker missed, and then cursed.

He'd struggled to manhandle the gun in that confined space. He laughed. "His cock's too small!" So, he fired through his penis and testicles into the man's perineum, between his legs.

Barker ignored the man's screams. He was concentrating on getting the next one right. He wasn't going to make the same embarrassing mistake with the MP.

"My word, you're a meaty beast aren't you," he said to the powerful gun.

He pulled the MP's penis up, pressed the gun against the skin, and fired. This time there was a crack as the nail smashed through his pubic symphysis.

He couldn't hear June's screeching above the wailing and screaming of the MP.

He gave June a self-satisfied look. "What's that you said? Any other comments you'd like to make?"

She couldn't speak from the shock of what she'd seen. She shook her head as a no.

"I'm getting the hang of this. A bit out of practice these days. I so much appreciate you and your jolly kind friends giving me this super opportunity to try out my new toy," he mimicked what he thought was a posh voice.

She stared back. Her eyes were full of loathing.

He'd learned his lesson. Now two-handed, he started with the easy stuff, the hands, then the forearms. He moved between each victim, building his confidence and skill level before he moved to heavier tissue.

Barker ignored the screams from the three victims; June, forced to watch, was also a victim.

161

She cursed and threw expletives.

The two male victims pleaded with him to stop.

What none of them realised, the more they pleaded and cursed, the more satisfaction he got from the exercise.

Now confidently using the gun, he started to work on the more substantial parts of their bodies. Barker loved the sound of the whoosh, thwack, and sometimes crack.

Whenever she turned away, Barker walked over and struck her angrily. He remembered to only punch her body, legs, and arms. Sometimes he'd slap her in the face, smashing her nose, bursting lips, and tearing tissue with his long manicured nails.

Give Barker his due, June's beating only went as far as was necessary to get over his point of view and retain her attention. He avoided permanent, visible damage to his property. Although, years later, she still suffered creaks and aches, especially in damp, cold weather.

It was such agonising torture that the elder of the two, the MP, mercifully died of a heart attack before Barker could exact his full revenge. So, he focussed his efforts on the ACC.

He never liked the police, and it showed that evening.

The spectacle was unbearable. Even though June eventually broke down, he made sure there was no respite for her. Both clients were not only regulars but also friends who helped her over the years.

And so it continued for almost an hour.

June got off lightly. She wasn't introduced to his plaything that night. She didn't come out into public for several weeks after that episode.

She swore that one day she'd get revenge for what he did to her and her clients.

Even three years later, as hard and mentally desensitised as she was from the prostitution industry, she still occasionally woke up in a sweat, thinking about that night. The visions were imprinted in her brain. No matter how hard she locked them down, they sometimes resurfaced.

:d to make sure she wouldn't forget. He succeeded.

She never did.

****

During Barker's and June's subsequent time together, she had enough sense to rethink her protection. Being dragged into that property to witness the two murders highlighted the failings of her security. It had to be ramped up.

She knew there would come a time when he'd have no use for her. She'd eventually become a liability, knowing too much about his business.

While she remained exclusive to him for some months after the incident, he still wasn't to her; he never was.

Over time, to her relief, he lost interest. She was pushed aside for her younger and more willing staff to satisfy his more extreme desires.

When they eventually parted ways, each had enough on the other for both to keep quiet. Her security by then was sufficient to discourage any attempt to eliminate her. They had a strained stalemate.

The dynamics of that impasse dramatically changed when she was arrested for people trafficking. Fortunately, those imported employees were willing participants, and none were underage.

June paid them and their families an advance. The families had the promise of regular transfers, which lubricated the negotiations. They all knew what they were getting into.

So, the CPS could only proceed with people smuggling and living off immoral earnings. With her record, she was still looking at a prison stretch of several years.

All was not lost.

With help from a senior friend inside the CPS and a hint from her solicitor to senior members of the police, June Mitchell was able to barter a deal. She would help them convict the killers of the Assistant Chief Constable and the Member of Parliament.

At last, the authorities could rid themselves of the ongoing public embarrassment of being unable to bring the murderers to justice.

And she could get that long-awaited justice for her friends.

163

The police and the CPS knew Barker and Co killed the two men. The case was effectively solved but lacked sufficient evidence to gain a conviction.

Having a willing eyewitness to the murders gave them that missing evidence.

People trafficking is a serious offence. However, the heinous murder of two people is even more serious, especially when both were prominent members of the establishment.

Even though the CPS couldn't drop the charges, if June testified against Barker, the agreement was no prison time. That was fine for her.

The CPS also demanded she had police protection, which she treated with extreme scepticism. She had her own people for that.

There was an informal part to the deal. As long as she kept her business under wraps, the authorities would turn a blind eye. This part of the deal especially pleased those clients in the police and CPS who helped in the background.

June Mitchell considered herself a people person, and she had a people business to run. That business couldn't operate while she was sealed off from the world. Running a couple of brothels and travelling 'service representatives' required a direct, in their face presence. If she was out of commission, her business could very well collapse. Even existing regulars would move on.

June was confident enough in her team's abilities to look after her. She definitely didn't want the police snooping around the business. Her clients and customers would never be happy with a visible police presence.

So, June brought two red lines to the negotiation. She needed to personally manage the business and the police would not be allowed to accompany her during that time.

The second was the local police had to be excluded from her security arrangements. Everyone knew Barker had his little fingers stretched throughout the police, and no one could be 100% trusted.

The CPS had only one red line. It, unfortunately, was in conflict with June's number one. They wanted her in close police protection and hidden. The police had a lot riding on their star witness and were not going to rely on June's security. Any deal with her would be forfeited if she didn't comply with that demand.

The negotiations about that close protection were highly charged. Both had agendas that needed to be satisfied.

Eventually, both parties reached a compromise.

June could attend to her business personally, with her security, two days per week, without police presence. The rest of the week, she was in close protection. The days she was out and about would be kept highly confidential and be on a changing two-week rolling plan.

For June, this new working and access arrangement worked well over the weeks it was in operation. Little did she know it at the time, her business operation ran even better under the new procedures.

Her online day-to-day calls and meetings were more efficient, flexible, and secure. June realised she only needed to be present part of the time.

Operating this hybrid 'remote vs on-the-job working' pattern was the way forward for her business.

22. BASES OF OPERATION

During her 2-days per week outside police security, she'd visit both her properties.

One was Greystone Manor, a substantial old rectory, dating from the days when church-going was a popular activity.

Her daughter, April, ran this brothel. She was a 'Chip-Off-The-Old-Block' in terms of her ruthlessness and her mother's business acumen. She also had her mother's strikingly good looks. They were often likened to sisters when out together.

April never endured the sex worker's life. She never experienced the same pain of her mother's early years. As such, she didn't have June's emotional baggage that sometimes interfered with her business decisions.

Even at 24 years old, she had transformed this brothel into a more efficient and profitable operation than The Steadings, the brothel her mother oversaw. They didn't discuss why, it was just accepted.

On the positive side, there were excellent financial benefits. And in the same way as her mother, she enjoyed behind-the-scenes influence and power.

Being an only child, April was extremely close to her mother. She never knew her father, and June never talked about him.

When asked, June always replied, "it could have been anyone."

June and April loved their time together, chatting and comparing stories.

April's business was so well run those days, June never paid any attention to operational matters. This was their special time together, to just enjoy each other's company.

The second property, and the other visit of these days, was The Steadings. While June was the person in overall charge of that brothel, it had a resident madam.

The Steadings was set in a secluded location, as was her daughter's brothel. Both had to be.

Complaining NIMBY neighbours were a nuisance and attracted unwanted attention from the authorities. They were also bad for business. Visiting clients wanted anonymity and didn't like the raised visibility they created.

Even worse were those righteous individuals and groups who took upon themselves the task of monitoring and outing prominent clients.

"Can't a girl just run a quiet business?" was a typical complaint from June when accosted in the streets or in receipt of various physical and e-post.

Then June would strut around and complain to anyone around. "I remove all that fuckin' pent-up testosterone from the streets and out of the beds of those prude bitches. I do those frigid cows a favour, so they don't have to service their own blokes!"

While many of her representatives worked hotels and occasionally peoples' houses on demand, these brothels were also bases of operations. When her boys and girls weren't engaged, they were also places to socialise.

Here they compared notes on the performance of their various clients and exchanged anecdotes. If only their clients could hear what their paid sexual partners said about them.

Operationally, visiting the Steadings was a different matter.

The first thing June would do was to go through the books and staff medical records with the relatively new resident madam. Even having been in place for almost a year, she and the staff there still needed June's particular style of 'direct' attention to deal with staff issues.

Three of her minders were always on hand. Two would travel with her. The third would already be there, taking his turn on the house-sitting rota.

Sometimes a client might get a bit out of hand, but more often than not, the in-house minder was there to manage spats between her staff.

Typically, her security would spend most of their time waiting for June in the warmth of the kitchen. There was the agenda of a bit of flirtation with those female staff not currently horizontally engaged. Hard as they might try, all they got was a cup of coffee or tea and biscuits.

June's girls were expensive operatives, far too expensive for these three. Some of the boys might have shown a bit more interest though, but the heavies weren't interested in them, outwardly anyway.

While there was alcohol on the premises for punter entertainment, she banned her heavies from imbibing; they knew the risks of having a tipple while on duty.

She needed her minders sharp. Sadly, even at their sharpest, they could only be described as blunt weapons. June chose them for their cost, brawn, and willingness to protect and dispense her orders.

Once finished with the books and taken the report from the resident madam in the study, Mitchell left her. As usual, she headed upstairs to start the personal tour of those girls currently in residence but not servicing clients.

She liked everyone to think this one-on-one time with staff was her way of checking on their health and well-being. And in her defence, she did go through the motions of caring.

However, what she was really interested in was maximising income from the clients. Spending time alone with each of her girls and boys was to hear the gossip and the issues affecting her business.

It also allowed them to talk about each other and the madam in charge. As far as June was concerned, a bit of discord and vindictive gossip kept her in the know and was good for business.

****

Two things happened almost simultaneously at The Steadings on the fourth afternoon of her shared plan.

23. PLAN THE EXECTION

A week after Morris' interview with the police, Barker, Morris, and Bill 'n' Ben were having a planning session in Barker's office. It was the culmination of almost two weeks of work. Today would be the final touches in removing Barker's ex-girlfriend, June Mitchell, from the double murder case against him.

Removal meant killing, and they had no qualms about murder. For Barker and Co, this was merely the business they were in.

Ben was the bright one on Barker's team. There's no disputing that Barker was highly intelligent. However, he couldn't be everywhere and do everything. When not required for the run-of-the-mill daily enforcement activities, Benjamina was Barker's go-to man, or rather person.

She was the lead for anything requiring more than a modicum of intelligence. Also, when the situation arose, as in this plan, she was more than capable, physically and emotionally, to play her part in executing her part.

As soon as they received the information on Mitchell, Benjamina was the obvious choice to track June and the teams protecting her. Barker needed to make sure the information they received was valid, and for two reasons.

Firstly, they didn't want to walk into a police trap. The information had to be assessed from that perspective. For some strange reason, Barker and his team didn't trust the police.

Secondly, they needed to identify what opportunities might arise for the hit; when, where, and how.

The information given to Barker was simple. Over the following two weeks, they had four days when June was out of police security, during which a hit could be made. Those two working days changed every week, on a rolling two-week plan. There was no pattern to her movements. It was that simple yet invaluable schedule, which cost Barker one hundred and fifty thousand pounds.

169

The first day was the validation of the informant's information. Barker's team had three opportunities left.

Ben tracked June during the second of those days. She watched and tracked her movements until she disappeared back into the clutches of the official witness security. Ben wasn't able to safely track her when back in the clutches of the authorities.

The third day was a repeat of the same, except Barker was with Ben. They couldn't build an exact repeatable set of her movements. However, they identified one key piece of data; she visited both properties on her three days outside police protection.

They were located some distance apart in rural-cum-suburbia; close enough to reach from the city and quiet enough not to be visible. Clients didn't like to travel too far for their sexual fix.

Barker and his team identified two ways to execute the execution.

They could ambush her car on one of the quiet rural roads while the two heavies were stuck inside.

Ben identified several good attack locations on her possible routes. The downside was the variables of routes and timings. It also meant waiting in cold weather, with lookouts to check her movements and following her to ensure they were on the right route.

To catch June Mitchell when travelling required many people. More people meant more chances of loose tongues and a greater risk of being caught.

The alternative was making the hit at one of the houses. The houses were the riskiest since there were people around.

She was well protected by at least three heavies at The Steadings. April's house was even more problematic. As well as June's security, April had her own heavy protection.

Fortunately, another more realistic and safer solution presented itself in the guise of Sally Anderson.

Last year, Sally Anderson was operationally running The Steadings.

June and her accountant identified that money was missing and accused her of skimming the books. She dealt with that transgression in her usual business-like way. In a fit of anger, she threw a pan of hot oil over Sally Anderson, scarring her down one side, from head to hip.

Mitchell was well-versed in dispensing vicious forms of judgement. Many once pretty and successful prostitutes could no longer ply their trade. Scarred faces and disfigured bodies had a way of deterring clients. The fear of this happening to the others kept her houses running efficiently.

When Sally reported that attack to the police, all the witnesses testified it was an unfortunate accident due to Sally's clumsiness. Even her closest friends were too scared to offer any support.

Some months later, April's house was missing money. This time, June investigated thoroughly. There was no way her daughter would skim. June was right, it was her accountant. He'd also been the one skimming the books at the Steadings, for which Sally was mutilated.

The accountant disappeared.

June never apologised or tried to make restitution to Sally. June justified her behaviour as being the risks of working in this industry. Also, Sally had gone to the police, and that was unforgivable.

Sally, on the other hand, bore a deep-seated grudge. She didn't care how risky it was to grass on her old boss. As far as she was concerned, her life and career were over anyway.

It was common knowledge that Barker was looking to remove Mitchell from the witness list against him. Everyone also knew that Barker had no chance of achieving this. Her own and the police security were too good.

She knew Barker as well as any sex worker would know a regular client, which he was for a while. Sally still had his contact details and reached out to him with the offer of help some weeks previously. At that time, there was nothing Barker could do with it.

"Hi Tony," she said then. "I know you're looking for Mitchell. While I've no idea where she is these days, I hear she pops her head up now and then. If there's anything I can do to nail that bitch after what she did to me, let me know."

She added. "No charge darling, this one's on the house. Topping her is payment enough."

Sally was a popular and fair madam. She still kept in touch with friends at The Steadings.

Her friends felt guilty about not supporting Sally when she complained to the police. While no one was happy with what had happened to Sally, they knew better than to make comment, even privately.

Sally understood her friends' dilemma and bore them no malice.

Now with the information Barker had on Mitchell's plans, Sally's offer of help and connections in the houses were, at last, going to be of use.

He called her. "Hi Sally," he opened, then got to the point. "Do you still have contacts at the Steadings? Perhaps anyone who might offer some help? I need access to the place."

"Absolutely! And a few of the girls owe me. So yes. I can get you the inside track on whatever you need there. I've even got a copy of the keys. Ask and if possible, it's yours."

"Yer a doll. Once the bitch's gone, I'll make sure the place is yours."

He knew Mitchell was not popular, and many working there quietly held grudges. The plan was coming together nicely.

Sally had one particularly close friend in the Steadings. She was naturally too terrified to help Sally during and after the hot oil attack. However, the woman was racked with guilt about that lack of support.

Sally called in that marker.

24. EXECUTE THE PLAN

The first thing that happened on that fourth afternoon was two hooded and armed men burst into the kitchen. Well, as far as those on the receiving ends of the guns were concerned, they were assumed to be men. Benjamina wasn't one to argue the point.

They pointed their sawn-off shotguns at the three heavies sat around the centre kitchen table. Four of June's girls were also in the room but weren't considered a potential problem.

All knew better than to move. At close range, a sawn-off shotgun was lethal. Even the worst shot couldn't miss.

The kitchen, typical of these old country houses, was large. It had been tastefully updated, with new, traditional-looking, units and modern appliances. In the middle sat a large pine table that could comfortably accommodate ten people. Overall, it had a comfortable, old-fashioned, and homely feel to host clients. It was, however, efficiently laid out. Her girls were best employed on their backs, not wasting time preparing food and tidying up.

The two with the guns said nothing to the occupants; they didn't need to. All knew why they were there. Those on the barrel ends of the guns knew it was safest to wait and see what unfolded.

A wave of the shotguns signalled all to either sit or remain seated.

They threw a large canvas bag to the heavies, who knew the routine. Still seated, they emptied their pockets of anything that might be a weapon. The heavies had also brought sawn-off shotguns. Those guns lay on the large sideboard close to where they now sat.

One of the two with guns waved his weapon at the closest girl, then pointed to the guns lying on the unit. She slowly got up, picked up the guns by the barrels, and placed them in the bag. The girl calmly and gently placed the bag at the feet of the masked men.

They all waited for what might happen next.

****

June climbed the stairs to the first floor for the first of her ever-so-caring gossipy chats.

While those in the kitchen were held at gunpoint, she entered the first upstairs room on the right.

The room was not particularly large. It was, however, furnished to a high standard. It had the all-important large comfortable bed, and a well-stocked dressing table with a chair in front. There were also the usual fittings like a built-in wardrobe, dresser, etc. The comfortable armchair, which normally sat side-on to the electric fire, unusually had its back to the entrance.

One of June's girls sat on the bed, cross-legged, eyes closed, listening to music via earphones. She rocked to the beat that was a mere whisper to June.

The girl, a recent import from Asia, was a stunning nineteen-year old, with elegant poise, elfin features, and a tiny frame. She could have passed for fourteen years of age, and hence was in great demand.

June checked her watch. She had an appointment with an important and rich client and would have to leave in one hour. So, she needed to get cracking with the checks on the girls, then head off sharpish.

She entered the room and was about to tell the girl to put away her headphones when she heard a movement from behind. Before she could do or say anything, the second thing happened.

June was grabbed from behind and yanked backward. A hand clasped over her mouth. The attacker's other arm clamped around her middle.

By the time June recovered from the shock, she couldn't call out for help. Not that there was anyone who could have helped her, even if they could.

Barker's other two had the others under control downstairs.

Someone with immense strength lifted her off the ground as if she were a rag doll. She was completely immobilised.

Morris then walked into the centre of the room, carrying his kicking doll, and stood there.

The girl on the bed opened her eyes, said nothing, closed them again, and

174

continued to enjoy the music.

Barker, who was sitting in the armchair with its back to the door, stood up and turned to face June. He wanted to see her look of fear, knowing she was at his mercy.

June Mitchell faced the man against whom she was conspiring to put away. She was not going to show fear to this 'evil bastard'. It was what he'd expect and relish. So all he got was her well-rehearsed poker face.

Barker, now annoyed at her for not being scared to see him, pulled the killer's gun from inside his jacket and pointed it at her. He hoped that action would encourage some visible fear to surface.

All he saw was a smiling, taunting face and eyes through the fingers of Morris' hand.

The 'bitch' wasn't complying.

He took another tack. Ever so politely, as one does when bumping into an acquaintance in the street, he announced, how's tricks?" He grinned, thinking his play on the slang word, 'tricks', was a good one.

She rolled her eyes up; she'd heard it all before. June still said nothing, not that she could say anything if she even wanted. The large slab of meat that was Morris' gloved hand covered most of her face.

"June, so nice to see you again."

No reaction.

She wasn't playing ball! She should be terrified! In a now, not so-friendly tone he said, "if Morris removes his hand, are you goin' to bellow out?"

She signified no by shaking her head, at least as far as she could under the circumstances.

Barker said to Morris, "if she does try to scream, please be so kind as to break her neck."

"What the fuck are you doing here?" she screeched, although not loudly. She didn't want any of her valuable staff coming in and getting hurt.

"I'm not here to kill you, just talk." Barker was there to kill her, but he wanted to draw out the enjoyment of this moment. He wanted to tease her with the possibility of survival.

"Your lot is safe downstairs at the business end of a barrel as long as they play ball. As I said, just here to have a chat." He lied again.

She didn't rise to his bait but asked, "how'd you get in?"

"Now that's a long story. So, to summarise, your people kindly put us up for a few hours while we waited for you to arrive. They were all happy to screw you over. Once you were on your own, we just popped in for a chat."

He wasn't 100% truthful. Yes, Sally's friend did help, and the girl sitting on the bed was also aware. She also hated June, but that's a different story. So, she was happy to remain silent on the promise of being safe if anything kicked off.

Sally's friend let them into the house earlier that day. She gave Barker and Co a key to a room that no one would be going in; it was locked and about to be decorated.

Once the time was right, a simple knock on the door from her friend, and Barker and Morris went upstairs into the room where they currently were.

The second knock on the door meant that June was at the top of the stairs. It was then time for the other two to barge into the kitchen and hold up the people there. It was a simple and effective plan, and it worked well.

"I've answered your question and been polite. Why can't you be civil?"

"Because you've broken into my house and threatened my staff you little cunt."

"Ah, good point," he conceded. "Anyway, haven't you missed me?"

"Like cock up my arse I have. What d'ya want?"

Barker pointed to the chair in front of the dressing table and said, "Please sit down. We need to talk."

She had no choice but to comply.

"You need to stop saying those bad things about me in the next court case. Otherwise, I'll have to hurt you." He then held the gun to her forehead in a gloved hand.

If she was worried, she never showed it. Without flinching, she retorted, "the fuckin' bizzies have me for bitch traffickin'. My way out was to tell the judge how you fucked me over and killed two of my best-paying clients. I liked them. Anyway, it's just business; survival of the fittest and all that."

"Listen you old dried-up whore, no one fucks with me and walks away."

"And you're not walking away from this if anything happens to me," she replied. "Too many witnesses here and downstairs. You gonna kill 'em all?"

"Well, I am walking away. And people know not to talk." Barker fired a shot to the centre of her forehead at point-blank range. He then shot her in the heart, just like the killer would have.

"And to your point on witnesses," he turned and walked up to the girl sitting on the bed, still with her eyes closed and rocking away to her favourite music. He fired twice, again at point blank range, forehead and heart.

He turned to the corpse of June Mitchell and gloated at her. "See, no witnesses."

Barker and Morris pulled up their ski masks, left the room, and exited the house. They started the car and climbed into the back, ready for the two others. When they sounded the horn, his two balaclava-clad heavies hastily followed.

No one came after them, and no one overtly looked out of the windows. Any checking on their departure would have invited a direct gun blast. The warnings were clear, albeit not spoken. Barker was right. There were no witnesses from those in the kitchen or elsewhere in the house. With June now gone, there was no point.

Although he wore gloves, Barker nevertheless, cleaned any potential fingerprints off the gun and left it in the glove box of the stolen car.

They parked the car in open countryside, away from cameras and sightseers. As they drove away, Bill could see, in his rear-view mirror, the burning car fade into the distance.

177

25. DOWN THE PAN

DSU Merriman was livid when he heard. He still hadn't cooled down when he arrived at June Mitchell's murder crime scene.

The close security team had proposed the security compromise to him, and the Chief Superintendent signed off on it. However, she only approved once the DSU had confirmed he was happy with the arrangements.

On his watch, a judge was killed. And shortly after, the key witness in the case was also killed, leaving his team with no case against Barker. The promise of putting away the MP and ACC killers was now in the wind.

The responsibility was going to hit the top of the command ladder he was so desperately trying to ascend. Then it would trickle down to him, where the buck would stop.

If he was to stave off the hungry packs of press, anti-police, and social media wolves, Merriman needed answers, fast.

He went over to Wills, "give me some good news."

Wills, equally annoyed, blurted out, "Barker's hit man broke a prostitution ring."

Normally, breaking a prostitution ring would be good news. However, Wills had said this sarcastically. It wasn't aimed at Merriman, but everywhere and nowhere.

Merriman realised this was an out-of-character outburst. He said nothing, merely waiting for his DCI to pull himself together.

Recovering his composure, Wills quickly followed up with, "sorry sir, just pissed off at the moment. Everything we've worked for is now down the pan."

"I know," Merriman said with a shrug of understanding. He felt the same way. As usual, he was better able to control his emotions.

In answer to the question, Wills responded with, "Sorry, nothing to add, sir."

"I'll let you all get on with it," Merriman sighed.

"Call me if anything comes up. In the meantime, I'll be under the thumbscrews. The Chief Super, the ACC, and whoever else up there will be queuing to have a pop." It was not often that he exhibited humour or even sarcasm; this was about as close as he got.

Merriman would do his best to buffer the fallout so that his team could get on with their job.

As the DSU left, he said to Wills, "9 am my office tomorrow with an update? Anything significant beforehand, ring me. Anytime!"

"Yes sir."

****

The next morning, Wills and Hansen knocked on Merriman's office door. He waved them in. All three had a late night and were too tired for pleasantries.

"There were four assailants who entered the property. Two went into the kitchen and held Ms Mitchell's people at gunpoint there. At the same time, another two went upstairs and killed Ms Mitchell and the young woman in the room," opened Wills.

"We found a burned-out car resembling the one the killers left in. It was reported stolen a day earlier."

"The car was dumped and set alight seven miles away in open waste ground. They could have reached there by one of three routes."

"In the fire, there were remnants of what were most likely to have been overalls and balaclavas. The fire helped destroy all traces of gunshot residue and DNA from whoever made the kill."

"We found a SIG P226 in the glove compartment of that car. Ballistics confirmed it was the same gun used in the killings at The Steadings and also the murder of Judge Davidson."

"The injuries to both victims at The Steadings and the judge are the same. Both had one shot to the centre of the forehead and one to the heart."

179

"So, are we talking about the same killer?" queried Merriman.

"I don't know yet. The killer acted alone in the judge's murder and the two other known ones that Sykes identified from his research. However, four people were involved in this one; a deviation from his MO."

"By the way, Barker was playing cards all night yesterday, coincidentally in a foursome. That is with his brother, Joe Morris, and Benjamina and William Potts."

The DSU acknowledged with a short, "Yep, aka Bill 'n' Ben; I know them well."

"SOCO and Sykes are going through the evidence to build a clearer picture of what happened in that upstairs room."

"We are going through their alibis and CCTV footage from where they were playing cards."

"And we're checking CCTV and witnesses from the vicinity where the car was stolen."

"The road from Steadings is mostly countryside, as is the area around the burnt-out car. So realistically, little chance of CCTV coverage or witnesses."

The DSU waited for Wills to continue, hoping for more. But, Wills finished with, "that's all we currently have, sir."

"Keep me posted if anything happens. Whatever the case, I need a daily 9 o'clock morning briefing." Merriman had to report every day at 0930 to his superiors.

Merriman turned to the paperwork on his desk. That effectively meant meeting over.

"He doesn't stand on ceremony does he," commented Hansen after they left the office.

"Works for me. I hate prevarication almost as much as the boss."

His statement could have been interpreted in two ways. Hansen left it at that.

****

Later that afternoon, Sykes briefed Hansen and Wills on what he'd found.

"I now believe this was not the same killer as the judge. The killer shot June Mitchell at point-blank range, but without a suppressor. The previous hits I linked to the same killer used a suppressor, all at least from several feet away."

Hansen interjected, "it might be that the killer believed there was no reason to use a suppressor since he didn't need the sound to be quieter. The property was in a remote location. All the others were either in their rooms, frightened, or held at gunpoint. No one would be coming in and checking."

"I agree guv. But the earlier kills were also solo jobs. This last hit had four in the team. Going through the process; we had people held at gunpoint and too many witnesses. Also, there were too many variables and things that could have gone wrong."

"This kill wasn't as cleanly planned as the others. I believe that this was a gangland-style kill. Effective, well executed, yes. But risky. Not the killer's full MO."

"I agree. Just validating your reasoning. Good work Sykes," said Hansen.

DCI Wills followed up with, "if we now believe Barker did the hit, we need to find evidence. If we can pin this one on him, we've got him for the judge's murder as well; the same gun was in the car."

Sykes then added, "We can't get them on GPS coverage. Their phones were on, but all four phones were where they were apparently playing cards."

"Barker's car's currently locked in his garage so forensics can't do their magic. We don't have enough evidence for a search warrant. That means it's staying there."

We checked CCTV coverage in the area where they were playing cards. Those local shops with CCTV told us their systems were off yesterday and still off today. Strange coincidence, eh?"

"The murders took place in a rural area, so we initially thought there'd be no CCTV. The good news is a recent spate of robberies made some farmers put up CCTV around their buildings. Sadly, none covered the roads possibly used by the killers. We're still looking into this."

Wills then asked what initially appeared to be an off-track question. "How's your Miss Graham?"

The DS reddened a little at the question and the use of 'your'.

Sykes assured himself he had no romantic interest in Jennifer; her issues were too frightening for him. However, others seemed to have a different perspective on their relationship. Was he that obvious?

"Coincidentally, I'm popping round tonight. I promised to help Jennifer go through some crime stuff. She was particularly wound-up about yesterday's episode of 'Unsolved True Crime Murders'. It'll be an interesting exercise, and we owe her some support after the help she gave us."

"Of course we do, and you're the man to repay her, do your duty for king and country," Hansen jested with his sergeant, whose face started to take on a rosy embarrassed glow.

"Terry, stop winding up the lad."

Wills turned back to Sykes. "Seriously, here's what I was thinking. Why don't you bring the young lady down to the station tomorrow morning? I know this is a bit dubious in terms of sharing evidence with her. Perhaps her visit might be construed as an interview for a consultancy job? Just thinking she might have a bit of insight to share."

He continued. "That condition of hers has proven to be useful to us. If nothing else, she can see things in an unemotional, pragmatic light currently evading us. Let's be honest, we're all hot around the collar on this."

"Will do, sir. I think she'd jump at the chance of working on a case with us again."

"And for payment in return?" questioned Hansen. Then to Wills, "what do you think about helping her with one of her crime problems?"

Wills and Hansen grinned at Sykes who pretended not to be too enthusiastic.

"Since it's your idea, Detective Inspector Hansen," added Wills, "both of you can be at her disposal to review her TV anguish."

Hansen grunted in mock disproval to his boss' revenge for winding up Sykes.

Then with a grin, he said to Sykes, "sorry, look's like you've got a chaperone." He gently elbowed Sykes in the ribs.

Sykes ignored the teasing from his guv.

With both of them happily on side, Wills immediately called the Super for his thoughts and hopefully approval to use Jennifer again.

"Absolutely!" he immediately retorted. "Great idea. Approved."

With the meeting over and now back at his desk, Sykes called Jennifer.

"Been talking with the DCI and the Super. We were wondering if you'd like to pop down to the station tomorrow and go through another case with us? And in return, you get two for the price of one. My guv, DI Hansen, would also love to hear about your issues with 'Unsolved True Crime Murders'."

"Oh yes," was her immediate response.

Then hesitantly she asked, "are you still coming over this evening? We now don't have to talk about crime since I'll have the both of you later."

"Love to. I was hoping we'd still be on."

He didn't know where this was going, but he was realising he'd like to take the journey and see where it took them.

26. STRAINED RELATIONS

Every Wednesday, the evening meal at 15 Primrose Avenue was an Indian takeaway. Jennifer and her aunt always ordered the same thing, from the same takeaway, at the same time.

They liked consistency, and it also avoided conflict.

Jennifer needed routine to help keep her grounded. She suspected she was on the OCD spectrum, although Peter never said anything about this.

She thought about Peter. '*Now he was definitely OCD.*'

Since Sykes also loved Indian food, and they both liked him, it was a natural decision to invite him to today's dinner. She was looking forward to him coming over.

As the time approached when Sykes would arrive, she was becoming a little anxious. The aunt hadn't placed the order and was unusually procrastinating. Jennifer assumed Aunt Doris wanted to ensure he was with them when they ordered, even though he'd already told them what he liked.

Just when Jennifer was about to take over and place the order, the doorbell rang.

Sykes was standing there with flowers.

Jennifer smiled and reached out to take them, but he pulled them back out of reach.

He reached past Jennifer to present the old woman with the flowers. He addressed the aunt, who stood behind Jennifer. "Good evening Miss Price. Would you mind if I disrupted your evening and take Jennifer out to dinner?"

Jennifer really liked Barrie and pretending to be annoyed, hands on hips, asked, "shouldn't you be asking me?"

He grinned at Jennifer. Feigning afterthought, he asked her, "would you like to come out for dinner tonight? I've already set this up with your aunt. We've been teasing you. Sorry."

She thumped him on the arm, enough to hurt as a reminder, but not too hard.

"So that's how it is? You're both conspiring against me. Let me think about it," shouted Jennifer over her shoulder as she launched herself up the stairs, leaving the two of them in the hallway.

"Where are you going?" shouted a now worried Sykes to what was left of her disappearing legs.

"To get changed, of course. I can't go out to dinner like this."

They heard her whistling as she banged around upstairs, attacking drawers and cupboards in her haste.

Ms Price chuckled. "I think we're forgiven. You'd better come inside."

****

Sykes was by no means a ladies' man. Any relationships he did have, he kept away from the prying eyes and gossip of the station. Even his time with Tabitha Malanga was kept private, or so he thought at the time. Tabitha, on the other hand, liked to gossip with the girls.

He considered himself a serious career police officer. He didn't want station flings interfering with his work, relationships, and professional image. Many female officers in the station wished he mightn't be so career orientated.

Unfortunately, there was no way he could keep any relationship with Jennifer quiet. The station gossip channels were already buzzing about them. They were eagerly awaiting the next chapter of their relationship, not that there'd been much more than a prologue to date.

Sykes had never seen Jennifer in anything more fashionable than casual clothes. And he must admit, she looked OK in them. So, he couldn't fathom why she was taking so long to come down.

He assumed it would be just a matter of turning up, asking her out, and they'd be off for a bite to eat.

More fool him!

This was suddenly an important date for her, and she was going to make an effort. In any case, she was perfectly happy letting him suffer after his deceit.

When she eventually entered the room and he looked up to check if she was ready to go, his jaw visibly dropped.

"You'll catch a fly with that open mouth," laughed Ms Price.

Jennifer beamed at his reaction. She stood inside the doorway a little longer than necessary to let him take in the view, which she was so pleased he appreciated.

Her long dress accentuated every point of her figure. With her hair done up and no longer hiding her features, he could now see that she was quite beautiful. Adding in high heels and an elegant shawl to cover her shoulders, Sykes felt wholly underdressed in just an open-necked shirt, jerkin, and trousers.

His surprise backfired, and now he was at the disadvantage. However, he still had something up his sleeve that would help him recover. They were going to his comfort zone, which maintained consistency with their theme of Indian food for Wednesdays.

"I've booked a table at a wonderful Indian restaurant called Saksham. Hope you don't mind?"

"Of course not."

"I often go there. It's named after one of my best friends from university. He's the only son of the couple who owns it. When I was at university here, they were like second parents to me, and still are."

He explained that Saksham's parents treated him like a second son. As their surrogate son, that also meant trying their best to guide or rather, interfere with him in everything he did.

"His mother runs the kitchen with a couple of helpers. The father-son combination manages front-of-house when Saksham isn't working late or studying for his bar exam. Cousins help out otherwise. It's a real family affair."

"This is my special place to eat and hang out," he added.

Jennifer was now relieved she'd made the effort. Otherwise, she might have felt uncomfortable.

He didn't mention to Jennifer that as well as trying to set up their elusive son in marriage, the parents were keeping a lookout for Sykes. They'd already invited him to large family and friend dinners, showing him off. They weren't bothered about interracial marriages; he was one of them.

He especially didn't tell Jennifer that in Saksham's mother's view, to date, none of the ladies he brought to the restaurant were suitable. She expected the same disappointment that evening.

However, Saksham and his parents would do as promised. They'd make every effort to make this evening as pleasant as possible, with their best food and service.

Knowing Saksham and his parents, there was no doubt about the food. It was the mother's uber-service that worried Sykes. He pleaded, "Mamma," as Sykes always called her, "please don't hover around and eavesdrop. Can we have a quiet unobtrusive evening?"

Unfortunately for Sykes, she didn't do discreet when on a mission. And she was on a mission. His pleading for this date to be perfect only succeeded in creating intrigue that she was determined to get to the bottom of. He'd never made such a fuss about a previous one. Normally, he'd just turn up.

"Of course," she lied. "I'm only looking out for you, and anyway, she'll never notice me."

At only four foot ten inches, she reached up high to clasp his cheeks in her podgy hands as reassurance.

Sykes wrapped his arms around her well-proportioned figure and hugged her.

****

Mamma was now hyped-up for the start of this mission. She needed to watch this one. Mamma insisted on regular reports coming in from the front-of-house, on pain of death.

When Sykes and Jennifer walked in, Saksham was behind the bar, which was located next to the entrance. He came round to the front to greet his friend but was diverted. Seeing Jennifer, he ignored Sykes, took her hand, and kissed it, old-fashioned style.

"Hi, I'm Saksham, Barrie's best friend and confidant; and most available bachelor."

Still holding her hand and without giving her a chance to respond, he escorted Jennifer to her seat. Jennifer turned around and gave a questioning grin at Sykes, who just shrugged his shoulders.

The restaurant seating was simple, flexible, and effective. It comprised square tables that sat four but could be placed together for larger parties.

Saksham, under strict instructions from his mother, sat Jennifer at one of the closer tables facing the bar. The table was chosen to be far enough away to ensure Jennifer couldn't hear what was going to be whispered about her. Yet it was close enough to be in plain sight.

He then left with the words, "gotta deal with some customers, but papa will be over for the drinks orders."

He lied. This woman was big news. He had to update Mamma. We strode to the far end of the restaurant and into the kitchen. The kitchen had a large window for guests to watch the cooking. Through that window, Jennifer and Sykes could see the animated discussion Mamma was having with Saksham, with occasional glances in their direction.

Sykes was starting to think perhaps this might not have been such a good idea.

It was the father's turn to come over and check out the new woman in Sykes' life while he took their drinks order. Sykes introduced Jennifer to Papa, and they shook hands formally. From the look of the father's animated face and reaction, he too was impressed.

Jennifer beamed a smile at him. Then in Hindi, she asked for a glass of white wine. The father almost dropped his ordering book and pen.

After quickly recovering his composure and after also taking Sykes' drinks order, he gave Jennifer the biggest of grins. He rushed off, not to the bar, but also into the kitchen. Papa had another update for Mamma.

Sykes looked at her incredulously, "I didn't know you could speak Hindi?" Having known the family for some years, he'd picked up a smattering of the language, so recognised what she had said.

"Sadly, no. I only know a few words, and top of the pile was ordering a glass of wine. It's just fun watching them when they think you can speak their

188

language. They're then scared to say anything about you or the food, in case you understand."

"I can see I'm under the spotlight, so I thought I'd play with them in return."

"You're a devious blighter," chuckled Sykes.

"You can blame Aunt Doris. It goes back to a few years ago when we were in India on holiday together. We were lounging in a beach bar. A couple of local boys talked to us in English and then to each other in Hindi. They were laughing with each other while glancing over. We knew they were talking about us and not very politely."

"You should have said something to the owner," said Sykes, feeling annoyed on her behalf.

"Aunt Doris did something even better than that. She stood up and walked close by to where they were sitting. She delicately picked up a butterfly that was resting on a branch."

"Then she shouted over to me, "sundar titalee," which in Hindi means beautiful butterfly. She then stared at them with one of her earth-opening looks she'd honed over decades of teaching. They quickly drank up and left. They assumed my aunt was fluent in Hindi and overheard everything they said about us."

Sykes interjected after immediately catching on. "Who else but someone fluent in the language would know the word for butterfly?"

They both burst out laughing.

"So, I learned a few words in Hindi, Italian, Greek, and even Mandarin."

"I order in their language, then I like to sit back and see their reaction. There's another advantage, most appreciate the effort visitors make."

The parents came out of the kitchen and went behind the bar. Mamma stood there pretending to dry glasses, conspicuously not staring at this woman. The father and mother were deep in whispering conversation from the sides of their mouths.

It was Mamma's turn to discreetly investigate this new woman face-to-face. She came over to take their food order and Sykes introduced them to each other. Mamma took Jennifer's hand and gave her an all-over lingering look.

189

Satisfied with what she saw, she winked approval to her Barrie. Mamma warmly smiled at Jennifer. "Good evening. Welcome, and if there is anything you need, you call me. Forget these men here. I'm in charge."

She then released Jennifer's hand.

Jennifer ordered her usual Chicken Dhansak and boiled plain rice. Mamma tried her best to get her to sample their restaurant's specialities, but Jennifer couldn't be persuaded otherwise.

She did reluctantly delve into some of the many bites and side dishes offered up despite her protestations. Each was personally brought over by the, definitely not fussing or hovering matriarch.

Jennifer was checked-out throughout the evening and was clearly passing with flying colours.

Saksham, grinning from ear to ear, eventually came over and said to Sykes for Jennifer to overhear, "my parents think Jennifer's wonderful and asked if she had a sister for me?"

Jennifer stood up, walked over to the mother, kissed her on the cheek, and said, "thank you, Mamma."

Sykes was shocked at Jennifer's reaction. He'd never seen her so outwardly confident and with strangers! He was now able to relax at last.

Jennifer wasn't normally comfortable amongst people she didn't know. This was the first time she'd walked up to a strange woman and confidently kissed her on the cheek. Even more out of character, she did this in an unfamiliar place.

But with Barrie and amongst these lovely people, his friends and informally adoptive family, she felt completely at ease.

The food and drink came and went. The relaxed atmosphere of his comfort zone was now hers as well. She couldn't remember the last time she'd forgotten about her condition and how it impacted her relationships.

While she had boyfriends, it was rare that she let her guard down. Of course, she enjoyed sex, but only with the right person and in the right circumstances.

All too often, it all just ended up in all that verbal dancing around sex that had to be politely endured, before she could put a close to the sex-less evening.

With Sykes, she could be who she was; without hiding.

Sykes looked at Jennifer, perhaps it was the alcohol influencing him, but he no longer felt scared about being in her company.

Their first foray out together was enough, and both knew it. By mutual agreement, the end of the meal was the end of the evening. Perhaps both were scared of losing the magic?

After hugs and re-hugs with Mamma, they took their leave with the promise of soon returning.

The taxi stopped outside Fifteen Primrose Avenue, and Sykes walked Jennifer to her door.

Barrie hesitated. He was about to walk away, but she grabbed him and gave him a long, hard, tongue-searching kiss. The second time this evening she'd overcome her normal reticence.

Sykes walked back to the taxi with a spring in his step. He turned around and waved goodnight.

Aunt Doris was waiting in the hallway with a questioning look, but Jennifer said nothing.

She wasn't one to be ignored. "Well?" questioned the aunt loudly.

"I like him; very much."

A relief came over Ms Price. There was hope for this girl yet. In the back of her mind was the fear that this one would also run scared, again hurting her precious niece.

As they pulled away from the kerb, the old taxi driver said, "she's a cracker, that one."

"I know."

And at no time in the evening did Jennifer and Barrie discuss crime.

27. FURTHER INSIGHTS

It was cold, wet, and windy when Sykes pulled up at Jennifer's house the following morning. He was hopeful that if anyone could offer some ideas to help resolve the case of June Mitchell's murder, it would be Jennifer.

She, on the other hand, was looking forward to another foray into real-life crime. Seeing him pull up, she ran down the path while fighting with a half-opened umbrella. She jumped into the car with a flourish and a spray of water.

He again had no chance to get out of the car and do the gentlemanly thing of opening the door for her.

She leaned over and hastily kissed him on the cheek. And as quick, she sat back to fasten her seatbelt.

"I had a lovely evening, thank you again."

"When I set this up with your aunt, she was initially reticent with me. Once she realised that I honestly liked you and had no other agenda, she started to drop that protective shield she has around you. She's a lovely lady."

Jennifer leaned back in the seat, folded her arms, and smirked while looking forward. She was relieved that he reciprocated her feelings.

Then, coming out of her thoughts, she said, "what a wonderful place that was, such lovely food. And the family, they're just super!" she exclaimed.

"I hope Saksham was not too forward. He doesn't know about your, ahem," he stammered, "condition." He still felt uncomfortable thinking, let alone talking about it.

"He's a doll."

"His mother likes you, you know. They all do."

"And I'm already fond of them all, especially her," extolled Jennifer. "When you told me this place was special for you, I was initially scared. Actually, I was terrified of going there and letting you down."

They continued to make comfortable small talk as they drove towards the station.

Once signed in, Sykes took her up to the same team meeting room where they initially met. The judge's case pictures and diagrams were still on display at the end of the room.

The room now also contained all the information on the June Mitchell murder. Everything on the case was stuck up on all the windows of the partition separating the room from the main office.

Hansen was waiting for her with a beaming smile and shook her hand enthusiastically. "Welcome back, and looking forward to working with you again."

Hansen nodded to Sykes to take the lead.

Sykes opened. "The case we're now looking at," he gestured to everything plastered along the side of the room, "is the murder of a madam who ran a couple of brothels."

"She was the principal witness in the case of a gangland boss," he didn't give June's name at this time. "This case is related to the judge's case you helped us with over a week ago."

He went through the facts they had, plus their extrapolated assumptions.

"Even though there are similarities to the MO of the judge's murder, there are enough differences to make us think the perpetrators are different. Add in the MOs of the two others we linked to the killer, we believe June Mitchell's was a different one."

Just to confirm, and as additional background, Sykes also went through the two earlier murders attributed to the killer. He then walked her through the photographs and various diagrams, statements, and other pieces of evidence on the case. Every so often, Hansen added a point of clarification.

After walking through the murder in her mind, she remarked, "I don't think four men entered the house as you suggest."

"The evidence and witnesses said there were two of them in the kitchen, and after they ran out, they glimpsed another two in the car, that makes four," defended Hansen.

"Sorry, I'm not questioning the numbers of men. You're right, there were four. I'm just saying four people couldn't have entered the house and gotten into position simultaneously. And how would they know when would be the perfect time?"

"It would have been too risky for anyone to sneak into the house without revealing themselves to the heavies downstairs. From what I see, it would make more sense that the upstairs two were already there."

"If they all entered together, it would have been at speed. There would have been sounds and noise. June would have been warned not to enter the room. If they burst into the girl's room with June there, she'd almost certainly have heard them coming and called out."

Jennifer asked, "did anyone hear anything before the shots?"

Sykes replied. "The people downstairs heard no one walking upstairs apart from June walking and entering the room. They did hear some heavy movement after they were held up by the two downstairs."

"Ah, that helps," she responded. "It looks like the people were already in the house before June and her friends arrived."

She then rhetorically asked, pointing at the picture of the armchair facing the wall, "who has an armchair facing a wall?"

She followed up with, "I see someone waiting, with the back of the armchair facing the door to surprise her after she entered. The killer stood up from behind the armchair. Otherwise, he/she would have been hiding elsewhere. The armchair was a risky move that could have spooked the victim. That all works together if she knew her killer. And, this was very, very personal."

"By the way, it's not a big armchair. If I'm right, and someone was hiding in it, that someone was quite small."

Jennifer continued her train of thought. "She was taken by surprise as she entered the room. And that large bruising to her mouth and around it," she pointed to the pictures of the dead woman, "makes me think that someone strong and large covered her mouth."

"If that was me and someone barged in, my immediate reaction would have been to scream for my minders, or at least shout out in surprise."

"Her killer planned this to look like a professional hit, to distract you from looking in their direction."

She chuckled, "it wasn't actually that professional, was it?"

"The only way I can visualise this happening is that someone let them in. Not only were they let in, but someone hid them for some time before she arrived."

"The perpetrators would have known and trusted the helper very well. So, like the judge's murder, there was an inside person. And that means you've got a direct link to the killer."

"Told ya," said Wills behind them. He'd arrived as Jennifer was in full flow but said nothing to distract her.

Then to Jennifer, "we've been arguing about many of those pieces of evidence. I'm sure this time, we'd have gotten there, at least I hope so, eventually.

"However, you've quickly made sense of them and given us a confirmed line of investigation. Thank you, Jennifer."

Jennifer turned round to the friendly face of the DCI. Normally, when caught by surprise like this, she'd just clam up. Her mouth would go dry.

Not here with these people she considered as friends. They'd always been kind. After all, it was Wills who rescued her from that other Detective Inspector.

That confidence enabled Jennifer to quietly say, "do you mind if I have something more to add? It's not directly related to the evidence here but it might help."

"Shoot," said Wills with interest.

"I saw in the news that there's been a lot of stealing from farms; they've very expensive equipment and livestock. It's easy to have CCTV and other security around the main property." The problem that farmers face is the many buildings to secure away from the main farmhouse. They struggle to protect them."

Hansen sighed. "Yeh, I know where you're going. Sadly, we tried looking at this and asked farmers. However, they only secure the main areas. They say it's too expensive to do more CCTV coverage than in those areas. That was a

195

dead end."

Wills felt he needed to comment. "Miss Graham, if there is anything at all, no matter how insignificant, all ideas are on the table."

"Ah," responded Jennifer. "That was my idea. You're ahead of me here. I was going to add something but I'm not sure now?"

"Please go on."

"I was interested in this sort of crime, so I did a bit of browsing for some more background. One of the solutions proposed by some in the farmers union is they deploy CCTV to protect the main access roads and paths that thieves would use. The problem is that with GDPR, it is potentially against the law to record public areas. I had a big argument with Peter about this. I was right."

"So, when your police officers ask farmers if they have CCTV elsewhere on their property or even on the main road, they'd deny it. It's potentially against the law, and with big fines if caught."

"Anyway, just thought you might look around in obvious hiding places; or was that a contradiction? Or you could politely ask again and promise anonymity?"

The DSU standing at the doorway interrupted the proceedings with, "my word, nice idea. And yes, you're right. There have been circulars about this. If farmers have CCTV in those locations that can help us, they can land in trouble."

"Break the law to help the law. Welcome to the joys of modern-day policing." Wills added.

"Thank you very much, young lady. You need to run a Master Class in accuracy and brevity to my officers."

Hansen and Wills looked at each other. Was this another effort at humour from Smiley, or was he serious?

After a few questions and points of clarification from both sides, she was done.

Wills noticed Jennifer smiling and tapping her briefcase. He nodded to Hansen and Sykes that payment was due.

Hansen knew what was going on and said, "right my girl, let's sort out the mess that 'Unsolved True Crime Murders' have gotten themselves into with you."

As Wills left with the Super, he said, "Miss Graham has you for two hours. In the meantime, I'll kick off this new line of investigation. Join us when Miss Graham's finished with you."

To Sykes, he added, "please ensure Miss Graham is dropped off home first though."

Looking at Jennifer with a friendly grin as he spoke to them, "we don't want this young lady exploring other cases on her own around here. Our lads and lasses in the station would end up with nothing to do, and we'll have a strike on our hands."

The three of them trundled off to a room with a TV and watched a re-run of a crime TV programme in a police station. Could this be a first? At least in this station, it was. If watching that programme wasn't a first, using the services of two police officers as bartering for payment, definitely was.

****

Wills delayed the next day's three-way internal briefing regarding the murder of June Mitchell until late in the afternoon. He wanted to give the team time to get out and investigate Jennifer's line of thinking, then report back.

Merriman joined their briefing. He was getting severe grief from his bosses and needed something to keep the wolves at bay.

Wills opened with, "Hansen, Sykes, how did your 'True Crimes' session with the marvellous Miss Graham go yesterday?"

"She's an interesting character," replied Hansen. "First impressions are quiet and shy. However, once she warms to the situation, she gets so focussed, she takes over. She can be quite assertive!"

Sykes smiled inwardly at hearing his guv speak about Jennifer.

He thought about their meal the previous night. It all ended with everyone relaxed. His nagging doubts about getting involved with her seemed unfounded that night.

Mamma approved of Jennifer, and Sykes valued her judge of character; she was always right. "You'd have made a great policewoman."

She'd respond with, "if I had stilts."

Hansen broke Sykes' thoughts as he continued. "Miss Graham basically threw the TV programmers' evidence-to-crime-process rationale up in the air," he paused, then continued, "yet again."

"It was also fascinating walking through another case with her again and seeing that mind in action. I'd love to use her again. If nothing else, challenging our thinking would be another check and balance for us."

"That's good to hear," said Wills. "I think we are sometimes too close to cases like this one. As they say, 'can't see the wood for the trees'."

"The Chief Inspector and I have an idea on that very point," interjected the DSU. "However, let's keep that separate and to the end of this briefing."

He gestured for Hansen and Wills to continue.

"Thank you, sir," said Hansen. "OK. So, the killing of Ms June Mitchell."

"Miss Graham's line of thinking proved correct. One farm eventually admitted to having external CCTV cameras. We challenged a second one when we found secreted CCTV cameras on the most vulnerable accesses to their farm. All were monitoring roads and the comings and goings of people up and down them."

"Even caught a couple having a bit of 'how's-yer-father' behind a bush. They were hidden from the road but in full view of a camera. Could make a couple hundred selling the video to …" he paused, trying to remember. "What's that show called? Bugger! Can't remember the name."

"That's a relief," cut in Merriman, "let's get back on track if that's OK with you?"

"Sorry, sir. As a result, we've got camera footage from an entrance gate that showed a similar model of car heading in the right direction at the right time; four people inside. Unfortunately, we can't make out faces, just figures in the car."

"However, one of the people sitting in the back was definitely Joseph Morris. You won't find many three-hundred-pound gorillas being driven around country lanes. The upshot is all this is only really useful as supporting evidence."

Merriman sighed in disappointment.

"But there's good news." Hansen paused.

Merriman leaned in. "Hansen, cut the drama and give."

"Sorry, sir," he again apologised. "We extended her idea of challenging farmers' CCTV locations. This time we looked for cars leaving the scene of the burning car."

"Guess what, we've got Barker's car reg. plate. So, we've got him in the frame. The CPS is looking at this, but may not be enough. At least we've another big nail in his coffin."

Hansen nodded to Sykes for his turn to speak.

"We've followed up with those who might be coerced into giving access and a hiding space in the house. There were many suspects. Our Ms June Mitchell was not a popular character. Almost everyone disliked her or had a grudge."

Sykes let that hang for a moment, but not too long in case Merriman had a dig at him as well.

"However, only the house madam had the keys and access to hide the perpetrators. Unfortunately, she's quite new to the job, internal promotion and all that. She'd nothing to gain but everything to lose from her boss' death. So, she's out of the frame, for the moment at least."

"We've got a strong line of enquiry. The previous house madam, Miss Sally Anderson, had been badly disfigured by Ms Mitchell, over money. There was an incident with hot oil that badly disfigured Miss Anderson. She wasn't the first of Ms Mitchell's employees to receive a similar fate."

Merriman added, "I remember Sally Anderson from when I was a young DI and she was pretty new to the game. She was quite some woman. She'd be in her early to mid-forties now. I'm assuming it's the same woman?"

"It is, sir," Wills put in.

"Ah, yes," Merriman continued. "Ms Anderson made a case made against Ms Mitchell for assault. All unproven and was quickly closed as I remember."

"And, sir, she's still hot," added Hansen, "even though scarred on one side."

Wills ignored Hansen's comment and continued the thread. "She'd know the house, its comings and goings, the people there, even possible access. She's got a grudge against Ms Mitchell the size of Wembley stadium."

"She's on her way to the station to be interviewed as we speak. She could even be one of the gang who murdered June Mitchell."

"I want to sit in on her interview," interjected their Super with surprising enthusiasm. "I want you with me," he said to Wills. "If we get this one right, and she did put June Mitchell in Barker's sights, we've pretty much got him."

"Oh, and by the way," said Wills to Hansen and Sykes. "As mentioned earlier, we've got an idea to use our Miss Graham again. But let's put that on hold until we're done with Miss Sally Anderson.

Hansen and Sykes looked at each other, wondering what these old blighters were up to.

28. A WOMAN SCORNED

When Sally Anderson entered the station, waited in reception, then walked down the corridor to the interview room, both male and female eyes followed her well-practiced, elegant and understated walk.

She had the proverbial hourglass figure but nothing too extreme. There was no exaggerated sway of the hips or the obvious come-on-and-get-me motion that many of her peers employed.

She knew she was at the centre of attention and even now, she still loved it.

She just oozed sensuality.

When Merriman and Wills walked in, Anderson was already seated at the interview room table. PC Sherrard stood at the rear, by the door.

Sally didn't initially turn round to watch them enter from the door behind.

Merriman had remembered correctly. As they came round the table, he could see that she was still stunningly beautiful.

When she turned to face them, they saw the scaring down the other side of her face. Her blouse was closed at the top, suggesting it concealed more scarring below.

Merriman stopped Wills from starting the recording system.

Wills looked at his boss questioningly but said nothing.

Ignoring Wills' look, he addressed Anderson, "just an informal chat before we get started to clear the air, so to speak."

She said nothing but threw him a questioning look.

Merriman looked to PC Sherrard, who stood at the back of the room. "How's about making a nice cup of tea for Miss Anderson?"

The PC didn't know what to do. She wasn't concerned about being asked to leave and make tea, a request rarely made these days. It was the protocol that a female uniformed staff be present when male officers interviewed a female witness. It was Merriman himself, who insisted this be the process to protect the police. Now he was breaking his rules.

"Sir?" was all she could say.

"Thank you, constable," he said firmly. "On this occasion, you can be assured that it's OK to leave DCI Wills and me with Miss Anderson."

Wills caught his boss' severe expression and nodded a confirmation to Sherrard that she should leave.

After the PC left, Sally said to the two senior officers, "I'm intrigued. All this secrecy? Get on with it then."

Wills waited, said, and did nothing. His Super clearly had an agenda. He was taking the lead without having pre-warned Wills; an unusual situation.

Merriman started, "Miss Anderson, thank you for coming."

Before Merriman could continue, she sarcastically stated, "whatever happened it wasn't me. Whenever it happened I've an alibi. So whatever I'm here for, you're wasting my valuable time."

She clasped her arms behind her head and leaned back grinning. There was no malice, she seemed to be enjoying herself.

The two officers saw the scarring on her left arm as the sleeve of her blouse rode up. The marks matched the left-hand side of her face.

Sally saw them staring at her injuries. She undid the top buttons of her high-necked blouse, leaned forward, and showed off further scarring.

"And yes, my left tit's also scarred, but it'll cost you to see that freak show."

Sally Anderson was no longer enjoying the moment. She did up the buttons and said, "that bitch June Mitchell did this to me. She said I was a two-faced bitch, and everyone would now see two different sides of me for the rest of my life."

She was still a stunning woman, albeit right-side on and from the back.

Unlike many of her fellow trades-people, she was university educated and came from a middle-class background. Her accent was middle England, neither posh nor heavily accented.

Sally's choice of profession was not through need.

However, abused as a child by both her aunt and uncle from her father's side, she was desensitised to any flavour of sexual act.

With Sally's looks and poise, and the regular offers of inducements, it seemed to her that a career in prostitution was an ideal profession to make lots of money. And it was, and she did.

That is until the fatal day when a frying pan of hot oil in June Mitchell's hands put paid to it.

"I'm not stupid and I know what this is all about. So, no, I did not kill her. Saying that, I'd have been happy to kill her if given the opportunity. But, there's one big difference between me and those who committed this crime."

She paused for effect, while again leaning forward. This time, it was to emphasise her next statement which she said slowly, her unbridled venom aimed at the deceased woman.

"I'd have taken my time to enjoy making her suffer."

Once Sally Anderson finished, Merriman continued. "We believe Mr Anthony Barker committed that crime with three accomplices. Here's the question, would you be able to help us put him away?"

"If that was the case, Tony did me a favour. You'll have to do more than appeal to my good nature."

"Why would I help?"

"If you do not help, we believe that we can make a case against you as an accessory to June Mitchell's murder. In addition, we will also put away the people in the house who helped them commit murder."

Merriman explained how they knew it was an inside job and her involvement.

If Sally was worried, she didn't show it.

"I know you've got an agenda with all the theatrics. So, what's in it for me? That is, assuming I can help?"

Wills was worried that Merriman had given too much away to Sally so early in the process. She could walk out of the station and they'd have less than nothing.

"I know how things work and I'm not stupid," Sally reminded Merriman.

"You've no leads, and you want me to put someone in the frame for doing what I've been dreaming about doing this last year or so. They did me a favour. Why would I want to put them in the frame?"

"We know you were directly involved," replied Merriman.

"Let's be honest with each other. You know nothing! You might suspect something, but you can prove nothing." She said this calmly and deliberately.

Merriman just looked at Sally, saying nothing.

She felt compelled to fill the gap in the conversation. "You're either not listening or don't get it. So, let me spell it out for you. What's … in … it …. for ... me?" she said deliberately, pronouncing every syllable.

Merriman smiled in response.

"I do get it but was wondering when you'd ask," he teased her along.

"So here's how we see it and how this could play out to your advantage. We believe Anthony Barker asked you for help so he could talk with June Mitchell; only talk. We're sure you believed he'd never harm her. All he wanted was to make her see sense in backing off as a witness."

Sally was no longer sitting back in her chair. Merriman had her full attention.

"Perhaps he told you he was hoping they could even try again? I don't know. If it was like that, I'm sure the CPS wouldn't push for custodial charges against you. After all, you only gave information on when she might be coming and help him with access to the woman he loved."

She realised Merriman was suggesting a route to grass on Barker while keeping herself and her friend out of the frame. It was indeed fortunate the interview wasn't recorded, keeping her vitriol towards Mitchell off the record.

She considered her options for a few minutes. "OK, agreed, let's get on with it." She nodded to the recording device. "Oh, and one thing more, I'll need a new identity. When this comes out, I'm dead!"

The Super stood up and said, "I'm off to confer with the CPS." He then left the room.

Hansen and PC Sherrard entered shortly afterward. There was no tea for Sally Anderson, but the PC sported a beaming smile. The DSU thanked her personally for trusting him and going along with his ploy.

Wills underestimated his boss. With Sally Anderson's statement and the other evidence they'd built, there was now enough on Barker to pull him in and squeeze.

This all rested on Sally Anderson and the CPS playing ball with the DSU. He knew they were in the safest of hands on that score.

He grinned inwardly, '*if there's one area where Smilie excelled, that's the lobbying game.*'

Wills now switched on the recording device and started the interview formalities.

Sally considered her options. Her get-out-of-jail-card, as suggested by Merriman, was her only way out. Before she said anything, she walked through, in her mind, how the story could sound; it sounded OK.

She started her preamble for the benefit of the recording device while waiting for Merriman's return.

"If I did supply any information to Anthony Barker, it would only have been offered as an unknowing and unwilling party to the sad death of June Mitchell. She was my boss and close friend for many years."

"Any information I supplied would have been based on his assurances that he was planning to persuade her to marry him. That would effectively negate the prosecution's case, or at least make it more difficult to pursue."

At that point, Merriman re-entered the room and made his presence known for the recording. He nodded an affirmative, plus a thumbs-up to Sally.

She then started in earnest.

"I've known Tony, sorry Anthony Barker, for many years; you could say that we have been intimate friends. Anyway, he wanted to talk with June to ask if she would marry him. He also said that he had a business arrangement that would be mutually beneficial if only she would hear him out. He could only speak with June when you lot weren't around. He believed you turned her against him."

She continued with a pleasant voice, supported by a believable smile. "Both were my friends, and I did it for them. Tony said you lot fitted him up and forced June to lie about what happened so she could get off with a trafficking case."

Wills interrupted, "how could you say you were friends? As I understand, June Mitchell scarred you for life. You're on record as hating her."

"No, no. That was an accident, said Sally defending herself. "If you check, everyone testified it was an accident caused by my clumsiness. I might have blamed June then, but I was angry at myself. I took it out on poor June and I'm still ashamed of myself for what I said then."

"June forgave me. But we could no longer be close. My injuries would always be a reminder of the earlier bad feeling. So, we parted as friends and went our separate ways."

"Had to sanity check that point, since a lawyer would do the same."

Sally nodded in understanding. "If I might continue?"

"Sorry, please carry on," encouraged Wills.

"Honestly, I don't know what happened between them on that sad day when she died. June could be quite vicious. Perhaps they argued, and she attacked him. After all, he's not a big or powerful man. June could easily have hurt him. Maybe whatever happened to her was in self-defence?"

Sally gave out a long sad sigh, "it's all so tragic what happened, and I suspect we'll never know what went on between them."

"And this is what you truly believe?" interrupted Merriman.

"Yes, absolutely."

"Please continue."

"Everyone knew June visited her houses when she could. As you know, both houses are quite far apart. And, knowing she'd be going to The Steadings after visiting her daughter, it was easy for Tony to know when she was heading there."

"All I did was give them a set of keys and arrange for one of the girls to give them access to the house. She looked after them until June got there."

Sally then continued to fill in all the details of where Barker and his people hid. Her helper also assumed Barker was there to talk and propose marriage.

Sally reinforced that her helper was also excited about being a part of this rekindling of love.

Then she wondered. '*Hope I've not gone too far with this premise, but gotta keep Mandy out of trouble?*'

After Sally's interview finished and her witness statement taken, she was free to leave. Witness protection was in the process of being set up. As far as the police were concerned, Sally was safe until her testimony was released.

It would be hard to press charges against Sally. Mandy, the sex worker accomplice, would naturally support everything she said about the day June Mitchell died.

Merriman and Wills took their time arranging for the confirmation interview with Mandy. Sally had plenty of time to brief the helper in advance.

After the others departed, and when Wills and Merriman were left alone in the meeting room, Wills said to his boss, "I sometimes forget the cunning sod you are."

They both laughed. They had history. In private, those words were acceptable, especially when they got a result.

****

April Mitchell's phone rang. It was one of her girls.

"Hi, April, one of my fellas in the station confirmed that Wills and Smilie have interviewed Sally Anderson. She's copped to helping Barker top your mother. The cow's spewing out some bullshit about trying to help them sort their personal problems, even getting together. She's done a deal with the fuzz and has walked."

"Fuck her, she's dead. The cow's a walking corpse," retorted a fuming April Mitchell.

29. DEADLY HISTORY

Soon after the Sally Anderson interview, Merriman hosted a planning meeting with Wills, Hansen, and Sykes. They were agreeing on the follow-up actions needed to put a case together against Barker for the murder of June Mitchell; one that the CPS could run with.

Once finished, the DCI suggested to Hansen and, by implication also Sykes, "now let's also try and get a completely different nail in Tony Barker's coffin. What do you think about using Miss Graham to have a fresh look at the Charlie Farmer killing? It was five years ago, but we think it's still worth a try."

Charles James Farmer ran one of the bookies that Barker owned. Barker was an out-and-out crook who could never rationalise honesty. As with his accountant, he accepted a certain amount of skimming by his people. To Barker, it was simply nothing more than normal behaviour.

Charlie Farmer had more expensive habits than any low-level skimming could sustain. He got greedy, the skimming got bigger and bigger. Instead of backing off large bets to other bookies to minimise the risk of a large payout, he pocketed the money. He'd always been able to cover payouts to date.

Charlie had taken a large bet to win; an outside chance. Unfortunately for him, it won. He now owed over fifteen thousand pounds but couldn't make the payment. Barker, as the owner of the bookies, had to pay up.

Charlie was going to pay up, one way or another. The 'one way' was cash, the 'another' would be painful and terminal.

He was picked up from outside his bookies and driven to one of Barker's warehouses.

Barker was going to enjoy making an example of him. He'd recently bought a new gas/electric framing nail gun which he'd been desperate to try out. Lo and behold, the perfect opportunity arose in Charlie. Much to Barker's disappointment, Charlie expired too soon before he could fully get used to his new toy on live flesh.

Barker had made some fundamental mistakes leading up to the killing of Charlie. His team was seen picking him up in broad daylight. In addition, Barker's car was identified at the warehouse when and where Charlie was killed.

With that core evidence, plus other supporting information, the CPS believed they had a sufficiently strong case to proceed. It almost put Barker and Morris away, but it wasn't enough.

The result was a hung jury. Barker's barrister did a great job extracting him out of that hole.

Being a hung jury in a murder case meant the case could be retried. However, the CPS could and would only proceed if they had new compelling evidence.

Hansen jumped in. "Love it. It's a great idea to have her reviewing old cases."

Then he calmed down after a thought hit him. "But, sir, DI Peterson would not be amused with our going through his old cases. He'd be livid! He'd see this as outside people checking up on him and his work. He's protective about his work. We all are."

Hansen felt he had to add. "Honest, sir, if you did this to me, I'd go ballistic."

"You're right. This was and will still remain Peterson's case," responded Merriman. "DCI Wills and I have already discussed this idea. We are proposing an approach that will not create waves."

"Sir?" asked Hansen, not sure where this was going.

"Barker slithered out of that case by the skin of his teeth," said the DCI, taking over. "I want to know if there's the slightest piece of evidence we might have missed."

"This is not a slight on Peterson's work. Our Miss Graham has shown that she can find or interpret evidence that even the best of us got wrong. She's proven that to us, including DI Peterson."

Merriman then took his turn. "The evidence was so close. If there's a chance of finding anything that was overlooked, the CPS would be up for retrying the case."

Now it was back to Wills to continue the argument. "I'm hoping that if anyone can help, it would be her. I want another link found. I want to lock up our Mr Barker." Wills emphasised the 'want'. It was personal for him since he was the SIO for that case, even though Peterson's team did the leg work.

Merriman then explained their approach.

"In summary, DI Peterson will take the lead on looking back. However, we know that DI Peterson working with her directly would be a non-starter. Even though he's profusely apologised, I don't believe we'd get the best out of Miss Graham if she worked with him directly."

"OK?" responded an uncertain Hansen.

"Now, if our DS Sykes acts as liaison with Miss Graham and leg-man for Peterson on this review, we think this would work. That means Sykes'll work directly for Peterson on this particular case."

"Peterson rates Sykes for some strange reason," added the DCI, while grinning at Sykes, signifying the comment was humour. "So I'm sure he'll be up for it."

To Hansen directly, he said, "you're out of the frame for this case. Sykes'll still report to you on the other cases you're working."

"Ah, now that makes sense." Hansen relaxed.

Sykes said nothing. He just awaited his instructions. And working with Jennifer, even though that old crock Peterson was involved, wasn't going to be that onerous. Thinking about it, he relished the idea.

"Glad we're all on board," said the Superintendent in a way that meant it didn't matter if Hansen bought into the idea or not. It was happening anyway.

"Jon, could you get David on board with this and start the ball rolling?" the Super said to Wills, referring to DI David Peterson.

Then to Sykes, "any questions?"

"No sir."

****

Benjamina caught Barker in the kitchen with Joe. "Boss, our snout in the station just confirmed it was actually that twat Forrest wot grassed on Morris. They want to use his evidence that says he worked with Joe, so they could link

210

it to you."

"We knew that," growled Barker. "Hope that fuck-useless information didn't cost me."

"Nah, that was just a bit of freebie clarification."

She gave a pregnant pause to maximise dramatic effect.

Barker gave an impatient, "humpf," as he waited, knowing there was more to come. She sometimes annoyed him, playing these mind games to be centre stage. He'd learned to be patient and tolerant with her, at least as far as his temperament allowed.

"For fuck's sake, Ben. Spill whatever shite you're holding in that gob of yours!"

He was so easy to wind up.

"Now what I'm about to tell you did cost," alluding to a forthcoming piece of information she was about to announce.

"Ben, I'm going to hit you with that fuckin' kettle if you don't spill, now!" Barker was now getting bored, as well as angry. There was only so much teasing he'd tolerate, even from her.

She hastily continued. "What we didn't know, is that Forrest was put in the frame by some new consultant bird they have. The wench's also put us in the frame for June's kill. 'Coz of her, they've your reg. plate after we left the dumped car."

"What the fuck! How'd they do that? How'd she do that!" exclaimed the small man.

"So, I've been sniffing around. She's some sorta genius that solves crimes. One of our guys on the murder team watched her in action on the judge's case as she put that fuck-wit Forrest in the frame. He was gob-smacked with how she pulled it all together from nothing."

He interrupted. "I don't give a flying fuck for Forrest. He's old news and in the morning, he'll be newspaper news."

"How much did we pay for that useless information?" he added out of impatience.

"That's not it boss. I was just setting the scene."

And she did another one of her pregnant pauses. However, seeing the look of impatience on Barker's face, she decided to cough up the information fast.

"Now, this is it. Word is, they're using her to look at Charlie Farmer's hit."

"How're they going to pin a five-year-old case on us?"

"Boss, that kill was a fuck show, and we all know it. You and the big man were lucky to get off with it."

"I thought it went smoothly," interrupted Morris. "There were no problems, easy peasy."

"Listen you dumb gorilla, she's right. We were lucky to get off with that one," retorted the small man. Only Barker could get off with such blatant abuse to Morris, who never batted an eye. Others like Fahmi tended to be indirect in their abuse.

"Yes, we know the actual kill was fine, you shit-for-brains. But afterwards, the forensics, witness, and CCTV evidence almost destroyed us, or more importantly, me."

Ben looked at the gorilla and sighed, then continued. "If anyone can pin it on us, or rather you, as you said, then find even the smallest piece of evidence those arseholes in blue missed, it's gonna be her."

To drive the issue home, she added, "and that wasn't the only case she helped with. There was a Doctor Hardcastle wot was topped. The fuzz thought it was a suicide and were going to close the case. She just walked into the room, and ZAP, she told 'em he was murdered and why, even before forensics got the results back."

"It was DI Peterson's case, and he's no mug. He initially thought it was a suicide until she set him straight. She's evil boss. She's gonna get you!"

"OK, OK," acknowledged Barker, after she eventually managed to get to the point. He thought about what she'd said and that worried him. There was already too much suspicion coming his way.

"Fuck. That means we're going to have to top that consultant bitch as well as Forrest," Barker blurted.

He paused, considering his options.

"Right, we'll need to keep a low profile, so it'll need to be done outside again.

Lemmie call that Engineer contractor bloke and get him to do it fast."

At the scheduled time, Barker called the killer's number. "Got another couple of jobs for you."

As Barker was explaining the contracts and their urgency, the killer interrupted him before he could finish.

"Unfortunately, our relationship is at an end. We will never do business again. I'm not open to another contract from you, let alone two."

"What the fuck do you mean? I'm giving you a job and paying you fuckin' well, too fuckin' well!"

The killer didn't normally explain himself. That behaviour opened him up to emotions; he didn't do 'emotion' while on a job. However, for this irritating client, he needed to get the point over. "I do not like people using my MO to disguise their kills. You tried to link me to June Mitchell's kill. If it had been a professional kill, I could almost have excused your actions."

The killer was angry and took some time to calm down before he added, "but you and your lot were incompetent and screwed it up. I've a reputation for clean kills and accuracy. I won't have that compromised by arseholes like the Anthony Barker joke factory."

No one had talked to Barker like that in a long time, and he wasn't used to it. Taken aback by what The Engineer had said, all he could blurt out in response was, "who the fuck do you think you are!"

"I'm the person who kills for a living, and I do not miss. Oh, and there's talk on the street about you arranging a hit on me; most unadvised."

"What are you gibbering on about? Are you taking the contract or not?"

The killer couldn't believe his ears. His ex-client wasn't getting it; so much for his explanation to satisfy his anger towards his little ex-client.

He now kept it simple. "Not! I have already returned the equipment. As per our agreement, this concludes my relationship with you as a client and supplier. I thank you for your business. I have other, more honest and trustworthy clients to service."

The killer did have another hit coming up. Thankfully it was for an old client who respected the professionalism he brought to the job.

The Engineer had never talked to a client like this before. Even though he was a killer, he was still human. While he prided himself on not reacting emotionally, Barker got to him, as Barker did to almost everyone. It annoyed him that he was drawn in to react in this way. Emotions in this job were dangerous and a sign of weakness. He needed to close this relationship for his own sanity and professionalism.

Worse still, two urgent hits were suicidal. Without time for proper research and planning, they would be unnecessarily risky.

Barker was just about to bellow expletives down the phone to the killer when the line went dead. Instead, he bellowed out his frustrations in general. He called the killer back but without success. The SIM was no longer in service.

Barker poured himself a large shot of whisky. He stood there sipping and thinking. He decided what to do, then gulped the remaining down and looked at Ms Potts.

"Ben, get the boys, and let's get eyes on that new police consultant. I need to know where she lives and how to get to her. Then she's toast."

"First of all, I want Forrest found and topped. Get the job done fast before the bizzies decide to put him into protection."

"No one grasses me up!"

30. DIRTYING THE SLATE

Weeks earlier, Alan Forrest's slate had not only been wiped clean by his new friend, Joe Morris, but he'd also cash burning a hole in his pocket. His mood was light as he walked with a spring to his step towards his foe.

Having given Morris the information on the judge's movements and entry access to the house, Forrest's life had now turned around. He was no longer looking over his shoulder, wondering when the bookie's boys would find him again. The next time, it would have been broken bones; that was always the way with this bookie.

He thought the people coming into the house were burglars and rationalised that this would be a victimless crime. '*The old bugger was insured after all.*'

As well as solving his financial woes, it would prevent an even worse crime from being committed, namely GBH to his body; a win-win for everyone.

'*It was all that fuckin' bookie's fault!*' As well as hating the bookie, he also blamed him for putting him in the position where he had to set up the judge.

It was only later he realised Morris and his lot had lied to him. He'd inadvertently set the judge up for a hit. Anyway, none of what happened was his fault. Even if he was in a very tiny way to blame, his need was greater than the judge.

Of course, Forrest was a little sad the judge had died. It wasn't because he liked the old man, but working for him was tax-free pocket money he'd no longer enjoy.

On the positive side, Forrest no longer lived in fear. And he had money. With that money, he could once and for all, screw the cause of all his grief; the bookie.

Forrest could never reconcile that it was his ineptitude in backing the wrong horses that were the cause of his problems. As far as he was concerned, it was a conspiracy by others.

He thought back to the previous encounter with his nemesis. Forrest remembered walking out of the shop. He saw the bookie sitting there, behind that glass screen, with a big, sneering, self-satisfied grin on his face.

Now, the tables had turned. Forrest just needed a few big wins, then it was all over for the bookie.

He had a new repeating vision in his mind, one he was enjoying over and over. Forrest was looking forward to the look of shock on that slimy turd's face. He could visualise the sweat running down the bookie's greasy, fat forehead while he counted out Forrest's winnings. Forrest would display a smug grin while patiently waiting and watching the bookie's shaking, reluctant hand delivering over his newfound wealth.

He entered the licensed bookies, checked out the races, and reviewed form.

Planning completed in his mind, it was now time to enact the demise of his arch-enemy, the bookie.

****

Ben was the careful one of Barker's crew. She took time researching and preparing for the hit on Alan Forrest. No way was there going to be another Charlie Farmer repeat; not on her watch anyway.

The following day, she contacted the betting shop to see how Alan Forrest was doing. The good news was that Forrest had been waving his newly acquired money around and had bet big. And joy to behold, Forrest had yet another bad run. He was in debt again, even bigger than before.

"And, if he doesn't pay up by Friday, his bones'll be mush once my boys have finished with him."

Ben chuckled when she heard that from the bookie. That meant Alan Forrest was going to be desperate.

Ben knew Joe Morris had sorted out Forrest's financial problems after he'd given the information on the judge.

Morris liked Forrest and felt sorry for him. He'd actually paid him extra after the tale of woe his new friend 'honest Alan Forrest' told him.

The big man's money had saved Forrest then. She could use that. Good. She hoped the bond Morris felt toward Forrest was also reciprocated. She assumed Forrest trusted Morris as much as the big man did him.

Ben asked the big man to call Forrest to see how things were.

Morris called Forrest, with the speaker enabled so Ben could overhear. Forrest gave him a tale of woe about how the races were fixed against you when you bet big. The bookie was in on it with the rest of them.

"That bastard took all your money and made sure I'm in debt again!" Forrest emphasised it being Morris' money to try and suck the big man into his story.

Morris offered sympathetic grunts and sighs. It wasn't that he was leading him on; he was actually feeling sorry for the poor man's gambling plight.

With Ben's coaxing and hand signals, Morris eventually asked if Forrest was OK. And, did he perhaps need some more help, perhaps some more money?

In response to further gesticulating from Ben, Morris told him, "listen, mate, we're not gangsters like that bookie. We're just businessmen."

"Yeh, I know and appreciated wot you dun for me before."

Ben continued the prompting and whispered guidance in Morris' ear.

"I trust ya. Happy to give you some money to get that guy off your back."

"Yer a gent!"

They could hear the voice on the other end relax.

"We could even make it an advance against some jobs. We've always places for trusted people like you to work off any debt, same as before."

Morris reassured him further that they were best of friends. He especially appreciated that Forrest hadn't put him in the frame with the police for the unfortunate 'accident' in the judge's house. He promised an extra ton for him as a thank you.

Forrest jumped at the offer. No way was he going to admit grassing on Morris and by implication, Barker "Yeh, a shame the old bugger was accidentally killed. But he shouldn't 'ave gotten in the way of the blokes wot were doing the house." Forrest kept up that pretence, even though he knew the truth.

But, Forrest didn't know, that they knew he knew the truth about what happened and that he'd grassed. That's what made him dangerous to Barker.

217

"As you said, it would only have been a few small and pricy things that were nicked, and the boys would have been in and out without the old bugger being the wiser."

Forrest continued with his pretence about still believing this was a burglary gone wrong. "They could have been replaced, and the insurance company would have coughed up, so why'd he interfere?"

"I know, stupid accident," Morris said. "The old guy musta' thought he was some vigilante or somethin'."

"Alan," said Morris as he started to read the few words Ben had written on a scrap of paper. He tried his best to read, but the words came out slowly and deliberately.

"I have got some work near your local pub, which I shall finish late. If you are around, I would be happy to bung you that dosh to keep you going."

Joe Morris wasn't the best reader in the world. Fortunately, he also wasn't the most articulate speaker. That's why it pretty much sounded normal. Forrest was also none too bright, so didn't notice anyway.

Ben nudged him again to finish what she wrote.

Morris continued, taking everything Ben said at face value. "And we can discuss a nice simple earner for you. This time it will be all legal. So you can repay us and no risk."

"That'd be great," said an excited Forrest. "I'm there most nights."

Still the voice for Ben's hand signs, Morris asked, "how much d'ya' need to clear that thievin' bookie's tab?"

"Five ton," said Forrest. He then hesitantly asked, "and the extra one you mentioned?"

"No problem, of course, I'll bung you the six."

They arranged to meet at 11:30 that evening in the same quiet alley as before, so no one could see the agreed financial transaction.

****

After closing time, the desperate Forrest arrived early for his meeting with

Morris. He positioned himself against the lee wall to protect himself from the rain. And in the shadow of the distant street light, he wasn't visible.

While he waited, Forrest saw two hooded men heading in his direction. Their heads faced downwards to avoid the cold, driving rain as much as possible.

Both were wearing long coats. Forrest thought nothing further of them as he hunched in the alley, trying to keep as warm and dry as possible. Being early, he was already on his second cigarette, struggling to keep it dry.

The two others paid him no attention as they approached. He assumed from his hidden position, they'd walk by.

When the two were only a few feet away from Forrest, they stopped and faced him. He knew he was in trouble and looked around for help.

Where was Morris? He'd sort these two out. He just needed to keep them talking until the big man arrived.

He didn't shout out, assuming these were the bookie's boys again. Instead, Forrest pleaded, "honest chaps, I'm good for it. Got a meeting in five minutes to pick up the cash, and I'll be right round to see him."

There was no response from the two men, who looked around as they walked toward him.

"We can wait together. He's on his way with my money, your boss' money."

Forrest kept looking around for Morris, who was nowhere to be seen.

As he explained the forthcoming monies, the two pulled out sawn-off shotguns. These were the same used to keep June Mitchell's security guards covered while she was being murdered upstairs at The Steadings.

They each discharged both barrels at point-blank range. They trudged off in the way that everyone does in heavy rain.

Long before the police arrived, the two perpetrators were long gone.

****

Earlier that day, Barker told his brother he'd be handing over the money as he was passing by anyway. So, no need to change the appointment.

He also told Bill 'n' Ben never to let Morris find out they killed Forrest. It would confuse matters for the big man.

When word got out the next day, Ben told Morris that Forrest was mugged for the six hundred pounds.

****

An unknown caller reported hearing gunshots but gave no further information. Since this was a rough neighbourhood, and there had been previous shootings in the area, a patrol car was immediately dispatched.

An Armed Response Vehicle (ARV) was also requested and expected a further fifteen minutes later.

By the time Hansen and Wills arrived at the scene of Forrest's shooting that night, the crime scene had already been sealed by uniform.

They soon realised there was little evidence to be collected. SOCO was already onto what little was still there. As well as keeping the streets clear of people, the heavy rain would have washed away most of any evidence that might normally have remained in dry weather.

The only items of evidential significance were pellets that had missed the victim, a spent cigarette near his feet, and one half-finished near his body. As usual, everything was photographed.

Very little information resulted from house-to-house canvassing. No one saw anything. If they did, they weren't talking. In that part of the city, few talked to the police.

All that uniform could ascertain was there were multiple gunshots, albeit conflicting accounts. Some witnesses were saying two shots, some three, and others heard four shots.

What security cameras that were in the area, were either not working or not of any use.

The motive, however, was clear. Being prepared to put Morris in the frame, put Forrest in the line of fire. Barker was quick off the mark with this one, too quick for the close security paperwork to be approved.

How did Barker's lot find out so soon? There was a leak in the station.

The police didn't buy the bookie being responsible story.

31. UNORTHODOX WITNESS PROTECTION

Hansen knocked on Wills' door early the next morning, as requested in the voice message.

"Guv, nothing more to report on Forrest's killing last night. Barker's and his mob's alibis were as sound as usual. They love their card games, especially when something like this has gone down."

"I didn't expect anything to come from the inquiries," admitted the DCI.

Hansen continued with the briefing he thought he was here to deliver. "This was a simple and typical gangland kill. Barker's lot is good at this. Even without that foul weather last night, these crimes are always hard to investigate, but we're on it, sir."

"Relax, you can brief me later when I know we'll have had more information."

Hansen looked questioningly at Wills.

"That's not the reason I called you. The Super and I have been talking. We're worried about Miss Graham," frowned Wills.

"Barker's jumped the gun, so to speak. He's cleared up loose ends with the Forrest killing. We believe there's a leak in the CPS or the station."

Hansen responded defensively. "Not my team, I know them!"

"Don't get your knickers in a twist," said Wills, trying to calm him down. "We'll deal with leaks and accusations later. Right now, we have more urgent matters."

Hansen said nothing more. He calmed down as his boss continued.

"Firstly, we're reliably informed that Barker was tipped off about Forrest spilling on him. Our same source, which we now think we can trust, told us that they're after Miss Graham next."

"Why? She's only been helping with evidence. She's surely not any risk to them. Any one of us could have come up with her reasoning."

"But none of us did," responded Wills.

"Mind you," said Hansen as an afterthought, "he's such a vindictive bastard, he might well have been after her in any case for the help she'd already given us."

"True, but he's not stupid enough to go after someone who's just doing their job. It would be like going after one of us. Just where would that get him and where would it stop."

"But, that's not the real issue, it's more serious than that. We now believe Barker knows we're looking again at the evidence on the Charles Farmer murder. They know we'll be using Miss Graham. With her track record so far, they'll be worried she'll find something we missed. Now, killing her is worth the risk."

Hansen couldn't respond. His mind was in a spin as he was taking all this in.

"Barker escaped that conviction by a hair's breadth, and he's not daft. As we've already discussed, even the smallest thing can put away that little turd."

Hansen conceded. "If they're in the know, I wouldn't put it past the bastards."

"Yep," acknowledged the DCI. "What she'd given us had truly buggered them. Sadly, it's raised her credibility and put her in their line of fire, so to speak. She could well be their next target."

"Bugger!" was all Hansen could say.

"Unfortunately, upstairs is not wearing her being at risk, since she doesn't have any particular incriminating evidence. She doesn't fit their nice-in-a-box criteria for close security."

"So, the woman who has helped us build a case for a gangland thug is at risk. And we can't help her? That's shite!" Hansen's face was red with anger. "We owe that innocent young woman! I'll put her up myself if that's what's needed."

"Whoa there Silver," said Wills using a version of the phrase from an old cowboy TV series. "We're going to protect her, and immediately. So don't worry."

Hansen leaned forward and enthusiastically waited for what was coming next.

"The Super needs a few days to work on the powers-that-be. If there's one thing he's good at, that's sorting upstairs' politics. For that job, there's no one I'd trust more."

Hansen thought for a moment, then asked, "so we'll be putting some of our people on her full-time?"

"I was just thinking one. Sykes."

"Surely that's too risky, sir! What happens if they come mob-handed? One man cannot fight them all," retorted the DI.

"Their best safety is in secrecy. We have to keep this one quiet amongst the four of us until officially sanctioned. We now know the station's leaking to Barker. The fewer who know, the safer she'll be. Too many people out of the station will raise suspicions, and word will definitely get back to them."

"Sykes could take a short holiday from his accrued annual leave. I've checked. He's got the days and is long overdue for a break."

"Where are you planning to send them?"

"The Super's signed off on enough budget for the likes of a holiday cottage, for both her and the aunt. Thoughts?"

"I'm not happy guv. Just Sykes? Have you spoken with him?"

At that point, an agitated Sykes knocked on the DCI's door. He was waved in.

"Guv," he said to Hansen, "I've been looking for you and heard you were here."

"And?" questioned Hansen.

"I've just arrived and heard from uniform that Forrest's been killed. I'm worried Jennifer's next." Both older policemen picked up on the use of 'Jennifer', but neither made any comment this time.

"What do you think about protection for her? Do you think upstairs would sanction it?" He looked at the DCI this time. He was clearly worried.

"This time, we're ahead of you. The Super's behind us and already lobbying for security for both of them. However, it'll take a few days t the meantime, we need them out of the way."

After those reassurances, they could see the tension releasing from the young sergeant.

"So how'd you fancy a holiday with 'Jennifer' and her lovely aunt?" added Hansen, while emphasising the woman's name to tease his sergeant.

"Thanks, guv," he said to Hansen, "and sir," to Wills.

In a now calmer tone, "I'm in. No question. When? Where?"

"Now," was the short answer from Wills.

The DCI continued, "for the where, can you ask Ms Graham if she has any preference in where to go out of the city for a few days to lie low? The quieter and more secluded, the better."

"Keep us both informed, but only us and the Super. This station leaks like my old Jag."

"We've got budget for this, so let's get cracking on this eh?"

As Sykes was about to leave, one of the admins popped his head in the door and said to Sykes, "sergeant, the Super wants a word, alone."

"What about?" queried the DS nervously. The Super never calls the likes of him to his office alone, without his guv or the DCI around.

"Dunno, he didn't say, I didn't ask. I'm just the ever so 'umble messenger."

The DCI and DI both looked at each other. It was most unusual indeed.

"Better head upstairs. Don't keep the boss waiting. And by the way, whatever it is, don't worry. If there's a problem, he'd already have blown in my ear, big time."

****

Sykes knocked on the open door, "Sir, you wanted me?"

"Close the door and sit."

Sykes did as requested, now extremely nervous at the DSU's curt response.

"Relax, sergeant. You're not in trouble." Merriman actually smiled as he tried to reassure Sykes.

Sykes visibly relaxed but was still wondering what was going on.

"I've signed for this," said the DSU as he handed over a small hold-all. "You'll need it over the next few days. Do not lose it. Do not tell anyone, and I mean anyone." He emphasised the 'anyone' and the 'not'.

Inside was an automatic handgun with an underarm holster. It was the usual police issue; a 9mm Glock 17 self-loading pistol. As well as its 17-round magazine, there was an extra one inside the bag.

Both officers were teetering on the edge of the rules. However, Sykes was a SCO19 Authorised Firearms Officer, as was Merriman. They had a strong case for this action if there was a problem with the paperwork.

"Remember, keep the three of us posted where you are taking the lady. No one else! I mean NO one!" Merriman again stressed the 'NO'.

"Safety in silence, son."

Sykes had never heard him talk like that before. He wondered if the boss was getting soft in his old age.

32. IN HIDING

From his car, Sykes called Jennifer en route to her house.

"How'd you fancy a few days away with me?"

He wanted to keep the whole thing relaxed. So he approached the discussion with a light-hearted upbeat question.

"We've had one dinner together, and you want me away with you?"

She was surprised and a little shocked. And, if she would admit it to herself, most pleasantly flattered.

So she played hard to get, but not too hard. "What sort of girl do you think I am," she said flirtatiously.

"In that case, how's about we bring along Aunt Doris?"

"I don't do threesomes," she teased back.

"As a chaperone, I don't trust you on your own."

"OK?" she said hesitantly, with the intonation of a question.

After a thought, and now in a serious tone, she asked, "right, what's going on?"

He needed to tell her enough, so she would understand the urgency to be out of the way. At the same time, he didn't want to explain too much, to minimise potential worry.

He definitely couldn't say why Jennifer was at risk. Sykes felt so guilty about being party to them being in the line of fire; all because they planned to use her skills to help solve the Charles Farmer case.

However, hindsight's a wonderful thing. No one initially thought it was going to be a problem.

"You'll remember the judge's case you helped with? Well, the person who paid for the kill is not a particularly nice man; allegedly, as we say. Because you helped us, we're worried he might think you were responsible."

"So, when are you planning this dirty weekend away for the three of us?"

"Now?" was his hesitant, questioning response. "We want to take just-in-case precautions while we're sorting out longer-term arrangements, should we need them. I've volunteered my services for a few days."

"Bollocks!"

He was taken aback by her response. He'd never heard her talk like that.

"Not too sure what you mean?"

"You know exactly what I mean. If you want us to go now, there's more to it than you're saying. I'll be expecting a full explanation later; a truthful one!"

Before he could respond with any platitude, she followed up. "In the meantime, thank you. We'll get packed."

And as an afterthought, "by the way, stick with that story to Aunt Doris. I don't want her any more worried than she needs to be."

He was surprised by her forceful challenge to him.

'Wow, that's one seriously complex woman.'

The gentle, scared young woman interviewed by Paterson had disappeared for the moment. This was no simple, sensitive woman with a serious condition, or two; or even three.

"Oh, and any ideas where you might feel comfortable going?" added Sykes. "I was thinking a quiet short-term rental in the likes of Norfolk. We can make the booking when I get there."

"I've an idea. Let me first chat it through with Aunt Doris."

When Sykes arrived at their house, an animated Jennifer opened the front door and waved him in. She invited him into the lounge with the mandatory cup of tea and slice of cake to which he was now getting used, actually looking forward.

He passed two suitcases in the hallway, plus other bags and accessories. They were ready to go.

"A few days?" he queried, looking at the myriad of items ready to be loaded.

"You're off with two women, what do you expect?" she retorted.

He could see that Jennifer was outwardly in her element, probably putting on a brave face for her aunt.

Sykes asked them both, "have you had a chance to think of any place you'd like me to take you that's out of the way? As I said on the phone, ideally, somewhere no one knows. If not, I'll arrange something quiet for us."

Doris Price answered, "Jennifer and I have already agreed the perfect place. We think my old cottage would be perfect. It's in Dorset, out of the way, and only a couple of close friends know about it."

"That'd work," said Sykes. It was only going to be for a couple of days. Anyone looking for them would take time to find out about the cottage, assuming they could. By then, they'd have a clear longer-term plan, if necessary.

"I love the place. We go there from time to time to get out of the city," added Jennifer, "and to check up on it."

"Aunt Doris has a gardener and a cleaner who come in a few hours a week, but it really needs us to come down and air it properly."

"We're due a visit there anyway, so this is convenient timing. Since the police are paying for everything, even better," said Aunt Doris. "I must admit, I love being here in the city with Jennifer."

"Yeh, she's always telling me that she gets city'd-out and needs to escape into the calm and solitude there."

The banter between the two continued.

Then to Sykes, Ms Price said, in a more serious tone, "going back to the old place with a new, more independent Jennifer might bring things into a fresh perspective. When I moved in with Jennifer, she needed me here with her. Here's where her support infrastructure was. Perhaps things will change now Peter's no longer with us?"

The aunt lightened up. "Even in the short time since Peter's death and being involved with your lot, she's a different person, more confident. At last, she sees her condition as not only a burden."

"I was worried earlier. I now realise you and your bosses have given her a genuine outlet for her condition. I'd like to think there's hope for the future."

"Outlet possibly," said Sykes in an uncertain tone." But I don't see a condition. I see a talent. And so do my bosses."

Ms Price then asked, trying to hide her fear from Jennifer, "how dangerous is this, really?"

"I don't know," was all Sykes could say, or rather, was happy to admit.

"The experts believe that because she has nothing on the suspect that is not open knowledge, he won't waste his time on her. But better be safe than sorry, eh?" he tried to reassure them.

There was fear in Aunt Doris' eyes when she requested of Sykes, "whatever happens, never worry about me. Please take care of her."

The powerful ex-school mistress was no longer so confident. She knew they were potentially in danger. She was trying to hide her emotions from Jennifer, exactly as Jennifer was doing for her.

"Aunt Doris, we'll all be fine. This is an adventure." Jennifer sounded like a character from a 60s children's book.

She always seemed to surprise Sykes. With Peterson, and in front of an audience, she could clam up. Now, here she was, excited about a possible dangerous few days. She didn't seem in the slightest bit worried.

Jennifer knew Barrie would look after both of them, no matter the cost. She felt safe with him.

After a quick snack of mandatory tea and cake, the three headed off to Dorset.

From his car phone, Sykes called Hansen and told them where they were going and the coordinates.

"Nice one Barrie, I'll tell the DCI and the Super. Remember, this holiday's on my budget, so you'd better enjoy yourselves. Send photos, bring me back rock, or whatever goodies they have there." He was upbeat for all to hear.

The three in the car grinned at each other, and Jennifer shouted out for him to hear on the phone, "it's a deal."

Hansen was about to say, "stay safe," but thought better of it. Sykes was on speakerphone, and the others would hear. He didn't want the ladies to be unnecessarily agitated.

He wished he was with them.

****

Later that same morning, Peterson searched for Sykes to help him and Bhatia prepare the evidence for the Farmer case. He was rather annoyed Sykes was nowhere to be found. Worse still, there was nothing in the rota about him not being available.

Wills and Hansen hadn't had time to amend the rota to Sykes being on holiday.

After angrily asking around, one of the PCs piped up that he overheard Hansen on the phone to Wills about Sykes' taking a holiday to Axecross St. Jude, in Dorset.

Peterson eventually tracked down Hansen.

"I hear Sykes is on holiday in Dorset," Peterson angrily challenged Hansen. "And when was I going to be told!"

"Keep your voice down. How the hell did you find out about that?" Hansen was shocked. He was also angry and worried to hear that Peterson knew. "No one is supposed to know."

"One of the PCs told me."

Peterson then angrily challenged Hansen, albeit now in a raised whisper. "He's supposed to be seconded to me. What the hell's going on?"

"Whatever, your beef, take it up with the boss," said Hansen, "but in the meantime, keep what you've heard about Sykes to yourself. I'm serious!"

Hansen rushed away to find Wills and tell him what's happened. They needed to shut up who heard what was going on, to try and minimise the damage.

Hansen knew there was nothing they could do about it now, apart from halting further gossip. They needed to warn Sykes.

****

After a long stop for various items of shopping en route, by the time they arrived at Ms Price's cottage, the sun was slowly descending toward the top of the hill to the west. It was still light, but not for long.

Dorothy Price's cottage sat just outside the hamlet of Axecross St. Jude, approximately half a mile west of the local store-cum-post office. The closest neighbour was several hundred yards away. So they were definitely secluded.

The picturesque hamlet was nestled in a shallow river valley, surrounded by woodland and rolling hills. It was almost halfway between Salisbury and Shaftesbury. Sykes knew from his MapApp that there was a roadway and tracks on the hillsides above them. While their location offered high seclusion, potential attackers would have a perfect view of their movements.

Sykes parked up in the driveway on the left side of the cottage. Jennifer closed and locked the large, heavy wooden gates behind it. There was a locked, brick-built, lean-to garage at the end of the driveway, butting up to the house.

There was no chance of parking the car inside the garage. It was Ms Price's storage room and glory hole.

Her house wasn't the tiny picture-postcard country cottage Sykes expected of her. He assumed the garden would be full of rose bushes, flower beds, and shrubs to attract various bird and insect life.

Instead, it was basic, functional, and well-maintained. The bushes and a lawn were due for their first cut of the spring.

He found out later that due to the aunt being an infrequent visitor during the many years she'd not lived there, she changed the garden for ease of maintenance.

The detached house sat in a plot that he assumed to be at least a quarter of an acre. The property occupied the corner of two narrow lanes and was surrounded by four-foot stone walls.

To the right of the driveway gates and on the other side of the substantial supporting post, was a smaller gate. It opened to a path that gave pedestrian access to the entrance door.

There was another gate around the right side of the house. A path led from there to the back door.

Another path encircled the house. All paths were of the same construction,

231

brick-edged, and stone-slabbed.

"You're the man with the muscle. Please take the heavy stuff and follow me. Jennifer'll sort out the kitchen."

Sykes unloaded the heavier objects as commanded. Laden with luggage, Sykes entered the house behind the two women. There would be at least another heavily laden trip back and forth.

The outside door opened into a large vestibule lined with coats and jackets on the walls. Boots, shoes, and wellingtons were on the floor, neatly arranged on both sides.

The vestibule door opened to a large long hallway. It stretched out on the right-hand side towards what he took to be the kitchen. The door was open, and he could see the work surface on the far (back) wall; Jennifer went straight ahead with the household shopping.

The stairs to the upper floor were on the left of the hallway. As he climbed the stairs behind Ms Price, a door faced him, which she ignored. She turned right at the top of the stairs and pointed to an already open door. "You're in here."

His small bedroom overlooked the back and the side garden.

There were three bedrooms, all located mostly to the right-hand side of the house, looking from the front.

Turning right again, and halfway along the landing heading back towards the front of the house, Ms Price pointed out another bedroom, which looked out to the side of the house.

"Jennifer is here, and by the way," she paused for maximum effect, "I'm a light sleeper! And the floorboards creek!"

At the end of the landing was Ms. Price's master bedroom, which overlooked the front of the house. He noted that her bedroom had two accesses, the bedroom door and another via the shared bathroom. It would be a challenge to secure, with two doors to protect.

The bathroom was to the right of her bedroom and over the stairs.

The aunt pointed out which each of the suitcases should go where.

On his way back for the second load, Sykes checked the door at the top of the stairs. It opened to a large, long cupboard that housed the boiler, towels, and linen.

He returned with the rest of the heavy load, which he deposited in the bedrooms as directed. The old woman was busy putting their things away, so he left her to it.

Back downstairs, he strolled to the end of the hallway, taking in every feature as he passed by. He was correct, the kitchen sat at the end.

To the right of the kitchen, through an archway, was what he took to be the breakfast area. It offered direct access to the back garden via French windows.

On the left of the kitchen back wall was a door to a utility room-cum-toilet situated partially behind the garage. It was a later add-on to the cottage and had its own access to the back garden.

Jennifer was still in the small kitchen putting things away. He couldn't help but give her a quick kiss on the cheek as he passed.

She grinned back in appreciation of the gesture.

Sykes was on a mission. Hansen had called, warning him that some in the station had been talking about their whereabouts. While not a definite threat, it raised the urgency of his preparations.

There was no time to chat, as much as he'd have liked to. Dusk was coming, and he needed to explore the rest of the house and its surroundings.

He wanted to check out those potential viewing points he'd earlier identified from his recently purchased maps and his mobile MapApp. One of the hills overlooking the hamlet had a small road.

Via his powerful field binoculars, he identified many vantage points for any potential onlookers. Some of those locations were hidden behind high bushes, giving hidden and uninterrupted views of the property.

Over the next few days, he knew he'd need to regularly monitor the hillside road and other potential viewpoints for any sign of movement. Being one man, Sykes couldn't venture out that far on his security patrols. It'd be too risky for the ladies if he wasn't close to the house.

He therefore had to focus his attention on making what security provisions he could, around and close to the house.

Once Sykes was satisfied with the initial layout of the house and the surrounding hillsides, he took advantage of the remaining light to explore the lay of the land immediately around the property. Later, he'd go through the house in more detail when there was less time pressure from the reducing light.

He walked up and down the roads that led to the property to get a feel of the area. In particular, he wanted to see the house as others might see it, should they venture closer. It would give him their perspective.

Sykes checked for tyre marks, footprints, and anything else that might be a clue to someone being there. He took photographs on his mobile phone for future reference. He didn't expect anyone to be there before them. However, by knowing what was visible now, any changes in the following days would signify people had been around. Those differences could still be normal traffic. On the other hand, if there were nothing, at least that would be reassuring.

As the sun slid up the top of the easterly hills, dusk became dark. A clear night sky arrived. Without light pollution, it was brighter than he expected. His eyes were now accustomed to the dark.

Sykes knew how he'd make his approach to attack them. He expected any potential attackers would follow a similar strategy.

As he secured the outside of the house, he didn't use artificial light in case anyone was watching and seeing what he was up to. The mass of stars was sufficient to help him secure the house.

He only needed torchlight when walking around.

He had some ideas about how he might disrupt any approach and to give him some early warning. As well as shopping for groceries, he also bought items that were more of a technical nature.

As a prior warning of intruders, Sykes installed two IP cameras. He linked them to a 4G router and positioned them front and back of the house. Being activated by both sound and movement, they'd warn him of anyone coming during the night.

Of course, the likes of prowling foxes and badgers could also set them off. However, it was better to have a false warning than nothing. Anyway, it was a simple matter to check the live-streaming image on his mobile phone.

33. CUTTING THE FINAL THREAD

Shortly after noon, Barker got a call from Fahmi. "Hi Tony, remember that helpful person who helped you try to re-kindle that old flame?"

"Fahmi, for Christ's sake, what the fuck are you talking about? Stop talking riddles. Tell me, what's festering in that little brain of yours?"

"Well, that same person would like to help you catch up with another woman. Do you still have the same phone you used the last time? Seems he's some useful information for you."

"Was that so hard?" An exasperated Tony Barker immediately terminated the call.

Fahmi grinned to himself as he put his phone away. He loved winding up his well-paying, arrogant little client.

Barker opened his desk and pulled out a 2G phone. He kept it from the last time this source had given him the tip on June Mitchell's security and her whereabouts; because, you never know.

He called the same plumbed-in number as he did earlier. "Fahmi said you had information for me."

"I believe that you are looking for a Miss Jennifer Graham. Would you like her location details?" said the same muffled voice on the telephone.

"What's it gonna cost this time?"

"Nothing at all. This one's a freebie."

"No one gives freebies, what's the angle?" queried Barker.

"Honest, nothing. Once you transfer the balance from the last deal as we agreed, I'll send you the information."

"You want another hundred and fifty grand!" shrieked Barker.

"No, just what we agreed on from the last time. Here's your opportunity to make things right from that oversight."

"How can I trust you?"

"You can't, but same as before, if you're compromised, so am I. Anyway, 'honour among thieves', as the saying goes."

The informant followed up., "It's a small group who knows where she is. There's no way you'll find her without me. I've access to her location that few outside that group does."

"You're going to have to give me more, as you did as last time."

"OK. Here's a freebie in good faith to prove I know what I'm talking about; she's got Sykes as a bodyguard. That's all you're getting for now."

Barker thought for a moment, then said, "Gimmie ten minutes and I'll call ya back."

He hung up and called Ben on secure messenger, as he always does. "Any info on where that consultant woman's gotten to?"

"Nothing boss. They've kept it watertight. She and her aunt have gone, an' no one knows where. It's all hush-hush between Smilie, Wills, and Hansen."

"That's all you've got? No one coughing up after what I've done for them?"

"Well, there is something that's interesting. Dunno if useful or not, but that Sergeant Sykes has also disappeared; last-minute holiday. It's suspicious. No one knows where. If you ask me, I think he's off with her somewhere."

"Fuck! That bloke wot grassed on June, says he knows where she is. He says Sykes is with her and the old dear. But he's screwing me for the money he says I owe from June's balance. Do you have any way of getting that information?"

"Sorry boss, no chance."

"What d'ya think?"

"Boss, if you want her, you're going to have to cough. If you do, don't worry. We'll hunt the shite and get your money back. There aren't many in the know, so we'll find him. And when we do, you can have some fun with him."

Barker inwardly sneered at the thought.

He called the accountant and instructed the payment of the balance.

"Are you sure boss?" asked the accountant.

Barker was changing his mind again, and she was very cautious; she had to be. But she didn't want to incur his wrath by querying again. So, she quickly recovered with, "OK, will do."

The accountant covered herself again. She messaged confirmation when the monies were on their way and again when the transfer had been completed. Once Barker received the confirmation of payment received, he called the burner phone again.

The informant picked up after two rings and immediately said, "thank you payment received. Got a pen and paper?

After a grunt of acknowledgement from Barker, the voice said, "Jennifer Graham and Doris Price are on their way to Buddleja Cottage, Axecross St. Jude, the other side of Salisbury. As I said, they've sergeant Sykes with them. And here's yet another freebie because you're such a generous client, he's unarmed. Enjoy Dorset."

Barker hung up and shouted for Morris, who ambled in soon after.

"Joe, get the boys, and this time, not my car. We're going for a trip to the West Country," said an unusually jubilant Anthony Barker.

Soon, everyone who could have pinned anything on him will be out of the way.

At last, he could relax.

****

The informant was extremely pleased with himself. He never thought the balance would be forthcoming. This was working out very well indeed, even more profitable than expected.

34. THE PREY

It was dusk when Barker, Morris, and Bill 'n' Ben arrived in the hamlet and found the cottage. They managed to get there in time to check the place out before it got too dark.

They drove past the cottage, taking in the surroundings. En route, Ben checked that the closest police station was Shaftsbury. Dispatching from there would take about 20 minutes, assuming they treated this as a priority call.

All her contacts in their station back home knew nothing, or at least weren't talking. If that information was locked down there, there's no way it would have been communicated to the police here. Knowing the police as well as she did, it was a safe assumption to make.

To be sure, they planned to wait and discreetly watch the house from a hillside location that overlooked their prey. If there were police patrols over the next six to eight hours, it'd be a sure sign the local police were notified and actively supporting them.

"If all's good, we're doin' them after midnight, once they've been settled for a couple of hours, and we know there's no one else with them. It could also be a police trap, so we need to be careful. They'll never expect the hit so soon."

"We know Sykes isn't armed, but we can't trust these fuckin' country yokels to be unarmed. Everyone seems to have shotguns. Fuckin' dangerous place, far safer in the city," Barker laughed at his joke. No one else did this time. Everyone was too tense.

"So, we'll approach carefully in case the old bird's got one."

"When do we cut the telephone wires to the house?" asked Morris, keen to show initiative and enthusiasm to his brother.

"We're not cuttin' no wires, you numbskull. They've got mobile phones and the signal's good. Do you want to stand up and fuckin' wave at them that we're here and comin'?"

Morris said nothing. He was used to his brother's condescending behaviour. But he still thought it was a good idea. And in reality, it would have been had Sykes not taken the initiative of a 4G mobile router link for the cameras.

"Anyway," interjected Ben to take some of the pressure off Morris. "From when that lot in the house clock us, we've got at least twenty minutes, possibly half an hour until a patrol car comes our way. The fuzz'll not be armed, so if they come too soon, that's their fault. It'll take longer for them to get an ARV here."

"Any issues topping a couple of porkies?" asked Barker. He knew they wouldn't, but in case anyone had a change of heart, better to ask now than find out later.

His brother's lack of conviction sometimes worried him.

Barker knew Bill and Ben had no scruples about killing; they'd done enough in the past. However, killing police is different; the penalties are higher.

The siblings confirmed with a shrug. Morris gave an enthusiastic thumbs-up to the idea. He always agreed to anything his brother said.

****

Inside the house, the three of them finished their dinner then retired to the living room.

While the aunt had internet, she didn't use pay-on-demand channels or streaming services. So, the evening's entertainment was a choice of terrestrial TV channels; mostly repeats.

For Jennifer and Sykes, it would be a boring few days stuck behind closed doors.

The ladies decided that enough was enough. At almost 10 pm, they retired.

Sykes, now alone, strapped on, and checked his Glock before heading out for a final reconnaissance of the area.

****

From the overlooking hilltop, the three men and one woman could see someone with a torch walking around and checking out the immediate surroundings. They assumed this was Sykes. They'd seen him earlier, before it became fully dark.

"Bro, I don't want to kill that old lady. It'd be like doin' our ma."

"We're here to do the bitch wot's gonna screw us and the coppa with her. She put you in the frame with Forrest and is out to get ya. And I'm not having that! You're my favourite brother."

The big man beamed a happy smile realising that his brother was doing all this to protect him from that woman.

"Honest, the old dear'll not get hurt," continued Barker. "If she gets in the way, then it'll be their fault and not ours."

When Morris hurt people for his brother in the past, it had always been people who needed it. He was OK with that. This old woman was an innocent, and he wouldn't like to hurt her; for any reason.

Barker knew he needed to keep the aunt out of it. It had nothing to do with his conscience or lack of quarrel with her. Unfortunately, his daft half-brother was a softie when it came to the oldies. If there was a problem with her, he suspected his brother might do something stupid, like protect her.

Since oldies were never muscle for anyone needing to be topped or merely smacked, it had never been an issue before.

They were all going in masked up, so as long as no one else got in the way, it'd not be a problem.

35. JUSTIFIABLE ACTION

Just after 2 am, after parking some distance down the road in a small lane, the four approached the house.

Some four hours earlier, they saw lights in the two front upstairs bedrooms. Shortly afterward, they extinguished. Almost two hours later, they saw the other lights going off. Sykes had finally gone to bed. They would wait a further two hours before making their entry.

A porch light partially lit up the front, so all four entered the property via the gate at the unlit side. The side access was concealed by shrubs, making this entrance doubly attractive.

The plan they used was similar to previously successful attacks on occupants in houses; a synchronised front and rear attack.

Barker and Morris veered to the left and would enter through the front entrance. Police would use a steel battering ram, and others used sledgehammers to force entry. However, Barker had the best mobile tool of all. He had a Joseph Morris to kick in a door. Once in, they'd rush up the stairs and attack while their victims were sleeping.

At the same time, Bill 'n' Ben would veer right. They'd follow the path to the rear of the house to cut off any retreat. If no one tried to escape, they'd break in through the French windows and be backup support to 'Little-and-Large'.

The four attackers silently waited by the side gate, hidden by the foliage. There was no noise from within the house.

All clear!

Ben led her brother as they carefully navigated the path to the back of the house. Gardens in the pitch-black were notoriously tricky to cross. People tended to keep walkways clear, so it was safest to stay on, and follow the path.

They were making good progress.

"Shit!" Ben screamed, followed by an, "argh!" of agony.

Her right foot went through a concrete slab, slewing to the right as she partially fell in. She heard the crack of bone and felt the tissue tearing around her foot and ankle.

Ben could hear she was seriously injured, from her cry and the sound of cracking bone.

He reached out to find his sister in the dark and stumbled over her. "Shit," he mumbled.

"Idiot!" she screamed a whisper.

Supported by Bill, she pulled her leg out of the hole. Ben winced in pain as she felt down to her misshapen foot and ankle. At a minimum, there was a severe break.

"Stop, you arse!"

Not realising the damage she'd done, he was doing his best to help her get to her feet.

"I'm fucked, and no way can I walk. I'll have to crawl back to the car. You need to get around the back now! Get in there and support the boss yourself. Go! I'll call 'em."

As he and Morris sneaked to the front of the house, Barker inwardly cursed when he heard Ben's scream.

Soon after, Morris' phone rang.

"Are you a fuckin' muppet?" he whispered to his brother.

Morris fumbled with it, eventually managing to switch it off.

"I told ya to put the fuckin' thing on silent or vibrate. Are you trying to get us killed!" he whispered loudly and hoarsely.

Then it hit him. That must have been Bill or Ben calling. It was now obvious something had happened. Maybe there was a trap?

He checked and saw the missed call from Ben.

When he called her back, Ben explained that she was out of the game and crawling back to the car as best she could.

Whispered expletives flew from Barker's mouth.

The three attackers simultaneously burst into the house at a revised time of three minutes later than planned.

If the occupants weren't aware of the attack before Ben's scream and Joe's phone going off, they were now.

****

During Sykes' patrol of the house in the dark, he tripped over a loose slab. It rocked as he walked on it. An idea hit him.

In the black of the night, he removed the offending slab and dug a deep, neat hole underneath. He covered it with a piece of accurately cut, heavy-duty corrugated cardboard he'd found in the garage. In the faint light, it would look just like a concrete slab.

As long as it didn't rain, he hoped the noise from someone stepping on it would give them a warning sound.

He expected the noise of crumpling cardboard, perhaps even a curse as someone fell through would give them a warning.

As it was, all six people heard Ben's cry. The element of surprise was lost.

Sykes' idea worked even better than he envisaged. From Ben's pained scream, he knew one of them was at least hurt; or rather, he hoped.

"One down," Sykes said to the ladies. All three were already barricaded in Jennifer's room.

The outdoor IP cameras worked as planned. They picked up the intruders' movements, giving Sykes the warning he needed.

Jennifer messaged Hansen to let him know the attack was afoot, while Sykes called 999 to request help as an officer in danger. They gave him an ETA of 35 minutes for a patrol car. It would be 50 minutes before an ARV could reach them from Salisbury.

Sykes warned the police coordinator, "tell the officers to exercise extreme caution. Our attackers are all armed, definitely with shotguns, possibly at least one handgun."

He looked at his watch, it was 0207 and Sykes knew they were on their own until almost 0245. They wouldn't have effective help until almost 3 am.

They'd have to stall as best they could.

****

After Peterson told Hansen the secret was out, albeit to a limited audience, Hansen knew if Barker was indeed after them, he'd get their location soon enough. He decided to take the initiative. Better to be shouted after the fact than have the risk of three dead people.

Hansen had a friend who was a uniform inspector in the Salisbury police, whom he explicitly trusted. He gave him the heads-up that, during the next few days, an armed response vehicle might be required. He didn't give the exact location or any further details at that time.

The uniformed inspector took Hansen and the limited information on trust. He arranged with his team for an ARV to be on standby. At that time of night, it would make it to their location in 25 minutes.

****

Sykes took a call from Inspector Ramirez from Salisbury police station. There was no fuss. Ramirez got straight to the point.

"Forget the control room status. An ARV is on the way, ETA 21 minutes. Hang in there."

Sykes said thanks and cut the line. His watch now showed 0219, and the ARV was due around 0240. He needed to focus.

Barker knew the element of surprise was up, so it was a matter of simple negotiation.

"Coppa, you and the bitch come down, and we'll leave the old bird alone!" he shouted upstairs.

Barker knew Ben's injury was down to Sykes. He was livid the sergeant had screwed up his plans. He was going to pay for it as well as that consultant woman. It never occurred to him Sykes was merely doing his job.

"If we come up, you're all fucked." Barker still had the niggling concern that Ms Price might have a gun. Better to err on the safe side.

244

"We'll be safe here," said Sykes. The police are on their way.

Jennifer matter-of-factly whispered to Sykes. "You are wrong. There are three armed men out there and it won't take them more than a few minutes to break into this room."

They had the bed frame, wardrobe, and dresser barricading the door. Unfortunately, Morris was on the other side.

Sykes had arranged for the mattress to be between them and the barricade. He hoped it would be substantial enough to stop the worst of the shotgun blasts.

He did his best to reassure the women. "I'm armed, and they don't know it yet. It will take them by surprise and slow them. That'll give us a few more minutes. By then, the ARV will be here. We're good."

Jennifer calmly replied. "I can count, and I know you're bullshitting us."

Now it was his turn for surprise. He'd never heard her coming close to swearing; this was a first.

Jennifer continued. "You know as well as me, your gun is useless here. You have no one to fire on. When they burst in, as soon as they see anyone, three shotguns will fire as they enter. You will not have a target to defend anyone."

Still without emotion, she said, "I've gone through it, I've seen it, and it's all quite straightforward. The three of them are now in the house. Now's your chance to leave! If you leave by the window, they won't see you."

"Not on my watch," said Sykes.

"Barrie," she said, taking his hand, "whatever happens, they are going to kill me, and you cannot stop them without being killed. I don't believe they will hurt Aunt Doris."

"I'm not going anywhere!" He was adamant.

"Listen, I know how you feel. But you must stop being emotional. I've walked through the alternatives and there are only a few moves in this game. And all of them leave me dead."

Jennifer even surprised herself with how unemotional she was regarding the whole situation.

Aunt Doris looked at Jennifer aghast but said nothing. There was nothing to say. She could see the truth of what her niece was saying.

245

"OK, I'll spell it out, since you refuse to get it."

"One. I go down myself, and they come up for you, and Aunt Doris could get hurt in the crossfire."

"Two. You and I go down, and both of us die; Aunt Doris is hopefully safe."

"Three. We stay here and fight it out. Do you really think we have a chance? All of us will die. You might get one, but that's small consolation."

"Four. You leave out the window and take your chances. They only have the two of us. I'll go down and say you escaped. They won't even have time to look for you with the police on their way, let alone find you. They kill me, and Aunt Doris is safe."

Sykes could see the logic in her thinking. However, she was right, but he couldn't eliminate his emotional pain of leaving them alone.

"I'm not waiting for your mates to come screaming down the lane, it's now or never! Make your choice!" shouted Barker.

From the sound of his voice, he was still downstairs. However, they could hear Bill near the bedroom door.

"You have to go now." Jennifer was adamant. She walked over to the window and quietly opened it; then stood there waiting for him to decide that she was right.

Ms Price said, "go!" She pushed him to the window.

He looked at his watch. It was now 0123. 17 minutes to the cavalry. There wasn't enough time, and he had no choice.

He reluctantly nodded and moved towards the window. She grabbed him, gave him another lingering kiss, then pushed him through the window. He eased himself out. Gun in hand, he silently dropped to the soft ground below, rolling to one side to limit the impact.

"Four-b," he mumbled. "Leave by the window, then go back, fight, and stall them for as long as possible, for as long as it takes."

He hadn't counted on Ben still being in the garden.

As Ben crawled towards the side gate, she heard the soft thump as he landed. She stopped and turned around. Seeing him in the now illuminated downstairs lights, she fired once where he was; before he rolled away.

"Oi Coppa?" she shouted in his direction, hoping he'd respond so she could fire the second barrel. She didn't know he'd a gun. It didn't matter.

He quickly moved towards the front of the house, then stopped to fire three shots in the direction of her voice. He knew this was risky, so he crouched and covered himself, in case he missed and she fired again.

"That'll do nicely, she mumbled. She now knew where he was. She fired the second barrel. Now at a longer range, the more widely dispersed buckshot hit its mark. She really couldn't miss.

The lower left of his body took all the pellets. He ignored the pain and focussed his aim to instantly fire a double tap to the right of the muzzle flash. In response, he heard Ben's second, "argh," of the evening. Then silence. He decided not to check on the woman. He didn't have that luxury. He needed to move fast.

Barker shouted, "Ben, you OK? What's happening?" She never responded.

Sykes now knew she was out of the picture.

Barker was now getting impatient and had to close this. If they were to avoid the incoming police cars, they needed to be away from that place, sharpish.

****

When Sykes tried to move after being shot, he almost fainted from the pain in his lower back, buttocks, and upper thigh. His shirt and trousers stuck to his skin. He didn't know how badly he was shot but when he put his hand to his back, it came back soaked with blood.

He could still move. His plan remained game-on, albeit excruciatingly. His left leg hurt but it could still take some weight.

He crouched as he limped as quickly as possible towards the open front door to the vestibule. The sweat ran into his eyes, and now it stung from where he wiped it with his bloodied hands.

As he approached the front of the house, he could see the all lights were on downstairs.

"Bill, wot's going on up there?" asked Barker.

Bill's voice replied from the landing at the top of the stairs. "It's all quiet inside here."

Sykes crouched low as he looked around the doorframe. Logic told him that Barker would have stayed below and behind Morris, out of harm's way.

Rushing in against two people with shotguns would be fool-hardy. Coming in from the dark would also be against him since his eyes would need to acclimatise to the light from the dark outside.

"Oi Pig, if you're out there, come and get us, coz we're on our way to fuck that bitch of yours. The old woman gets it as well." Barker had heard the gunshots and knew Sykes was armed.

Then to the women upstairs, he shouted, "fuck it bitches, we're coming up, and you're all done!" He knew this would bring Sykes to them, assuming he didn't run away.

Sykes could hear the stairs creaking as someone heavy was starting to climb them.

Jennifer then shouted, "I'm coming out and leaving Aunt Price here. No more shooting please?"

Sykes could hear the scraping of furniture as the barricade was dismantled.

He looked at his watch, it was now 0128. 12 minutes to the cavalry. There wasn't enough time.

He could also hear further creaking as someone, most likely the monster Morris, was climbing the stairs. He wouldn't be looking back. Turning around would be difficult for the big man, assuming it was him.

Sykes knew it had to be now. There was no way to stall them if Barker was up the stairs.

His plan was simple, dive into the vestibule, and shoot whoever was at the bottom of the stairs. He stood up on his right leg against the doorframe, then pushed forward onto his left leg to lunge forward.

His left leg gave way!

The dive turned into an agonising flop. His gun fell to the ground, just out of reach in front of him.

He lay there in the vestibule, agonisingly on his left side.

Barker had positioned himself to the hallway side of the bannister should someone from above fire down at them. Barker turned around at the noise of Sykes' entrance. His face beamed with glee. About fifteen feet in front of him lay Sykes, injured and unarmed. Barker ever-so-slowly raised his gun, savouring the moment.

Sykes knew he couldn't reach his pistol in time before being shot. But he had no choice; his plan was always going to be a do-or-die stalling matter. He was always going to be dead from this course of action. So there was nothing to be lost by trying.

And you never know, he might even get off a shot.

Sykes reached out for his gun. He heard two shots in quick succession; both barrels.

But, Sykes was still alive and able to move?

Barker, still grinning, dropped his sawn-off shotgun, and slowly fell to his knees before slumping forward to the ground.

Morris stopped halfway up the stairs. He half-turned and seeing the prone Barker, he screamed for his brother.

Sykes, now gun in hand, and still lying on the ground, shouted, "armed police, stop or I fire."

He dropped his weapon on the stairs and rushed as quickly as his bulk could take him down to where his brother lay. He sat next to him in the hallway and heaved the little man onto his lap. The big man cried as he cradled his brother in his arms.

Seeing Sykes with the pistol pointing in his direction, he shouted, "you killed him, you killed him."

Morris gently lowered Barker to the floor. Suddenly, he roared in anger. He then stood up to charge at Sykes. Sykes knew that shooting an unarmed man was wrong, but he had no choice. This man could, and would kill him with his bare hands.

Again Sykes shouted, "armed police, stop or I shoot!"

As he prepared to fire, several shots rang out from further inside the house. The shots were to his lower legs, shattering bones, and the big man collapsed.

Morris gave up on attacking Sykes. Wailing like an injured animal, Morris used his arms to pull his bulk back to his brother.

Whoever shot both men was a marksman. The police were early, he realised with relief.

Sykes couldn't see from where the life-saving shots came. Barker and then Morris were in the way. Now, with a clear view of the kitchen, he saw a slim hooded figure dressed in black. It wasn't the police. With a wave of his hand, the man in black dashed towards the breakfast room.

Whoever it was, saved his life.

Now was not the time to think of his hooded saviour. He had to focus on the job at hand.

"William Potts, Barker's dead, Morris is disabled, it's over. I am an armed policeman. Drop your weapon and come down the stairs, hands in the air."

There was no response.

"Potts, this is your last warning. I'm armed and coming up the stairs. I will shoot. I'm bloody pissed with you lot. I've warned you!"

William Potts responded with, "OK, OK. I'm coming down."

He placed his shotgun at the top of the stairs. Then with hands in the air, he slowly walked down the stairs.

When Jennifer heard Sykes shouting, then Bill announcing he was coming down, she knew it was over. They were all safe.

She ran to the top of the stairs, excited to see Sykes alive and well. What she saw wiped the glee from her face. The sight of Sykes below stunned and immobilised her. His lower left side was all red. His blood had soaked the floor all around him. She had never seen so much blood, even in her crime stories!

She saw Sykes swaying in an awkwardly seated position. His gun arm quivered as it pointed at Ben coming down the stairs.

Sykes tried to focus, but the image of Bill faded in and out. He couldn't move, so just told Bill to sit on the bottom stair until the police arrived.

And three minutes later, he could hear the wail of sirens.

It was starting to get fuzzy, then dark. Sweat was now streaming down his face. Sykes squeezed his injured thigh. The excruciating pain gave him another burst of adrenalin to keep him conscious. Through the mist, he could see Potts watching him for any sign of collapse.

Slowly Bill turned into a vague outline. Sykes heard a click. Bill now had a gun that he'd cocked. Sykes couldn't fire since he knew Jennifer was somewhere behind Bill. Why hadn't Bill fired?

Nevertheless, he kept his position.

Two minutes later, a police car screeched to a halt outside. Armed police officers announced their presence as they ran up the path.

Sykes croaked a shout that he was a police officer with one man under guard, another dead, one disabled, and another in an unknown condition near the side gate.

They took Sykes' gun. He could now allow himself the luxury of collapsing. Everything went dark.

The police saw Jennifer with the cocked sawn-off shotgun a few inches from Bill's head.

They ordered her to lower it.

She complied and held up her hands. Then ignoring the commands from the armed police, she rushed to the prone Sykes.

"Sykes!" she screamed as arms dragged her from him.

In the distance was the sound of ambulances.

36. CONSEQUENCES

The killer warned Barker there would be consequences for putting a hit on him. Even worse, he tried to imitate his MO and pin an unprofessional hit on him. Barker's death would be a reminder to all his clients, past and future; they needed to respect his privacy and integrity.

Saving the policeman from Morris' attack was not going to do his reputation any good at all. Any hint of compassionate behaviour toward the police would worry his clients.

However, he needn't have worried. The story that got out was that the killer saved Joe Morris' life before the armed policeman could kill him. The Engineer's reputation remained intact; his clients respected that story.

Those who knew Morris would know that he was just a simple brother-worshipping fool in all this.

  ****

When the local police arrived, they engaged their local district Murder Investigation Team in the killings in the cottage.

They and the city's MIT coordinated their efforts to bring the matter to the CPS, charging Morris and William Potts.

Benjamina died almost immediately after being shot by Sykes.

  ****

Sykes had collapsed due to hypovolemic (or low-volume) shock from excessive blood loss caused by the many shotgun wounds.

Once in the ambulance, the crew managed to stabilise his life-threatening bleeding and gave him plasma.

After receiving blood in the hospital, his body was ready for the operating theatre to remove the shot. All he now needed was a lot of bed rest.

When he recovered consciousness, Jennifer was waiting for him at his bedside. He stifled the pain from her exuberant hug.

****

Two days after the gunfight, Merriman held a meeting in his office. With him were the two key officers involved in the conclusion of the judge's case, plus Peterson.

"Somehow, Barker and his team got wind of Sykes' location," opened Merriman.

"For the last few months, I've been quietly investigating moles who have been feeding Barker's organisation. I now know that Barker had a hold on certain elements within this station."

The three officers sitting in front of Merriman looked at each other questioningly.

He continued. "There's no excuse for us allowing fear, coercion, bribery, and you name it, to run rife on our patch. Barker's gone. And I now expect this to stop."

He paused to look at each of his officers in turn.

"I have closed my case files on this investigation. There's no reason to pursue this inquiry. However, I'm still holding onto them."

Merriman was rarely angry, but he was now. "You all knew about Sykes' location, and it got to Barker. In addition to leaks, sensitive conversations were overheard. Clean up your acts and your people! If there are more leaks, I'll share the files with the ACC."

All three again looked at each other but said nothing.

Merriman nodded to the door. The meeting was over.

He expected this matter to be closed and without repetition. Merriman wasn't just protecting his officers from repercussions. He also didn't want his bosses to know the extent of the corruption in his station. Any investigation would reflect badly on his reputation and career progression.

EPILOGUE

The Engineer sat at his wife's bedside, holding her hand as he watched the life flicker in her frail body. The high doses of painkillers kept the pain at bay while gently extinguishing what little life she had left.

After her life at last expired, he continued to sit by her bedside, remembering the joys of their long shared lives. They had no children or nearby family. He'd been living alone for over a year while she was in the hospice. There were also many earlier times when he lived a solitary existence for long periods.

Her various treatments took her far away, sometimes out of the country for long periods. His day job didn't allow him sufficient time off to be with her as she endured the many painful treatments; some conventional, others expensive trials.

There was little sexual intimacy for some years before that. However, the bond they had was stronger than anything physical. And now, that bond had finally been severed.

His wife pestered him every day in recent years to find someone else after she had gone.

"You're still young enough to find new happiness."

She knew death was coming, but he refused to admit it.

He pushed for any promising treatment, no matter how low the chances of success.

She only endured the agonies of the various treatments as a comfort to him. But it was coming to an end. There was nothing more they could do for her.

She knew him; he needed someone to replace her.

In his mind, no one could replace her, ever.

However, he did start to seek sexual gratification to stem the physical urges.

So, he resorted to using prostitutes since that was an emotionally safe business transaction.

Over time, he became a regular client to one who kept herself safe from diseases as much as anyone in her job could. She was kind, understanding, and a good listener.

He often sought her out merely to talk when the emotional pain was becoming too much. Slowly, over time, they became close friends.

Not long after he killed Barker, his wife died. Over time he and his regular prostitute became more personally intimate. She became his partner, at last leaving the life of a sex worker.

His wife was correct. He needed someone. While she could never be replaced, he could now open the next chapter in his life.

Since her demise, he used his contract money to help his now girlfriend to eliminate her baggage.

Sitting with his new partner in the two business-class middle seats, he inwardly thanked Barker for the extra three hundred thousand pounds. It was an added bonus that helped fund his comfortable early retirement.

Little did Barker know, but he had effectively paid the killer to kill him.

It was The Engineer who sold Jennifer's location to Barker, luring him to the cottage. While Barker was in the open and focussed on killing, he was an easy target. The hunter didn't realise he was the hunted; sadly, he never would.

There were some last-minute adjustments to his plans for the 'righteous' killing of Barker. In this plan, The Engineer's protégé, Sykes, and the two women were never in danger. However, Sykes' unexpected leap from the room, then the aftermath, almost ruined his plans for a clean kill.

The Sri Lankan Airlines A340 plane steeply banked as it turned to head east. Looking across the cabin, he could see the English countryside, which now seemed almost below them. It would be some weeks before they both returned. This was yet another trip as part of their round-the-world exploration.

The Engineer didn't feel sad about giving up his career in the police. Soon after the successful conclusion to the Barker and judge cases, the killer, professionally called The Engineer, aka DCI Wills, made the next rung on the ladder to Superintendent, replacing Smilie.

Without the support of his wife by his side, he didn't have the political guile to navigate the upper echelons of the police force. He began to hate his new job. He knew it was time to retire on a healthy Superintendent pension.

And so it started, a new chapter in his life.

****

Merriman was promoted to Chief Superintendent, continuing his rise toward becoming Chief. This vacancy enabled a reshuffle that would find Wills promoted to Superintendent.

****

After his encounters with Jennifer, DI Peterson realised that the city's streets no longer needed prehistoric police officers, as Wills alluded. Survival of the fittest necessitated a new breed of tech-savvy, politically correct officer to take over.

The aged policeman, with his wife, now had the countryside as his domain, enjoying walking its lanes and paths. His gut (instinct) was no longer needed and shrank to manageable proportions from all the exercise.

It was now long walks, instead of the station, that preceded his forays into hostelries.

****

Hansen is still a DI, but his promotion would come shortly.

In the meantime, and after the retirement of Peterson, Bhatia joined his team to learn policing in the 21st Century.

****

April Mitchell went to jail for running a brothel, or rather, 'Living off Immoral Earnings'.

She swore vengeance for Sally's part in her mother's murder and testifying against her for running prostitutes.

Her time would come.

****

Sally Anderson went into witness protection. After the failures in protecting key people and witnesses, the authorities could not take any risk of her also being compromised.

She was given a new identity as part of her deal with the authorities for testifying against April and Barker and Co.

With cosmetic surgery, it wasn't long before she finally felt able to get into the world, to be seen, and to live a new life.

****

Morris received a reduced sentence due to mitigating circumstances. Fortunately, William (Bill) Potts was in the same prison, albeit serving life. He was able to look after the big guy and vice versa.

After two years in prison, Joseph Morris was released early with good behaviour. He moved in with the accountant and her husband into their new and larger house. At last, the accountant could openly spend "Barker's abuse money," as she called it.

****

Sykes and Jennifer? Well, that is a whole different story.

The End

ABOUT THE AUTHOR

The son of a Scottish father and an Austrian mother, Max spent his informative years as a military brat in Malaysia, before returning to Scotland. He and his wife spent many years living and working in the Middle East and Asia.

Writing was the most enjoyable part of his work as an international marketer. With several thriller and murder novels bubbling around his head and desperate to pop out, the time had come for him to exit the rat race and write his own stories.

Now a full-time writer, Spectrum is his second novel. He hopes you enjoyed reading it as much as he enjoyed writing it.

He is married with two children, a football team of grandchildren, three dogs, and three cats.

Home is the south coast of England.

You can visit him on Facebook: Max.Holden.Author.

Printed in Great Britain
by Amazon

17216889R00148